# Solo Blues

Also by the author

*Fair Game*
*The Zero Trap*

*Paula Gosling*

# SOLO BLUES

*Coward, McCann & Geoghegan*   NEW YORK

Library of Congress Cataloging in Publication Data
Gosling, Paula.
  Solo blues.

  I. Title.
PR6057.075S6   1981      823'.914      81-5403
ISBN 0-698-11107-9                     AACR2

Printed in the United States of America

To Elaine, Ilsa, Janet, Frances, Liz,
Abbie and Emmy—for putting up with my
talk, my nonsense . . .
and all that jazz.

# 1

He wasn't a small man, but he walked small.

Head down, collar up, he stopped under a streetlight to light a cigarette, ducked to the match and threw it away. The rain had stopped at half-past one, but the air was still damp with its memory. Within the circle of illumination he saw an iridescent smear in the gutter, stepped over it and crossed the street against the signals that flashed for no one. His footsteps echoed briefly from an alleyway, then were only the sounds of grit scraped and a tin can kicked, to counterpoint the still of the night.

Walking was good for the legs and, anyway, cabdrivers always wanted to talk in the dark. After he'd played for hours, silence was another kind of music, good to hear.

Light still spilled from the open door of the American fried chicken place, but nobody was buying. He saw a face peer through the opening to the kitchen, then turn away as he passed by. Several paper napkins fluttered, caught under the propped-back glass door, and the neon sign buzzed faintly. He paused for a moment to catalog the sound. Maybe he could use it. Or maybe, like the chicken, he couldn't.

The stairs to his place were dark, but he knew the count by heart. He smelled her before he saw her. Perfume hung like invisible words in the air, told him she was waiting inside the flat. He almost went back to the chicken place, but accepted in the end and put his key in the lock. He should have asked for hers back, last time, but he'd been asleep.

She hadn't turned the lights on and he didn't bother. The glow from the streetlights was enough to make her out, curled up in the big leather chair that backed into the curve of the piano. And he heard the faint jangle of her gold charm bracelet as she moved, pushing her long blond hair back from her cheek.

"You're late tonight, Johnny," she complained, softly.

"Yeah," he sighed. "Sometimes they want more."

"Like me?"

"Like you." He tossed his keys into the Japanese pottery bowl on the table by the door and went into the kitchen to get a Coke from the fridge. The bulb inside had gone again and he knocked over half a can of beans before he felt the ring-tab he was searching for. Silently he mopped up the mess with a handful of paper towels, dumped the lot into the wastebasket, then opened the Coke with a hiss. After drinking half of it he went back into the sitting room. "Leave your key this time, Lisa. You know I don't like to talk when I finish working."

"That's not very friendly. Besides, I didn't come to talk."

"Even so, leave it, please. Or I'll have the lock changed. Either way, no more." He took off his jacket and tossed it over the back of the sofa, loosened his tie and pulled it through his collar. He hadn't meant it to sound so tough, but he'd played it every other way with her, and she still hadn't recognized the tune. What they'd had together had been good. If he hadn't cared about that, if he still didn't care about her in some ways, it wouldn't hurt the way it did. His problem was to cauterize the wound. There'd been a time when his resentment had been hot enough to do it. Now it was cold, and it was the only thing he had left to use against her. "Coming back the way you do is too easy. I'm not a bloody tap."

"Meaning I don't turn you on?" she asked archly.

"Meaning nothing. You wanted to go, you went. Fine. You have a life to lead, so do I. Let's get on with them and stop this stupid game of Johnny-yes, Johnny-no. I'm getting pissed off with playing a reprise of 'Bittersweet' every time you get bored or randy or just plain sorry for yourself. It's not my style, love. It shouldn't be yours either."

"You don't have to be so mean about it," she pouted. "Some men would be flattered. Some might even be *polite.*"

He set his jaw. "What you really mean is that some men would be grateful, right? Well, you're not offering me anything I couldn't get for myself. I don't have to beg for it and I don't have to buy it, thanks all the same."

Even in the shadows he could see her mask fall away. The Lisa who'd been hiding behind it was as clear-eyed and straight as ever. "You wouldn't be so angry if you didn't still want me, Johnny. You always will. Maybe that should make *me* the grateful one."

"Don't be." He could handle it when she was coy, he could handle it when she was aggressive, but he couldn't handle honesty. He didn't want to think of *her* being sad, *her* being lonely. He didn't want to think of her at all, but she made him. Every time. Every bloody time. "What's the matter—he gone out of town again?" he asked brusquely.

"Birmingham." Her dress rustled as she swung her legs down, and the bracelet tinkled again.

"Why didn't you go with him?" He went over to the window and finished the Coke, approving of the wet glistening of the pavement below. The empty well of the darkened street was marked by two lights burning, one out, three more burning. Syncopation.

"Because it was a house sale and house sales are boring." She was kicking off her shoes, now, unzipping her dress, the gold charm bracelet keeping up its obbligato all the while.

"Sales are where he makes all that money you appreciate so much."

He unlatched the window and pushed it up a little. Her perfume suffocated the fresh scent of the rain that had begun to fall again, needling the puddles in the street. Suddenly he felt the warmth of her body against his back. "I appreciate other things, too. Things he can't give me, things you can. You're so good at it, Johnny."

He put the empty Coke tin down on the windowsill. "No, I'm not," he said wearily. "No better than anyone else, no worse. I just do it the way you like it, that's all."

"Yes, please." Her hands came around to slide under his belt. Turning away, he walked back across the room and wondered what to do when he got to the other side. The flat wasn't *that* big, he couldn't run around it forever like some coy virgin, bouncing off the walls.

"Please, Johnny," she said again, putting that little catch into her voice she thought made him feel important. Once, yes—now only irritable. Well, that worked, too. He could feel his belly tightening. It had been a couple of weeks. Close off your head, she'll do. Anyone would. And you'll sleep better. Maybe.

"I don't want to see you again after this."

"Okay." She was coming across the room slowly, expecting him to turn around to enjoy the show. For him, like most things, it was better listened to than seen. He didn't turn.

"And leave your key."

"All *right.*" The edge in her voice satisfied him. He wouldn't have to talk anymore. In the morning light she'd see that he really meant what he said. This time was one time too many. And she knew he hated that perfume, thick, heavy, oversweet. It would take longer to get rid of that than to change the lock.

He intended to make it lousy for her, but forgot.

Later he awoke, realized he was alone, and wondered if she'd left her key in the bowl. It must have been the sound of the door closing that had wakened him, although perhaps she'd called goodbye. More probably it had been a dream.

He'd just about drifted off again when there was the sound of a car engine roaring from the street below. Hell hath no decibel level like the departure of a woman scorned.

He lay there for a moment, tangled in the sheets, then cursed aloud. He hadn't made it lousy for her, but for himself. Her perfume was all over him. He got up and took a shower. Never go to sleep dirty, his mother had always said. She was right.

# 2

$H$e went to bed and woke up as John Owen Cosatelli.

Sometimes he could go on being John Cosatelli all day. But it was a luxury.

Sometimes he'd be J. Owen, accompanist.

Or Owen Johns on Rhodes Electric Piano, Moog Micro-Moog and Oberheim Polyphonic Synthesizer.

If the Jacey Trio had laid down some studio time he could lie in bed and listen to himself playing cocktail piano on Radio 2 until he fell asleep or threw up.

And sometimes, when the Johnny Cosy Four were booked into a live gig he'd sit up on the stand while other people's smoke got in his eyes, smile at girls who were bored with their escorts, and wonder who the hell he was.

That's when he'd have to check his diary, in between sets.

Professional schizophrenia had begun fourteen years before when he'd come home from a concert tour to find that Wendy was pregnant and there would be no real money coming in until the following autumn. Unlike clinical schizophrenia it was profitable, regular, and you were booked instead of committed.

Otherwise, the same.

By the time the divorce was final the baby was three, he had session dates booked solid for eighteen months ahead, and there was no reason not to play them out and make more. He'd accepted there would be no more serious concerts and just the one recording of the Ravel G Major. He kept up his lessons once a week with Liebensohn simply to remind himself of what he was meant to be before he'd split.

His bank manager loved him but his agent blamed herself for ignoring what she called The Big Mistake. To most people The Big Mistake looked like success, but to her it was failure. Sometimes in the dark hours it looked that way to him, too, but he couldn't deny it was a pleasure to write a check he knew wouldn't bounce.

They'd done it for fun, that was all. A laugh. He and three friends from the London Symphony Orchestra had got into the habit of jamming in a few clubs after hours, sitting in with the guys who did it for blood. One day when it was raining they'd booked a studio and made some tapes—"just to hear ourselves stink," as Baz had put it. But a rep had been in the box and heard them. He duped the tracks and signed the group for his company. Four months later, for two unbelievable weeks, a latin-jazz hybrid they recorded called "Samba Break 6" knocked the Rolling Stones out of Number One in the charts. The Big Mistake had been made.

They'd gone into the recording studio as classical musicians, come out as the Johnny Cosy Four, and found themselves rich.

For a while.

The follow-up disc to "Samba Break 6" also made the charts—it went to Number 47 and then dropped out of sight. So did the Johnny Cosy Four, temporarily. But the damage had been done. They'd tasted money and the other three had bought nice big houses on which mortgage payments had a habit of recurring monthly. Bookings began to be made, wedged in between LSO rehearsals and concerts, and one by one the others dropped out of the orchestra and stuck to jazz full time.

It became imperative to keep the money coming in.

They built up a following and their albums sold respectably if not spectacularly. The success of "Samba Break 6" was never repeated, although separately as session musicians on other pop discs they were occasionally (if anonymously) in the charts.

Meanwhile Johnny's agent, Laynie Black, took her ten percent with a practical professionalism that had nothing to do with her personal feelings in the matter. Her only consolation was that he hadn't used his real name. She never ceased nagging him about "going back," because she cared more about him than her ten percent. He told her that attitude was pure emotionalism. She told him to shut up, made sure he kept up his work with Liebensohn, and bided her time. If he, like all her other clients, hadn't been so crazy about her the continuing campaign would have been irritating. As it was, Johnny Cosy smiled, took the money, and ran.

He found it wasn't so bad, really, if you kept moving. He became Cosy by name, cosy by life-style. And it had a certain air of inevitability about it. Of course, if being successful in monetary terms made life easier in terms of no dunning letters coming through the mailbox, it also exposed areas in which you were *not* successful. Such as why you couldn't sustain a relationship for more than a year without blowing it, or why you sometimes caught arrogance creeping into your conversation, or why you still got depressed without warning, and so on.

That was the kind of thing that kept Baz Bennett boozing.

Those were the things that got them through five drummers in ten years.

Those were the things that Moosh Bailey ate his way around.

Those were the things that Johnny paid himself well not to think about.

\*

The light coming through the gap in the curtains was dim and still tinged with the orange of the streetlights when the phone rang. He flailed at the alarm clock several times before he realized it was innocent, then staggered muttering and goosefleshed into the sitting room.

"Mmmmph?"

"Lemme speak to Miss Lisa," said a gruff, hurried voice.

"What?"

"Lisa . . . put her onna phone, quick."

He blinked and rubbed at his eyes with the back of his hand. "Lisa doesn't live here anymore. Sorry."

"Don't give me that . . . put her on."

"She's not here, I tell you," Johnny said, still sleepy but starting to become irritated.

"Listen, stud, I *know* she's there. Tell her to get her

little ass home before she gets caught. He's coming back a day early."

"Who *is* this?"

"Doesn't matter. Tell her if she doesn't want to get tossed out of a cushy number she should come home *now*. Okay?"

"Get the hell off my phone," Johnny snapped, and slammed down the receiver. That had to have been George, the octopus Lisa told him about, her new boyfriend's "butler." Blearily he peered at his watch. She was taking her time, she must have left the flat a good four hours ago. It didn't take that long to drive back to Berkshire. Was she playing more games somewhere, drinking at one of the all-night clubs, or just tooling around in that juiced-up Mercedes the old fool had given her? Probably that was it. Sailing, she called it—she loved to go sailing up and down the highway in the dark with the windows open, the radio blaring, and the heater blowing up her skirt and between her legs.

He crawled back into bed, wrapping the blankets into a cocoon and waiting for metamorphosis into something resembling a man who'd had enough sleep for once in his life. It didn't work. It never had.


Three hours later he was wandering around the flat stuffing handfuls of dry Quaker Cereal into his mouth and searching for his other shoe when there was a knock at the door.

"Baz?"

"Yeah," came the voice from the other side.

"It's open." He spotted the shoe under the piano and got down on his hands and knees to retrieve it. As he jammed his foot into it and crawled back out, Baz regarded him quizzically from the door, closing it behind him.

"You always put your shoes on under the piano?"

"Only when there's no room in the refrigerator."

Baz looked more hollow-eyed than usual. His short-clipped reddish hair clung damply to his wide forehead, and his mouth was pale. He had a high-angled delicate face tapering to a pointed chin over a body long in bone and short on flesh. "Have we got time for some of your lousy coffee?" he asked edgily.

"We'll make time." Johnny went out and flicked the kettle on, measuring out the coffee powder by feel as he watched Baz wander around the long sitting room. After a moment he disappeared and Johnny could hear him shuffling through the sheet music on the piano.

"What's Liebensohn got you working on this month?"

"The Franck Symphonic Variations."

"Kind of a comedown from the Hammerklavier, isn't it?"

"Not really." Johnny smiled to himself, thinking of the old man crouching like a spider in the corner of that cluttered stuffy living room of his, fingering a faded photograph he could no longer see clearly through his cataracts, talking softly about the music.

His reverie was interrupted simultaneously by the kettle clicking off and Baz's question.

"Why the hell do you go on taking all the crap Liebensohn hands you? You'll never use it . . . and you're always saying how impossible he is . . ."

"Keeps me humble," Johnny said lightly, watching Baz moving around the living room again, tapping things with his fingertips and mumbling to himself. To anyone who didn't know him, Baz might have seemed merely bored, but Johnny's eyes went years deeper than that. Baz was in a bad way, as ready to snap as an overwound string on Moosh's bass fiddle. Johnny added extra sugar to one mug and handed it over.

"The house rule is sit before you drink."

Baz sat and concentrated on the coffee, sipping it rhythmically until it was half gone, then sighing. "It doesn't get any better."

"My coffee or the daylight?"

"Both." Baz slid back on the sofa and balanced the mug on his knee. "How much time do we have to lay down over there?" The Jacey Trio had a taping date at the BBC for some easy-listening spots on the all-night show for Radio 2.

"Only ten numbers. We should be finished by lunchtime if there aren't too many retakes. You going to be okay?" He leaned against the piano and washed down the last of the dry cereal with the scalding coffee.

"I am going to be brilliant," Baz said. "I am *always* at the very peak of my performing ability at eleven o'clock in the goddamn morning."

"Uh-huh. And tonight? What about tonight?"

"Sure. Why not?" Baz quickly drank more of his coffee. Johnny decided he'd better ring Jack Scoular and ask him if he'd stand in. If they were lucky Baz would only disappear for a couple of days. They weren't always lucky.

"How's Molly?"

"Fine."

"The kids?"

"Noisy." He glanced at Johnny, then away, quickly. "They started out being noisy because they were happy, and ended up crying because I'd yelled at them. I don't know which noise was worse. I didn't mean to let fly at them . . . I never mean to hurt anyone. It just happens. And I never know what to say, afterwards."

"'Sorry' usually works."

"Sometimes it's too late for that. I wish . . ."

"What do you wish?"

Baz shrugged as if something were pressing down on his neck. "I wish I knew how to control it."

"People who want to change themselves usually end up changing more than they intended to," Johnny observed wryly. "That temper of yours gives your horn playing a nice, sharp edge. No such thing as a sweet-hearted brass man. Never met one, anyway. Deep down, you're all just as nasty as hell. We put up with you, though."

Baz looked up, startled, then smiled a little as he realized Johnny was just trying to take up some of the strain. "Is that what friends are for?"

"So my old man always tells me. By the time you get home tonight the kids will have forgotten all about it."

Baz sighed and nodded. "I guess I was just tired."

"Musicians' kids learn to lay low in the morning, eventually. Yours will, too. Give them a chance, they're still young."

"The Wise Old Man of Music speaks," Baz said in a sarcastic tone, then peered into his coffee mug. His knuckles were white where they encircled the handle, and Johnny could see that he was nearly choking on all the things he wanted to say and couldn't get out. That had always been Baz's problem, as long as he'd known him. The man was full of pain, but he could only get rid of it through the music, and to him that was its only respectable outlet. What he called his "temper" was mild compared to some Johnny had seen, but every minor outburst made Baz feel guilty for weeks. No doubt he'd simply told his kids to shut up and settle down, no more savagely than any father from behind his morning newspaper. Because he only did it occasionally, they were probably just startled into tears. And yet he was obviously convinced he'd torn them limb from limb, to judge by his reaction. When the pressure mounted up, as it was obviously doing now, his mouth went tight and he couldn't blow a note for release. Then only booze would help. And the moment was here, unfortunately.

"You got anything to go with this coffee?"

"Milk, sugar, aspirin, orange juice."

Baz gave a short laugh. "And if I looked for myself?"

"You'd find milk, sugar, aspirin, orange juice. Sorry."

"Any decent man keeps a bottle around for his friends."

Johnny didn't say anything, just swallowed more coffee and worked a wayward raisin out from behind his molar. Baz looked up.

"You used to."

"Used to what?" He put his empty mug down on a pile of Chopin scores.

"Drink."

"I still do, sometimes."

"No . . . you don't. I've been watching lately. A little wine now and again with a meal, but mostly it's Coke or plain tonic water. Not the boozer I used to know and match—what's the matter, you joined Alcoholics Anonymous or something?"

Johnny grinned. "No, I just got bored with having numb hands." And turned off by seeing what it's doing to you, he added silently.

"Oh." Baz finished his coffee but didn't get up. "You think I should join the AA, Johnny?"

"Can you say it?"

"Say what?"

"I am a drunk. Can you say it?"

Baz opened his mouth, waited to hear if anything came out, then shook his head. "I'm not a drunk, I don't drink *that* much. It's just I have a funny metabolism, sometimes it affects me more than others, that's all."

"Then you don't qualify."

Baz looked relieved. "That's what I told Molly."

Johnny went on. "You don't qualify because you're a liar as well as a drunk. The way I understand it, all the AA wants is your honesty—they'll give you the rest for free." But there was no point in making the point. In this condition Baz was deaf to it. Johnny looked at his watch and grabbed his jacket from the back of the sofa. "Come on, you big cluck—Auntie is waiting. She expects every man to play his best."

After a moment Baz got up, favoring him with the briefest of smiles. "Good old Auntie."

"Amen."

The Spitfire had collected a ticket as usual, and as usual Baz stuffed the offending bit of paper into the glove compartment with all the rest. The morning was bright and cold, the rain-washed air not yet reinfected with the dust and stink the wet pavements were still keeping to themselves. Johnny slid into the passenger seat and reached for the heater control while Baz started the engine. "I knew I should have worn my gloves," he groused, and Baz hesitated before pulling away.

"You want to go back for them?"

Johnny shook his head. "No . . . drive, James, drive."

Baz grunted and pulled away from the curb, automatically flicking on the cassette player when he'd shifted into fourth gear. The small cockpit of the sports car warmed quickly and Johnny stopped rubbing his hands as the strains of the Third Brandenburg filled in the corners. Baz made a turn without shifting down and narrowly missed a taxi. Johnny leaned his head back against the seat, hoping as usual that they'd make the studio at Maida Vale intact. He found himself thinking about Lisa, wondered why, then realized some of her perfume must still be clinging to his jacket.

She hadn't left her key in the bowl, but he didn't think she would be back again. It had seemed very final last night. Their bodies had performed as usual, but he got the impression her head was as far away as his had been.

After the divorce he'd tried burying himself in women. It had been interesting and educational, but not very satisfying, except that he slept better. They did more for the soul but resulted in insomnia—will she? if I? would we? could it? why? why? He was really better off on his own, he knew that. Alone he could keep his head together. He played better, worked better, did everything better. Yesterday morning he'd actually added two pages to the "serious" stack of manuscript paper on the piano and felt good about them. No illusions—they weren't great; he'd long ago accepted his limitations as a composer as he'd accepted a lot of things. Not great, no—but too good to flush away as he usually did, dropping them cere-monially down the toilet, pulling the chain and intoning, "From John thou camest and into the john thou goest." Lisa had resented his composing more than most, but she was totally jazz oriented. Why did all his women resent it when he sat down at the piano and worked at breaking down chords and harmonics instead of playing "Blue

Skies?" It wasn't the noise, he knew it wasn't. The shutting out, that's what they couldn't stand. If he sat down at the piano, or anywhere else in the flat for that matter, Lisa had always taken it as an automatic signal to come over and start playing her own favorite instrument. Flattering, but unproductive, musically speaking. He wondered if she'd got back home yet, before her rich and boring antiques tycoon returned from cornering the market in carved what-nots.

The taping session went as well as could be expected, perhaps even better than expected. Sometimes it was like that, when you didn't give a damn the stuff you threw off sounded right. Or maybe it was the fact that they were all doing it with half a mind and their instincts and experience served them more truly than they might have otherwise. Certainly Baz was riding close to the edge of his control and played with frantic concentration, simply in order to finish the job and get to the nearest pub. Moosh had given Johnny a lifted eyebrow across the piano and mouthed "Call Jack?!" during one of Baz's solos, and Johnny had nodded resignedly. It was getting harder and harder to hold Baz together, and sometimes he found himself wondering if it was worth the effort. Then, as often happened, Baz pulled off something incredible and he decided it was worth it after all. Baz's ability to play not only sax and trumpet, but also nearly every other brass and reed instrument was a major factor in their success. They could work in flute and oboe effects on ballads, even a tuba bounce on a bossa nova if they had a mind to. Baz could handle it all. In fact, the previous night they had been one of the groups featured at a benefit dinner

sponsored by their record company and Baz had made the
audience freeze with their soupspoons halfway to their
mouths by suddenly producing a bassoon solo during
"Moonlight in Vermont" that was enough to bring tears to
the eyes of a stone giraffe. He got jazz licks out of the
damnedest instruments. If he needed booze to do it, he
wasn't the first and he wouldn't be the last. So be it.

In the pub later Moosh and Johnny watched Baz at the
bar surreptitiously pouring a double vodka into his pint
and Moosh made a face.

"He's off schedule. According to my calendar he isn't
due for his period for another couple of weeks yet."

Johnny raised an eyebrow as he wrestled with a bag of
potato chips and succeeded in scattering half of them
across the table as the cellophane suddenly gave way.
"You're keeping track, now?"

"Somebody has to. You're so busy playing footsie with
the famous these days . . ."

"What the hell is that supposed to mean?" Johnny
asked, surprised at the edge in Moosh's voice.

Moosh's eyes rolled in his dark face. "Appearing soon at
the Wigmore Hall, seated at his py-ana, little Johnny Cosy
and his amazing flying fingers, count 'em, folks, only ten."

"Very funny. You know Gessler asked for me as a
favor."

"Yeah—I guess Horowitz was all tied up."

"What am I supposed to do, apologize for the fact
that—"

"You've canceled maybe four or five gigs just so you
could *rehearse* with the old man. Good gigs, too."

Johnny watched Moosh devouring his double helping of
shepherd's pie and beans, the loaded fork disappearing
with such speed and regularity into the cavernous mouth

it was doubtful that Moosh even tasted the food as it passed by on its way to his stomach. Suddenly even chips seemed too much to swallow. "I see. You're coming up short again this month, is that it?"

Moosh shrugged. "I got a lot of mouths to feed, Johnny."

Your own most of all, Johnny thought, then was annoyed with himself for the disloyalty. Moosh had four children and another on the way. Johnny knew Jenny Bailey was a frugal housewife and an excellent manager, yet Moosh always seemed to be in debt, despite the fact that he was constantly busy and well paid. Certainly his work with the Trio and the Quartet weren't his only sources of income, he also worked regularly with the NSO and other outfits. Of the three of them Moosh performed the most, yet was always broke. He made a mental note to send a check to Jenny via Laynie, disguised, as usual, as "royalties," but he was damned if he was going to give it to Moosh direct. He'd made that mistake before, and regretted it. Not the money, he never regretted that, only the fact that Moosh never seemed to pay it back, or even seemed inclined to remember it. The mystery was, where the hell did it all go?

Impulsively, he asked, and got a scowl in return for his curiosity.

"Shoes . . . that's the worst. Shoes and bicycles."

Which was nonsense, and they both knew it. Johnny guessed Moosh had started gambling again, and had probably run up a debt to some shark or other, trying to get even. He started to say something, then thought better of it. He'd have enough trouble playing without Baz that night, there was no point in antagonizing Moosh as well.

"Anyway," Moosh went on, scraping his plate with a

piece of bread crust. "I'm okay for the moment, it's only the *principle* of the thing, that's all I'm saying. Giving up good solid work in order to make union scale sitting behind some old poop playing a fiddle. You've gone past that, Johnny."

"I wouldn't call a Guarnerius del Gesu a 'fiddle,'" Johnny protested mildly. "And I wouldn't call Walter Gessler an 'old poop,' either."

"No, maybe not. Point is . . . jazz is making a comeback, John. Pop is sagging. The kids who don't want to break their ankles in discos are getting into jazz more and more. Schemansky re-released 'Samba Break 6' and is talking good money for next year's contract. People are ready to *listen* again, and we're better than ever, we can get back on top, no trouble."

"I wonder," Johnny said dryly.

"I don't," Moosh said, pushing away his plate and picking up his apple pie in one hand and his pint in the other. "I *know*."

"Well, then my missing a few gigs here and there won't make much difference in the long run, will it?" Johnny asked. "I don't intend to make a habit of it, after all."

"Let's hope not," Moosh said. "I mean, I know you still got serious music in your gut and I respect you for that, but playing Mozart never paid the kind of bills *I* got, that's for sure."

"Mozart did all right out of it, for a while, anyway."

"Then he was the first and last. Come on, Johnny, see sense. Some people make music their life, the rest of us make a living from it. Or try to. All I'm saying is—"

"You've said it," Johnny finished.

Moosh's face drew up like a prune. "No need to get all uptight . . . I got your best interests at heart."

"Sure, sure."

"I mean, maybe you think jazz is beneath you, but you can't complain that it hasn't got you—"

"All *right,* dammit," Johnny snapped. "If I'd thought jazz was 'beneath me' I'd never have gone into it in the first place, as you bloody well know. What's got into you, anyway?"

"Ah . . . nothin'. Sorry. Don't mean to take it out on you, just blowing off my troubles. Pay no mind."

"If you're really strapped . . ."

Moosh had the grace to look embarrassed. "No, I told you, I'm okay now." He glanced up as Baz came toward the table carrying another pint for himself and Moosh, and Johnny's Coke. "Just don't like it when everybody starts getting unpredictable, that's all," he muttered. "Like to know I can count on people."

"Don't we all?" Johnny said quietly.

*

Johnny had arranged to spend the afternoon with Walter Gessler going over the numbers for the recital, but in his early-morning haze he'd forgotten the music and had to ask the cab to make a detour to his flat to collect it.

For all that he had in the bank, Johnny did not live in what could conceivably be termed a luxury neighborhood. Instead he'd bought himself a commercial building on one of the less salutary back streets of Islington. He leased the ground floor warehouse accommodation to a nearby commercial caterer and had the entire second floor for himself. He'd put a lot of money into converting the premises to a flat because it had the great advantage of neighbors who didn't complain when he got up and played Beethoven Sonatas in the middle of the night. They were, respectively, a speciality buttonmaker and a book bindery and were inhabited only from nine to five. He didn't want the upkeep of a house and garden to bother with, and took cabs everywhere after working out it was cheaper than owning a car he couldn't park closer than three streets from where he lived, no parking zones being the rule almost everywhere in London these days.

Two men were leaning against the door of the stairs to his flat. He'd never seen them before, but they seemed to be watching for him. He asked the cabby to wait, climbed out and started searching for his keys.

"You Cosatelli?" one of the men asked. He recognized the gruff voice from the early-morning phone call.

"Yes . . ." he said cautiously, standing by the cab.

"She still inside, sleeping you off?" George was a bull-necked type with no forehead, lots of wiry black curls, and an impressive line in jaw structure and scowls.

"I told you on the phone, Lisa isn't with me."

George looked him up and down like a buyer at Smithfield's. "Yeah, sure." He turned to his equally unprepossessing friend. "I guess what *he's* got don't show when he's put his pants on." The other man muttered something in return and George laughed.

Johnny turned to the cabby, who was watching this confrontation with interest. "I'm going up to my flat to collect something and I'm going to allow these two beauty queens to go with me to prove something. If I'm not back down in three minutes, would you please call the police on that radio of yours?" He reached into his pocket and handed the cabby a fiver.

"Sure, mate." The cabby took the fiver and osten-
tatiously looked at his watch. "Three minutes . . . you're
on."

"Gentlemen . . . since you don't believe me, why not
see for yourselves?" Johnny suggested, pushing between
them and unlocking the door. They thudded up the stairs
after him, made a show of looking around the flat while he
gathered up the various manuscripts from the piano.
"Satisfied?" he asked blandly when they emerged from the
second bedroom that was rarely used except to store things
he was too lazy to throw out.

"I see you like to dress up in girl's clothes," George
sneered.

"They're some of Lisa's things. Maybe you'd like to take
them, since you're here. If you think you're strong enough
to handle a duffel bag."

"Lissen—" George began angrily.

"I *have* listened, and I'm bored to the teeth with it. Lisa
is not my woman or my responsibility anymore, so you can
just get yourselves the hell out of it before my friend
downstairs puts in that call. And if he asks you can tell
your boss that as far as I'm concerned, Lisa is all his and
he's welcome to her." Lisa had told him about Mark
Claverton's insane jealousy and he was damned if he was
going to cause her trouble. It looked like she had enough
of that already.

George started forward, but his companion grabbed his
arm and hustled him down the stairs. By the time Johnny
had locked the flat and reached the street, they'd disappeared. He climbed back into the cab with an irritated
slam of the door. The cabby glanced at him in the mirror,
then pulled away from the curb.

"Okay?" he asked, after a minute.

"As okay as it ever gets," Johnny grumbled, then looked up. "Thanks."

The cabby shrugged and pulled out to go around a truck that was unloading at the curb. "They didn't look like insurance salesmen."

Johnny laughed. "Neither do you, but you sold a little."

"Looking for some girl, were they?" the cabby probed.

When Johnny bent his head to sort through his music without answering, the cabby blew his horn at a bus and shrugged again. "Cheyne Walk, you said?"

"That's right," Johnny said absently, shuffling pages. "Cheyne Walk."

# 3

"A man is helping the police with their enquiries."

God knows he'd read the euphemism often enough, nodded, said to himself "They've got him," and slept easier, comforted by the strength of the long arm of the law.

Well, he now knew the law consisted of a small bleak room with a table and chairs, empty paper cups that had once held metallic tea with too much sugar, a very bright overhead light, sounds of people talking and typing somewhere down the hall, and a man with a very cold pair of green eyes.

And he didn't feel one damn bit comforted.

He kept looking at his watch, which was probably a very bad thing to do under the circumstances, but he couldn't help it. It was either the watch, the empty paper cups, or the green eyes. He preferred the watch, even though it seemed to have stopped.

They'd found the battered body of Lisa Mary Kendrick in an empty lot somewhere in Highgate. Her purse was gone and it had taken them thirty-six hours to identify her. She had been beaten and her neck had been broken.

According to the preliminary medical report she'd died of the broken neck around five in the morning of February 26. Some two hours, in fact, after leaving Johnny's flat.

It had taken them a few more hours to get around to Johnny, and for reasons they still hadn't spelled out they seemed to think he was the murderer. They'd picked him up outside a theater where he'd been rehearsing. He cooperated because it didn't occur to him not to. They'd been extremely interested in the state of his hands, especially the fingernails, his face, and had even asked him to strip and had taken scrapings and samples from his body. They seemed disappointed to find that under his clothing there was only the hairy chest he'd always had, unmarked except for three small chickenpox scars on his left shoulder blade.

Detective Inspector Gates—he of the cold green eyes— had informed him that he had a right to call a solicitor, didn't have to perform any of the indignities they requested of him, could spit in their eyes if he wished, although the implication was that it wouldn't look terribly clever.

Johnny neither refused, spat in their eyes, or called a solicitor. He simply did what they asked, answered their questions, and stayed locked inside himself looking out.

From the time he was a child anger had turned him to ice.

No bellowing, no screaming, no red-faced grimaces. Cold, just cold, all over. It had stood him in good stead with the bully boys of the schoolyard who found it laughable that someone with his build could actually prefer Rachmaninof to rugby. Especially in the Rhondda. The games of "get Cosatelli" never lasted long, however.

Not if they looked him straight in the face. If cornered he would fight, could fight, did fight. Fortunately for his hands, it rarely came to that.

Now, however, he met his own eyes in Gates' face. Green rather than blue, but cut from the same glacier.

It was "get Cosatelli" all over again.

"Let's go over it once more," said the thin mouth that went with the green eyes. So he went over it once more, carefully, neutrally, as calmly as he could, as if reciting lessons in a language he'd learned by rote. A language other than his own.

"I met her about two years ago. She came into the club with friends of my trumpet player. We got introduced and talked between sets, nothing much. A few nights later she came back on her own and we talked some more. She got in the habit of coming in, staying after. Maybe a month later, she moved in with me."

"You fell in love?"

He thought about it, shook his head. "Not the way you mean, no hearts and flowers. There was a strong physical attraction, we got on well . . . it just happened. You know how it is."

"No, tell me how it is."

"How it was." She was dead, she was dead, she was dead.

"How it was, then."

"It was easier than saying 'my place or yours' every goddamned night, that's how it was," he said harshly.

"Did you want to marry her?"

"No. She knew that, there was never any question of marriage. I'm divorced and I don't intend to make another mistake. Anyway, she wasn't the kind of girl you put in an apron and expect to knit you a pot roast every Sunday."

"She was a very beautiful girl, from her pictures," the Inspector said softly.

"Tall and tan and young and lovely," Johnny agreed evenly.

"Incredible body. Fantastic body."

It was a probe, they both knew it, and he didn't let it get inside. "She was a very beautiful girl because she worked at it. It was all she had going for her. She wanted to be an actress. I offered to pay for drama school, but she couldn't pass any of the auditions. So she did some modeling."

"Nude modeling?"

Johnny smiled briefly. "No. Too skinny. She was ideal for high fashion, a racehorse, she called herself. All cheekbones and long legs. She moved well, had that narcissistic thing about her body the good ones have. Being looked at turned her on."

"And did looking at her turn you on?"

"It turned most men on. There was a kind of animal sexiness in her, standing up with her knees together always looked like a temporary occupation as far as she was concerned. Even so . . . there was nothing cheap about her. She was a very classy bird . . . as long as she kept her mouth shut. And she didn't come easy, no matter what she looked like."

"She came easy enough for you . . . a month, you said, and she'd moved in."

Johnny shrugged. "I got lucky." He moved one of the empty cups around, set it into another. "All we had was good sex and a few laughs, okay? She liked me, I liked her, but I wasn't what she intended to do for the rest of her life and we both accepted that, no illusions."

"And then she walked out on you for somebody else. That must have hurt, illusions or no illusions."

Johnny looked at Gates and tried to figure out how he could explain that it hadn't hurt at all, without sounding either callous or a liar. "Look," he said, leaning forward onto the table. "Let me ask you something, Inspector. Did you ever have a woman who wanted sex more than you did?"

"I've led a very sheltered life," was the dry reply.

Johnny gave a short, rueful laugh. "Yeah, well I haven't, and believe me, that was a problem I'd never had to deal with before. I even started to understand the Women's Lib bunch—that stuff about being a Sex Object, you know? At first . . . great, terrific, all for it. But after a while . . ." He sighed, seeing Gates' disbelief and amusement. "I guess it doesn't do a lot for my macho image, does it? But I've got a brain and I've got talent and I've even got a heart, how about that? Very touching, very meaningful. All Lisa wanted from me was my cock and you know what that's like, after a while? When you've done it every which way but at separate tables . . . and there's nothing to go with it, for God's sake? I'll tell you—it's boring. Just that. Boring and tiring and even some kind of ass-backwards insult, come to think of it. I liked her, I liked taking her to bed, and I liked it even better when she left because I could actually sleep all through the night once in a while without having to perform. *That's* what it was like." He stared at the nested cups and smiled, briefly. "Or maybe it's just that I'm getting past it, hey?"

"Maybe." Gates didn't seem amused somehow. If there was anything in his eyes, it might have been recognition. Of what, Johnny couldn't have said.

"Anyway, when she met Claverton and he started coming on with the big presents and all that crap, I was almost relieved. I was also actually glad for her. She was like a kid let loose in Harrod's with all her father's credit cards. The big house, the flashy friends . . . all that made her feel important. It would hardly have made her feel important if I'd told her she was boring me out of my mind. When she left, it was good for both of us."

"But she came back," Gates said.

Johnny sighed. "Yes, she came back now and then. Claverton is nearly sixty . . . she couldn't get everything she needed with credit cards."

"That must have done *something* for your macho image," Gates observed.

"It was cheaper than paying for it."

"Oh?"

Johnny's hand suddenly crushed the paper cups. "I didn't mean that the way it sounded. I told you, I *liked* her. And with me, well—she didn't have to pretend to be anything except what she was. Sometimes I got the feeling it wasn't for sex at all, but just for . . . comfort. None of Claverton's friends liked her and they sure didn't 'approve' of her. I think she was lonely out there in that big house. The only people she had anything in common with was the servants, and Claverton didn't think much of her spending time with *them*. She was just an ordinary girl, no matter what she looked like. Just an ordinary girl."

"She had a juvenile record," Gates said, glancing at the file on the table.

"Two counts of shoplifting," Johnny snorted. "Big deal, she was only a kid when that happened. Teenage rebellion, isn't that what they call it?"

"*We* call it thieving," Gates said.

His tone annoyed Johnny. "If you look at that file a little closer, you'll see that both her parents died in a car crash when she was fourteen. It hit her hard, she had to go to live with her grandmother and it took them a little while to get it together. When Lisa got pulled in for that shoplifting business her grandmother came through in spades, stood by her all the way. Lisa didn't get into any trouble after that."

"No trouble with *us*, anyway," Gates said, turning over a page. "Her social worker said her morals left a lot to be desired."

"I'll bet. Social workers can be a pain in the ass. Lisa was a beautiful girl . . . she learned early there are other ways of getting what you want than stealing them. I don't condemn her for that, why should you? And if you're trying to imply she was a whore, forget it. She wasn't."

"Just 'high-spirited'?" Gates said wryly.

"*Yes*, as a matter of fact. That's *exactly* what she was."

"I thought you said you didn't love her."

"Of course I loved her, but there are lots of kinds of love. I loved her honesty about herself, her realistic attitude, her sense of humor, her hunger for luxury, her natural good taste . . ." He saw Gates raise an eyebrow. "Does that surprise you? She could spot a phony a mile off, people or things. She told me once that Claverton said she had 'the eye' . . . and in his business that's a valuable commodity. He's an antique dealer, pictures, furniture . . . that's how they met. She went into his gallery to buy me a birthday present. There was a framed piece of music manuscript in the window and she thought it would be nice for me, but when they took it out for her, she told them it was a fake."

"Did she know about . . ."

"She didn't have a clue. She just *knew*, that's all. So they had somebody check it out, and damned if she wasn't right. That impressed him. That and her knockers, I suppose."

"I gather you don't think much of Mark Claverton."

"I never met the man. Haven't a thing against him . . ."

"Except he stole your girl."

"In which case, I should be in here for murdering *him*, not her."

"I see the grandmother died last year," Gates said abruptly.

"Yes. Last June." The memory hurt a little, even now. It had been the one time in their relationship that he'd been able to give Lisa more than the usual. Her grandmother's unexpected death had really broken her up, and for a while she'd needed him. They'd been close, the closest they ever were. But it passed. "She—the grandmother—was only sixty-seven. I got the impression bringing up Lisa had shortened her years a little, although she was a hell of a woman."

"You knew her?"

"You could hardly know Lisa and not know Nicki . . . we saw her a couple of times a month, mostly on Sundays. Lisa saw her more often, of course. She only lived in Harrow."

"You mean you went home to her grandmother's for Sunday *lunch?*" Gates asked, raising an eyebrow.

"You mean when we weren't screwing or lying around drunk or shooting up with the other junkies? I see you have the usual ideas about musicians and models. Let me lay out our wild life-style for you, Inspector. Maybe two Sundays we'd see Nicki . . . Lisa's grandmother. Maybe one Sunday a month we'd go down to *my* parents for the day. And one Sunday a month we'd have my daughter over or take her out someplace. Cops aren't the only people with families. I'm still very close to my parents, and Lisa was close to Nicki, and I love my daughter very much. I'd see her more if I could, but . . . her mother makes the rules. It doesn't matter what I do for a living, I'm half Welsh, half Italian—family counts with me. I don't see what's so damn funny about that."

"I didn't say it was funny—" Gates began.

"But it wasn't what you expected, right? Sorry to disappoint you."

"You don't disappoint me, Cosatelli, you interest me. Italians can be very passionate people, the men can be very possessive about their—"

Johnny started to laugh, partly from amusement, mostly from exhaustion. "Next you'll be saying I'm in the Mafia. For crying out loud . . . I'm an ordinary, middle-class middle-aged middle-sized guy. You won't find 'Omerta' printed on my underwear, just St. Michael's hundred-percent cotton. What the hell are you trying to build up here?"

"I'm trying to build up the facts in a murder enquiry, Mr. Cosatelli," Gates said sharply. "I'm trying to find out the kind of woman Lisa Kendrick was, the kind of friends she had, the reasons why somebody savagely beat her to death and left her sprawled in a patch of weeds for a milkman to find. That's what I'm trying to do."

Johnny closed his eyes. "Okay, okay."

Gates darted his thin fingers into the file and extracted something, sliding it across the table. "That's what I'm working on, Mr. Cosatelli. Take a look."

Johnny opened his eyes, looked, wished he hadn't. It

was a full-color eight by ten glossy photograph of Lisa as she'd been found. At least, he assumed it was Lisa, there was little to recognize in the battered half-clothed thing that lay spread-eagled among the frozen stalks of ragweed. "Jesus Christ," he breathed, closed his eyes again, and tried to close his throat against the impulse to vomit.

After a moment Gates drew the picture back and replaced it in the file. He regarded Cosatelli thoughtfully. That he had been shocked and horrified was obvious . . . it's difficult to fake every ounce of blood draining from your face. On the other hand, murderers could be as shocked as anyone by being shown what they had done in darkness and rage. And she *had* been with him that night.

"You say she left your place about two A.M.?" he asked after a minute had passed. The color hadn't returned to Cosatelli's square, strong-jawed face, but he'd stopped swallowing so convulsively.

"About that . . . I was asleep but I woke up when she went out. I guess she slammed the door."

"Why would she slam the door?"

"*What?*" Cosatelli's voice was ragged.

"I said why would she slam the door. Did you have an argument? Was she angry?"

"No," Johnny whispered. He cleared his throat and repeated it. "No . . . not an argument. I'd . . . I'd told her that I didn't want her to come back like that anymore. I didn't think it was any good for her, and it sure as hell wasn't any good for me. I never knew when she was going to turn up . . . she'd walk in and expect . . . I work hard, I need to concentrate . . . and . . ." he trailed off.

"And?"

Johnny took a deep breath, glanced quickly to see if the photograph was still there, then kept his eyes open, relieved. When he spoke his voice was a little stronger. "And it played merry hell with my social life. Once I brought someone home and Lisa was already there . . ."

"A woman?"

"Yeah, a woman. *She* didn't stay around for explanations."

"So from being someone you loved, Lisa Kendrick had become an annoyance to you, is that it?"

"If you like."

"Someone you wanted to get rid of?"

Johnny looked at him coldly. "Someone I preferred to ring me up before coming around. Someone who no longer had a right to barge in and out of my life whenever she felt like it."

"Well, she won't be doing that anymore, will she, Cosatelli?" Gates asked softly.

"No." Johnny shook his head. "No," he said bleakly. "She won't be doing that anymore."

"So, either way, you're rid of her."

"I didn't *want* to be 'rid of her.' I told you, I liked her. I just wanted our relationship to be on a different basis, that's all. Dammit, she left my place around two-thirty in the morning on her own feet, alive as hell. I didn't kill her, I had no wish to kill her, but frankly I would be very happy to kill whoever *did* do that to her, and you can put that into your goddamn notebook if you like."

"Why?"

"Why what?"

"Why would you want to kill whoever murdered her?"

Johnny stared at him. "Let's just say I have a highly developed sense of social responsibility. I don't like people who litter up the city with dead bodies, it lowers the tone of the environment." Suddenly, as Gates stared at him, unsmiling, the concept of confessing to something just to get it all over with didn't seem as farfetched as when he read about it. And he did read about it, saw it in films and on TV, and my God, here he was, right here in this hard room on this hard chair with this hard bastard across the table thinking he was a killer and it was just the way they said it was, just exactly the way they said.

Nasty.

"I didn't kill Lisa," he said firmly, and decided not to say any more. He kept imagining the way she must have lain there in that filthy field while he slept in his bed, perhaps with her eyes open to the sky but blind, perhaps with some of himself inside her, perhaps her dress . . . he couldn't even remember the color of her dress, they'd never put the lights on, he couldn't even . . .

"Mark Claverton seems to think you did," Gates said.

"Does he?" he asked, dully. So Claverton thought he killed her. Well, why not? Everybody else did. "And that's why I'm here, is it? Because some rich toffee-nosed bastard tells you I should be?"

Gates' mouth tightened and he seemed suddenly fascinated by one corner of the ceiling. "No, Mr. Cosatelli," he said evenly. "You're here because we're conducting a murder investigation and to the best of our knowledge you are the last person to have seen Lisa Kendrick alive. You have both a possible motive and clear opportunity against you. We would have asked you for a statement whether Mr. Claverton had accused you or not."

"Wow. You'd have thought of it all by your little selves, would you?" Johnny said sarcastically, and Gates faced him again.

"Don't," he warned softly.

"Don't what?"

"Don't play smart-ass, Mr. Cosatelli. It won't get you anywhere and it might just change my impression of you."

"Oh? What's your impression of me, then?" Johnny asked wearily. Five hours he'd been in this bloody room. Five years, five centuries, maybe.

"My *impression* is that you're a man who would like to cry and doesn't quite know how to let go enough to do it. My *impression* is that you are shocked and stunned by the death of Lisa Kendrick. My *impression* is that you did not kill her."

Johnny looked at him for a long time, then sighed. "Got it in three, Inspector. I guess it must look like I don't care she's dead, but I do, I care like hell about it. I just don't seem able to—" He closed his eyes. "I guess I feel guilty because it seems she deserves more from me than she's getting. More than just regret or sorrow. I want to feel rage and pain and anger . . . I want to feel *bad*, but—"

"You will, eventually. It's shock, that's all. I see it all the time. You said you have a heart, didn't you?"

"I'm very poetic under stress," Johnny said, tasting bitterness.

"You're better off without one, sometimes."

"Oh?" It seemed an odd thing for a police officer to say. He seemed an odd cop altogether, in fact. Johnny took another look at him—tall, blond, skinny, well-dressed but tired. Suit, shirt and eyes, all tired. A better class of accent than he would have expected. Gates was obviously educated, intelligent, articulate, and tough as hell. No getting around that. Tough as hell and then some. "You've got a heart, have you?"

"Only on my days off," Gates said.

"Where do you put it when you go to work?"

A smile suddenly compressed the corners of the green eyes. "In a jar by the door, where else?"

Song lyric references to suit the suspect, yet—Gates was a changeling and no mistake. Or was he just trying another ploy, using sympathy to catch his suspect off-guard? Johnny said nothing, and Gates leaned back and fished a pack of cigarettes out of his jacket pocket, offered one. Johnny shook his head—his mouth was so dry a cigarette would have simply sealed his tongue to the roof of his mouth. Gates lit one and blew a long stream of smoke that bounced off the cover of the open file on the table between them. Finally he spoke.

"I don't like to waste time, Mr. Cosatelli. I've wasted something like—" he glanced at his watch. "Something like five hours questioning you when I could have much more profitably been doing something else."

"Wasting time? You mean you finally believe I didn't do it?"

"I think it's possible . . . but unlikely."

"Then I can go?"

Gates stood up. "As soon as you've signed a formal statement, yes. But don't go far without telling us, Mr. Cosatelli. Just in case."

"Just in case what?"

"In case I'm wrong. I've been wrong before."

"I'll keep that in mind, Inspector."

"Good. Then that will make two of us, won't it?" Gates said quietly.


He was coming down the steps, looking into the cold shadows of the near empty street for a cab when an old but immaculately maintained Rolls Silver Cloud pulled up at the curb and two men got out. Turning up his collar, Johnny moved diagonally away to the foot of the steps, glancing at his watch. He would be late for the gig, but a phone call had calmed the club owner. He'd spotted a cab and was about to wave it down when a violent blow between the shoulder blades sent him lurching into the side of a police car parked on the double yellow line in front of the station. A uniformed officer in the passenger seat looked up from the report he was filling out on a clipboard, as startled as Johnny.

Somebody grabbed his left arm and whirled him around. One of the men from the Rolls was behind him, moving in to stand nearly nose to nose, glaring, shouting, drops of spit flying from his mouth into Johnny's. The attack was so sudden and unexpected that he couldn't for the life of him make out what the man was screaming. The car door behind him pushed against his back as the uniformed officer tried to get out.

"You killed her . . . you bastard . . . killed her . . ." the man was screaming. In the yellow glare of the iodide streetlights his face had a ghastly purple hue, his teeth like gray stones in a cave, his eyes bulging with the pressure of his rage. Johnny tried to pry his arm free but couldn't.

"Killed her . . . killed her . . ." the man raved on as his companion tried to pull him off. The uniformed officer, who had apparently crawled across and got out of the driver's side, was now also dragging at Johnny's infuriated accuser. With his free hand the screaming man suddenly struck at Johnny's face, one of his big-stoned rings drawing blood.

"Jesus . . ." Johnny gasped, ducking his head back

before the hand could strike again. The uniformed officer twisted the man's arm behind him. Panting and struggling, Mark Claverton—for this had to be Mark Claverton—stared wildly at Johnny, hate twisting his handsome features into a gargoyle mask.

Wiping at his face with his sleeve, Johnny gaped at Claverton, too dazed to do anything more constructive. The uniformed officer danced a gradually suppressive accompaniment to Claverton's gyrations as he attempted to strike at Johnny once more.

"Take it easy . . . just . . . bloody . . . stop it . . ." panted the cop.

"For heaven's sake, Mark . . . control yourself," said Claverton's companion, a sleek handsome man several years his junior. Claverton's vicuna coat and white silk scarf were already askew on his big frame and his carefully shaped homburg had fallen to the pavement.

"What's he doing out here?" Claverton demanded wildly of nobody in particular. "He should be in a cell . . . I was told they'd arrested him."

The officer tightened his grip and looked at Johnny. "What's your version?"

"Inspector Gates' version, you mean," Johnny answered, eyeing Claverton warily as he straightened from his undignified sprawl against the police car. "I came in voluntarily, made my statement, and was told I was free to go. *I* didn't kill her, Claverton. Did you?"

The cop nearly lost his hold as the big man made another sudden lunge which Johnny managed to sidestep.

"Kill who?" the cop wanted to know.

"Mr. Claverton is stricken with grief, officer, he doesn't know what he's doing or saying," the other man intervened smoothly before Claverton could begin another tirade. "His fiancée has been murdered . . . I'm sure you understand . . . the shock . . ."

"All *I* understand is that he attacked this man. It was an unprovoked assault and he can be charged with it. Do you wish to make a charge, sir?"

"No . . . forget it," Johnny said, the cut on his face continuing to bleed despite the constant application of his sleeve. "He's obviously off his head . . . forget it."

"*I* won't leave it, you can count on that, Cosatelli," Claverton snarled. "If they don't get you, I will . . . I swear . . ."

"That's enough of *that!*" the officer snapped. "You're only making it worse . . . *I* can prefer charges if nobody else wants to."

"What's all this?" The driver of the police car had returned.

Tersely his partner explained and the second officer, older and more cautious, looked carefully at Claverton and then at Johnny. "You better come inside, all of you."

"I don't want to press charges," Johnny protested. "I'm already late as it is . . . just forget it, for God's sake . . ."

But the second officer wouldn't wear it. "That's a bad cut you've got there, sir, somebody'd better take a look at it."

It was easier to go in than to stand there arguing.

Claverton pulled away angrily and retrieved his hat from the pavement. He and the other man marched up the stairs without a backward glance, and Johnny followed, accompanied by the officer who had pulled Claverton off. He looked sideways at Johnny.

"Looks like you got yourself an enemy," he said carefully.

Johnny wiped at his face once more and inspected his

sleeve. "Looks like I'm going to have a big bill for dry cleaning, too. I guess it just isn't my night."

"That wasn't a very clever thing to do, Mr. Claverton," Gates said quietly. Claverton didn't reply but sat hunched and sulky in a chair in front of the desk.

"I'm sure Mark regrets it already, Inspector Gates," Lewis Manvers said silkily, giving a good imitation of sincere disappointment at the actions of a recalcitrant child. "Miss Kendrick's death has affected him deeply . . . it was an impulse born of grief, nothing more."

"The officer said he also verbally threatened Mr. Cosatelli," Gates commented.

"Again . . . words spoken in the heat of the moment, quite meaningless. Mr. Claverton is an emotional man and—"

"Why haven't you arrested that little bastard?" Claverton interrupted suddenly. Gates looked at him coolly.

"Because I have no evidence on which to base a charge, Mr. Claverton. None whatsoever."

"She was with him that night, wasn't she?"

Gates glanced at Manvers briefly, then back at Claverton. "Yes, she was. But she left several hours before she was killed."

"Or so he *claims,* you mean."

"There's no evidence to indicate otherwise."

"Evidence? *Evidence?* What evidence do you need . . . the man's a fly-by-night musician, probably some kind of pervert, they all are, junkies and drunks . . ." Claverton was working himself up again and Manvers reached across to put a precautionary hand on his arm. Claverton shrugged it off.

Gates sighed. "On the contrary, Mr. Claverton, Mr. Cosatelli is a respected member of his profession, a decent man who works hard and has achieved something of a reputation, to say nothing of a considerable income, both as a performer and as a composer."

"Who told you *that* . . . Cosatelli?"

"No. As a matter of fact I've spoken to his agent and to an official of the Musicians' Union, both of whom said the same thing."

"Next you'll tell me you talked to his mother about him," Claverton sneered. "Did his agent, whom he pays, I might point out, tell you about his reputation with women? He goes through them like salted peanuts. He's insatiable, a goat. He was always calling Lisa, getting her to come around, he had some kind of hold on her . . . some kind of sexual hold . . . he's—"

"Mr. Claverton," Gates snapped and Claverton halted in midflight at his tone. "I am quite capable of conducting an investigation into Mr. Cosatelli and anyone else connected with this enquiry. I need neither your accusations nor your instructions."

"Mark didn't mean to imply—" Manvers began.

"I certainly *did* mean to imply," Claverton said sharply. "Lisa has been dead for almost two days and nothing has been done about it, nothing at all. I pay taxes that pay your salary, Gates, and—"

"Mr. Cosatelli pays taxes, too," Gates responded. "Even if he didn't, even if he *were* what you call a 'fly-by-night' he would be entitled to the full protection of the law. I don't like men who behave as you're behaving, Mr. Claverton." He waved a hand at Manvers, who started to protest. "I have every sympathy and I'm assuming that grief has temporarily made you forget both good sense and good manners. Cosatelli has every right to lodge a complaint against you and frankly I'm surprised he hasn't. That alone should tell you something about him."

"Perhaps he'd simply prefer to avoid *any* involvement with the law, in case it throws a spotlight onto him," Manvers suggested.

Gates stared at him. "Perhaps."

"I mean to say, the girl was attractive, I don't deny that, but frankly she was not all she should have been," Manvers went on smoothly. "Cosatelli may not have been her *only* extracurricular activity." There was a wordless growl from Claverton. "Well, I'm sorry, Mark, but you knew my opinion before and I won't change it now to suit come convention about the dead. She wasn't good enough for you, no matter *what* she looked like. No background, no education . . . appearances can be deceiving, that's all I'm saying."

"Which is why we stick to facts," Gates said flatly. "As yet there is no evidence to connect Cosatelli with the act of murder itself, although he could conceivably have had a motive and he undoubtedly had an opportunity. Theoretically so did everyone else in London, of course."

"What do you mean . . . no evidence 'as yet'?" Claverton said, his sulk changing to interest.

"I meant the investigation is proceeding . . . there are forensic reports not yet completed, people not yet interviewed, that kind of thing."

"Then some evidence *could* turn up . . ." Claverton murmured.

"Oh, yes," Gates said. "Things are always turning up; one way and another."

"I did *not* 'keep calling her,'" Johnny protested as the duty police surgeon put butterfly strips over the edges of the wound. Claverton's ring had cut his cheek to the bone just under the left eye. "As a matter of fact all my calls go through an answering service. I suggest you check with them to see how many times she called *me*. I don't even know Claverton's number, for Pete's sake, and if I had I wouldn't have been dumb enough to call her there because she told me what a jealous nut he was. So where did I 'keep calling her'?"

"That's quite a cut," Gates observed, sidestepping the question.

"I always wanted a saber scar," Johnny muttered around the medic's ministrations. "Think it will impress people?"

"I doubt it."

Johnny twisted his face a little to feel if it still worked. It did, but it hurt. As the surgeon went over to wash his hands, Johnny looked at Gates speculatively. "Claverton seems awfully eager to get me arrested for this, doesn't he?"

"Does he?"

"Hell, yes. I mean, that was an outright lie about me calling Lisa. So what other lies is he telling . . . was he really in Birmingham when she was killed?"

"Yes, he was. We checked with the hotel."

"Oh." Johnny hitched himself down from the treatment table, staggered a little and grabbed for the edge to steady himself. Gates reached out, too, but missed. "I'm all right," Johnny said irritably. "I just lost my balance. Thanks for the patchwork," he said to the medic.

"Sure . . . it makes a change from taking urine samples," the surgeon said. "I'll just give you a tetanus shot."

"A . . . what?" Johnny said uneasily as the doctor

selected a disposable syringe from a drawer. He went a
little paler as the needle was uncapped and caught the
light from overhead. Glancing over at Gates, who now
looked amused, he leaned back against the treatment table
and folded his arms.

"Do I get a sweet afterward?" he asked obstinately.

"Only if you don't cry," the medic grinned.

"Always a goddamn catch somewhere," Johnny muttered and closed his eyes.


His arrival at the club caused a minor sensation
backstage because they all assumed the police had caused
the damage to his face. They seemed almost disappointed
to hear it had been Claverton. He told them what had
happened, wearily, then went out and played some really
rotten sets. He was past caring.

He kept waiting for the reaction Gates had promised
would come, but it didn't arrive. Moosh offered him a lift
home but he said he'd rather walk. At every streetcorner
he paused, searched the street and himself for some sign
that Lisa was dead, couldn't find it. There were no ghost
riders in the sky, no stars falling on Alabama, nothing.
Come on, you bastard, he urged, let's shed a tear, let's
vomit, let's do *something*. She's dead, murdered, gone. Just
two nights ago you were doing what's called making love to
the lady—where's the love now? And got stuck, for his
efforts, with the song going through his head over and
over, spinning like a top: Where is the love? In the
morgue. Goodbye.

Again he didn't turn on the lights in the flat, got himself
a Coke from the fridge without spilling anything this time,
wandered around holding the tin. He didn't want to sit

down. As he passed the window he paused and looked down into the street.

There was a car parked across the street. He saw the glow of a cigarette in the dark sedan and stifled an irrational impulse to lift the sash and shout a friendly "good night" to the two plainclothes detectives in the front seat.

Gates *was* a cop, after all. No evidence to hold him? Relax, Cosatelli, relax, you're off the hook? I think you're innocent, I think you're swell, I think you're the nicest piano player in town? Uh-huh. *Sure.*

Well, he could stand there all night, staring down at the men staring up at him, or he could go to bed. He went to bed, found he was still surrounded by her perfume on the sheets, got up, started to pull the sheets off, found he was crying, found he was cursing in Italian, Welsh, and Anglo-Saxon, found he cared after all, found he didn't have any clean sheets in the linen cupboard because the laundry didn't come until Friday, wore the blankets like a hair shirt all night long, found that if you itched it meant you were alive and that made it even worse.

He went to bed as John Owen Cosatelli and woke up feeling like hell.

# 4

His father called just after nine. Italian by birth, Welsh by virtue of having settled there permanently after the War, Dom's words had an odd mixture of intonations and accents that were totally unique. "We saw about Lisa in the papers this morning. I'm sorry, son."

"Was my name in the papers?" Johnny asked apprehensively. There was a long silence.

"No . . . should it have been?" Dom asked carefully.

"Well, the police questioned me. I saw her just a few hours before . . . before she was killed. It was nothing," he added hurriedly. "I just made a statement and signed it, that's all."

Another moment's silence. "Would you like to come home for a time, John?"

He closed his eyes. For an instant, just an instant, there was nothing he wanted more. "No need, Da, I'm fine. I have a lot of work, probably better to get on with it. Thanks."

"If you need anything, you'll ring." It wasn't a question.

"Yes."

They talked for a while longer, and then Johnny said

goodbye, cutting his direct line to comfort with a slight ping as he replaced the receiver. He didn't have anything scheduled until later that afternoon, so he pulled on some jeans and a sweater and went out for fresh bread and the papers. There was still a car parked across the street but it was blue instead of dark green. The men inside suddenly made a big deal about sharing a newspaper.

Pantoni's, the little shop on the corner, was so out of place in the neighborhood that he often wondered how it survived. It was a fragrant cave, narrow and dark, so jammed to overflowing that the shelves seemed to lean together overhead. The only cans that ever shone bright were of baked beans, soups, canned peas and carrots. All the other rare and exotic offerings seemed as permanent as the shelves themselves. Facing the door was a glass-fronted refrigerated counter holding thick-rinded cheeses, fresh salads, dark knobbly salamis and fat-studded mortadellas, wonderful pickles and olives. They all scented the cave and invariably made his mouth water the minute he entered, whether he was hungry or not.

Piled high next to the cash register and scale were crusty rolls and loaves that steamed slightly in the cold air he brought in with him. Along one wall was a shallow wooden rack with newspapers and magazines, and on the floor in front of it were boxes holding melons, green peppers, onions, potatoes—vegetables that changed from season to season, some of which he had to ask Rosa to name and explain how to cook.

After Lisa had left him Johnny had suddenly decided to punish himself for past sensual indulgences by becoming a vegetarian. The simple truth was that the taste and texture of meat had begun to repel him. He'd begun sampling the cans with indecipherable contents and more of the odd things in the bins. Week by week, he and Rosa were adventuring down his alimentary tract. Long ago, when she'd learned he was half Italian, she'd adopted him. Lisa had not been approved of, naturally—she bleached her hair, she wasn't Italian, and she hadn't looked after him properly. He had mothers all over the place.

This morning, however, Rosa was occupied when he came in. He was glad to see her toothache was better—the other morning her face had been swollen lopsided with it. She looked up and smiled, then went back to her conversation with the woman at the counter. Johnny glanced at them as he collected the papers. He'd seen the woman in the shop several times before. She occasionally bought something, but she was not really a customer. She looked businesslike and efficient and always put her purchases into the briefcase she seemed to carry instead of a handbag. He'd decided she was probably some kind of inspector from the Department of Health or something, but she and Rosa seemed on friendly terms. What had always interested him was not her face, which was nice enough he supposed, or her figure, which was always hidden under bulky clothes, but her legs. Despite the sensible shoes she seemed to prefer, she had the most terrific pair of legs he'd ever seen, and he was a leg expert. He wandered down the shop collecting a few cans. He took some Boursin, a couple of pints of milk, and a carton of sour cream from the dairy freezer, keeping an eye on the legs and half an ear on the conversation.

"He hasn't had the results, yet," Rosa was saying. "But I think he's pretty sure it was okay."

The other woman nodded. "So is Mr. Withers . . . I spoke to him yesterday, I think he's had some kind of hint from the Board of Examiners. Unofficially of course."

"But they talk to him . . . friendly, I suppose?"

The other woman smiled, and Johnny realized she was probably younger than he'd thought. Under forty, not over. "We call it the Old Boy Network in this country. You tell Gino to call me the minute he hears . . . I think I'm as nervous as he is," the woman said.

"Okay," Rosa promised placidly. "And if you hear first, *you* call us, yes?"

Johnny put his bits and pieces down onto the counter as unobtrusively as he could, but a tin of ratatouille rolled off and dropped into the woman's open briefcase which was standing against the cabinet. "Ummmm . . ." he said tentatively, and she turned to glance at him. "I'm afraid I just dropped my lunch into your pending file," he told her, gesturing toward the briefcase. She looked down, then looked up, puzzled. He tried again. "One of my cans fell into . . . sorry . . ."

Her face cleared and she looked amused. "Now, if you hadn't told me, it could have been *my* lunch. Pity." She smiled and retrieved the can for him.

"Hope it didn't do any damage," he murmured.

"I keep all my eggs in my *other* basket," she said.

"Hell of a way to run an omelette," he grinned, and she flushed. He didn't see anything in his remark for her to get all hot and bothered about. "I've seen you in here before, haven't I?" he asked, nearly wincing at his scintillating originality.

"Possibly," she admitted, the flush receding rapidly.

Rosa looked from one to the other and smiled. "This is Mrs. Fisher. She helps Gino with the school. This is Mr. Cosatelli, I tell you about the other day."

"Oh." Something in the efficient Mrs. Fisher's face

altered slightly. Johnny wasn't certain if it was interest he saw in her eyes, or wariness. "The musician."

"Now why do I feel guilty all of a sudden?" he asked the wheel of cheese on the cutting machine. He glanced at Mrs. Fisher and saw the blush had returned. She seemed to have a faulty thermostat somewhere under all those tweeds. "You don't care for music?"

"Hah!" Rosa put in. "She love music, she and Gino talk music all the time. Talk, argue—you know how Gino is." She smiled at Mrs. Fisher. "Gino, he argues with Mr. Cosatelli, too, as if he should know better than a real artiste. Music, music . . . what is to argue about music? Is to listen, that's all, I tell him. To enjoy. But . . ." She smiled fondly. "Is Gino talking, is argument. Like his papa. Too much, maybe." The smile darkened to a scowl.

"Nonsense," said Mrs. Fisher briskly. "Gino argues from a lively, enquiring mind, not from a short temper."

"And he's not always easy to beat," Johnny said ruefully. "He knows a lot." He met Mrs. Fisher's eyes again. It *was* wariness. "If it isn't music you dislike, then it must be musicians. We're not such a bad bunch, really. Somebody has to play the stuff, after all."

"I *don't* dislike musicians," she said, startled. "Whyever should you think that?"

"Oh . . . vibrations." He gave the word a melodramatic overemphasis. "We're very sensitive to vibrations, you know."

"Your own most of all, I should imagine," she responded tartly. "I assure you, Mr. Cosatelli, I have nothing against musicians. Some of my best friends have perfect pitch."

"Ouch," he grinned, and winked at Rosa. "I think

maybe I should buy an apple for the teacher—she's cross with me."

"I'm neither cross with you nor . . . anything else," Mrs. Fisher said impatiently, and glanced at her watch. "But I *am* late. Goodbye, Rosa. I'll ring you if I hear anything."

She started toward the door and gave Johnny a brief, chilly smile. "Nice to have met you, Mr. Cosatelli."

"Well, it was nice for *me,* anyway," he drawled with a glance downward. "I never had a teacher with legs like yours, Mrs. Fisher. If I had, maybe I wouldn't have grown up to be something as unacceptable as a musician."

She stood still, then turned, slowly, her briefcase held against her body like a shield. "If you'd had a teacher like me, Mr. Cosatelli, you probably wouldn't have grown up at all." His eyes met hers, stare for stare, and then suddenly, unexpectedly, she grinned at him. "The ankles are Steinway, the knees are Bechstein, but I promise you, the thighs are pure Boesendorfer."

"All the way to the top?"

"*All* the way." It was a very impudent grin.

"I'm impressed." He was, too.

"No doubt that makes a change for you."

"You don't think I impress easily?"

"I think . . ." She faltered under his steady gaze. Whatever impulse had caused her to accept his challenge seemed to dissipate, suddenly. He felt as exhilarated as a burglar who'd slipped a diamond ring from the hand of a sleeping countess, and couldn't understand it. They looked at one another, perplexed.

"What do you think?" he asked quietly. He really wanted to know.

There was a flash of red outside the window. "I think I just missed my bus," she said desperately, and fled before he could take anything else away from her.

He stood where he was, staring at the closed door, feeling slightly unhinged. The shop had seemed crowded a moment before, and now it was very, very still. It was amazing the way a bad night's sleep could affect a man, he decided. Hallucinations and everything. It was too much on an empty stomach. He stalked irritably over to the vegetable bins and picked out some oranges and some big Cyprus potatoes for baking. When he brought them back, Rosa reached under the counter at the back and produced the wholemeal loaf she always kept back for him.

"I got some new salami in . . . really strong," she offered.

"No meat, Rosa, you know that." It was a bone of contention between them. A man *needed* meat, she insisted. He tried to keep looking as healthy as possible to prove her wrong, but he could tell by her expression that this morning she was ahead on points. He looked lousy and they both knew it. He changed the subject before she could start in on him. "Gino having trouble at school?"

"Gino? Never. He's doing good, like always." She seemed a little affronted that he should even suspect her precious son of having difficulties. Because Rosa always wore black and he never saw a man around the shop, Johnny had deduced that she was a widow. He knew very little about her personal life, although over the years they had seen each other at least once a day. They were friendly strangers across the mile of countertop. Gino, and Theresa, her daughter, often helped out in the evenings and on weekends. He had struck up a friendship with the boy through their common interest in music, but he'd never heard Gino mention his father either. Yet Mrs. Fisher had referred to him as if he were still alive, and it puzzled him.

"Gino's lucky to have such a devoted teacher," he said.

Rosa looked confused, then her face cleared. "Oh, you mean Mrs. Fisher? She's no his teacher, she's more a friend . . . a family friend, you say?" She was about to continue, but as she began to ring up his purchases she uncovered the newspapers and stopped. Under the potatoes the edge of Lisa's photograph was visible.

"Your lady . . . I saw this morning. So terrible," she said awkwardly. "I'm sorry, Mr. Cosatelli, for you."

"Johnny," he corrected her automatically. "Thank you, Rosa . . . but she wasn't my lady anymore. Not for months, now."

She sighed. "Yes, but still . . . terrible." She finished ringing up. He paid her, gathered up the brown paper bag and the newspapers, smiled goodbye and went out into the cold.

Gates was standing in front of his door and watched him come down the pavement. He didn't smile.

"You want to see me, Inspector?" Johnny jammed the bag onto one hip and dug in his jeans pocket for his key.

"If you've got a few minutes."

"I've got the whole morning . . . come inside before you freeze your backside off." They mounted the stairs single file, Gates catching the newspapers when they slipped out from Johnny's elbow.

Johnny took the bag into the kitchen, put the milk and cheese into the fridge, flicked on the kettle. When he looked over the breakfast bar he caught Gates looking around him with an air of surprise.

"What's wrong?"

Gates shrugged and unbuttoned his topcoat. "Not what I expected, especially from outside."

"There are several ways I could take that."

The detective almost smiled. "I suppose there are. People get fixed ideas about musicians, same way they do about cops. The piano, records, stereo system . . . I expected that."

"Sure." He got out coffee and mugs. "What didn't you expect?"

"The luxury, I suppose. The . . . comfort."

Johnny smiled. "We're not all junkies and drunks," he said mildly, in unconscious imitation of Claverton. Gates glanced at him.

"I'm still not really clear on what it is you actually *do*," he complained. "I know you're a jazz musician, that you make records and so on, but . . ."

"I'm not a 'jazz musician' as such," Johnny explained. "I'm a 'session man,' mostly. Also I compose a little, advertising jingles and theme tunes. If you've ever watched *In Town* or *Pinky's Circus* or *Update* you've heard my music. Also frozen peas, shampoo, jeans, milk, cars . . . that kind of stuff. Sometimes a song or two for somebody's cabaret act. Pop stuff, too. And I do a little accompanying when I have time. Not so much of that, anymore, though. And I've been musical director on a couple of small jazz and folk festivals, nothing spectacular. There's a lot of music around needs doing . . . you'd be surprised."

"I am. I would imagine all that brings in a lot of money."

"Enough," Johnny admitted.

"Enough to afford a really good solicitor?" Gates asked blandly.

Johnny felt his gut clench. "Do I need one?"

"It might be a good idea," Gates said softly as he leaned forward to peer at a framed piece of musical manuscript with small pen and ink drawings in the margin. "This yours?"

"No," Johnny said, drily. "Man named Satie."

"A cartoonist?"

"No, French composer, one of The Six, influenced Ravel and Debussy among others."

"Oh." Gates turned. "I don't know that much about classical music."

"I don't know that much about the law. Why do I need a solicitor all of a sudden?"

"Everybody needs a solicitor." Gates had moved on to another piece of framed manuscript. "This Satie, too?"

"No. An up and coming young composer named Allegra Anne Cosatelli." Gates turned, puzzled, and Johnny explained. "My daughter. I've always composed a piece of music for her birthday and last year she did one for mine." Gates nodded. Johnny looked down and saw that he'd got out a tray and set it with sugar, milk and teaspoons. Regular bloody little hostess he was turning into. Might as well go all the way. "Look, I haven't had breakfast. Mind if I make some toast before you arrest me?"

"Go ahead."

Rather unsteadily, Johnny hacked some slices off the fresh loaf, ending up with an array of half-burned wedges which he carried through and put onto the coffee table. He dropped into a chair. Gates finished wandering around the room and sat down opposite him. He helped himself to milk and sugar, took a slice of toast. Johnny watched him nervously. Gates hadn't said he was going to arrest him, but on the other hand he hadn't said he wasn't going to, either. He leaned forward and rested his elbows on his knees. "Tell me why you think I should call a solicitor."

Gates spoke with difficulty around the toast. "We got the final coroner's report this morning."

"Oh?"

Gates nodded, drank some coffee. "Lisa Kendrick wasn't beaten and killed. She was killed and *then* she was beaten."

"You mean . . . after she was already dead?"

"That's right. To make it look like a mugging, maybe. The killer, not being a pathologist, wouldn't realize that was useless. Wounds made after death are very different than those made while the victim is alive."

Johnny swallowed. "You think . . . you think *I'd* do something like that?"

"Would you?"

"Jesus . . . no. *No.*"

Gates reached into his jacket pocket and produced his notebook, flipped through the pages, stopped. "You said you spent Tuesday afternoon 'working out' with a man named Pascal Lebrun."

Johnny stared at him, confused, and then it hit him. "She was kicked?" he whispered. *"Kicked?"*

"What made you take up sabot, Mr. Cosatelli?" Gates asked.

Johnny's mouth and throat had dried up and he couldn't get his voice to cooperate for a moment. He felt sweat gathering along his body. "I . . . I studied for two years in Paris and I shared a flat with a cellist names Paul Desault. He was from Marseilles and he was into sabot, got me interested, too. He said if you earned a living with your hands it was better to learn how to fight with your feet so you could defend yourself without destroying your livelihood. It was fun but I'm not really much of an athlete, so when I came back home I dropped it. But when I started doing late-night gigs and so on . . . it seemed a good idea to take it up again. I wrote to Paul and he asked around and sent me Pascal's name. That's all . . ."

Gates closed the notebook and stood up. "We assumed it was a beating and that there had been a struggle. That's why we examined your body and hands. But most of her injuries—the ones inflicted after death—were done with the toe of a shoe, according to the pathologist." He walked over and opened the door of the flat. Two men were standing outside, one with a large suitcase.

"We'd like your shoes, Mr. Cosatelli. All of them, please," Gates said gently.

They left him his slippers. Too soft, they said. Too soft to have kicked in the face and body of Lisa Mary Kendrick.

# 5

Gates was reading the surveillance reports on Claverton, aware that Sergeant Dunhill was watching his face to get a reaction. Finally Gates looked up.

"What do you want me to say?"

"Are we going to let it pass like all the rest?"

Gates dropped the flimsies onto his blotter and scowled. "We'll have to. They're riding our backs and tying our hands at the same time."

"You'll have to admit that for a so-called member of the upper classes Claverton has some funny friends."

"Obviously. But money has a habit of putting odd people in bed together. It doesn't prove anything."

"What about all these complaints he's making?"

"I told Manvers they couldn't have it both ways—if Claverton is so hellbent on us finding Lisa Kendrick's killer then he'll have to put up with everything that goes with it. And that includes surveillance and interviews with his friends and clients, anyone who knew Lisa Kendrick, in fact."

"Manvers is no dunce, he knows far more people are

being brought into this than normal. And all Claverton *really* wants is for us to hang it on Cosatelli."

"Uh-huh. He's made that very clear. Too clear, if you ask me. I'm not in the habit of expediting other people's vengeance."

Dunhill stood up and went to look out the window, jingling the change in his pockets. "Cosatelli *is* the best bet we've got."

"I know that . . . nothing is changed, we're still watching him. *He's* not complaining. But she had other friends, so she might have had other enemies."

Dunhill turned. "What makes you so damn sure Cosatelli *didn't* do it?"

"Ten years of looking killers in the face," Gates said.

Dunhill snorted and returned to looking out the window. "What I don't understand is how somebody like Claverton got involved with her."

"He's a fifty-seven-year-old man who liked to walk into a room with a gorgeous woman on his arm."

"A fifty-seven-year-old *married* man," Dunhill emphasized.

"Whose wife has lived in Switzerland for the past nine years," Gates amplified. "They're legally separated."

"Even so . . . from what we've got the Kendrick girl was just a great-looking bird, good for a screw. But he had her living with him, took her just about everywhere, the whole thing."

"According to Cosatelli she was more than just 'good for a screw' . . . she had some talent for the business Claverton is in."

"You mean Claverton *told* her that . . . he was just giving her a line. How could a girl who went to a secondary modern in Harrow know anything about antiques and paintings? You saw her school records, the social worker's reports, she was just—"

"Her mother taught art and her father was a master carpenter. They didn't die until she was fourteen."

"So?"

"So fourteen years is plenty of time to absorb whatever it is that gives you an eye for quality in paintings and furniture. And her grandmother ran an antiques shop."

"A junk shop, you mean."

"All right, a junk shop. So at least she knew how to recognize *junk* when she saw it. It doesn't seem farfetched to me. Cosatelli said she made a hobby of going around the markets and picking up things, selling them at a profit. A lot of people do that, but not all of them make a profit. He said one day she'd planned to put all her earnings as a model into something like that, a shop of her own. She knew her looks wouldn't last. He said she was a realist. And a lot of it *is* instinct. I asked Solly Mensch about it, and he said somebody like Lisa Kendrick could be a real asset to Claverton. They don't come that thick on the ground, he said, people with 'the eye.' Most people learn through their mistakes. She didn't make many mistakes, according to Cosatelli."

"Well . . . she must have made one, at least, to end up the way she did."

"Maybe it was as simple as walking down the wrong street at the wrong time," Gates said. "Maybe we're looking in the wrong places for the wrong things. After all, according to Claverton, she was wearing a small fortune in jewelry that night, rings, bracelets, diamond watch, so on. It was all missing, and we still haven't come up with anything on it. It may have been a simple mugging that got out of hand."

"Uh-uh." Dunhill shook his head. "Whoever killed her hated her . . . you have to know somebody to hate them that badly."

Gates shrugged. "Even so, maybe it was a bunch of kids, maybe they got carried away, kept it up until they got bored with it or heard somebody coming. I'm still not discounting that, Jim."

"If it was walking down the wrong street at the wrong time, how come it was a street in Highgate? Cosatelli lives in Islington . . . that's a hell of a long walk."

"Maybe she was going to see someone. Maybe she took a cab. We found her car in the pound this morning, didn't we?"

"Yeah . . . towed in off a no-parking zone about three streets away from Cosatelli's place. Maybe he drove her out to Highgate, killed her, then drove back and left the car to be found," Dunhill suggested.

"There were only her fingerprints in it," Gates reminded him.

"So he wore gloves. He was wearing gloves when you brought him in for questioning . . . a man makes his living with his hands, he wears gloves all the time."

"So did she . . . we found a pair of driving gloves under the seat, remember? It's March, it's cold out." He looked over at Dunhill. "Claverton wears gloves, too."

"I notice you haven't brought *his* shoes into forensic."

"He *was* in Birmingham, we've checked," Gates said wearily. "Besides which, I think the man is genuinely grieving. I admit he has a motive because she was cheating on him with Cosatelli, but I get the feeling he knew all about her little trips back there and chose to ignore them. She was a very demanding girl, sexually, and he probably accepted he couldn't keep up the pace. It didn't matter as long as she was discreet about it and came back to him. He wants revenge for her death, not her infidelity. I think he was really in love with her."

"Maybe. But he sure as hell wants Cosatelli's guts for garters." Dunhill sat down on the edge of his desk. "You don't suppose . . ."

"What?"

Dunhill rubbed the side of his nose as he tried to put his ideas together. "Maybe, like you say, Claverton loved her. Okay. But maybe her going back to Cosatelli all the time got to him, finally. I mean, *really* got to him. She must have talked about Cosatelli, sometimes . . . in the beginning, anyway."

"So?"

"So . . . maybe she mentioned this sabot business to Claverton, said that Cosatelli could defend himself with this kicking thing. So when he had her killed, he told whoever did it to use his feet in order to make it look like Cosatelli did it."

"It's occurred to me," Gates said quietly. "And not only for those reasons. I wonder if it's occurred to Cosatelli?"

*

It had started to rain by the time the cab dropped him at the artist's entrance of Wigmore Hall. He'd had to ask it to wait while he ran into a shoeshop and bought the first pair of black loafers that fit. There was a line folding itself in through the front doors, which made him even more nervous. Of course, a recital by Walter Gessler was a rarity nowadays. He had been astonished when Laynie had called him a month before and told him Gessler's usual accompanist had to go into the hospital and Gessler had asked for Johnny. He'd worked with Gessler once or twice many years before and was amazed that the old man had even remembered his name. However, Laynie had insisted that Gessler wanted him, and when he'd shown up for their first rehearsal Gessler's welcome was warm and approving. The work had gone very well, but he nevertheless felt about fourteen years old as he walked down the shadowy passage toward the dressing room. It's never easy, appearing with a legend.

Far less so when you're wearing stiff new shoes and wondering if this was going to be a farewell appearance before being carted off to jail.

He was relieved to see that Gessler, too, was nervous. He kept running his hands over his violin, humming to himself, loosening and tightening the bow abstractedly until Johnny wanted to snatch it away from him and hide it someplace before it snapped altogether. Once they were onstage, however, Gessler straightened up into something other than the nervous old man in the dressing room. His cockatoo crest of white hair floated over his pink scalp as he acknowledged the applause that greeted his appearance, then gestured gracefully to include Johnny, who was edging as inconspicuously as he could onto the piano bench.

Because Gessler's strength would be greatest at the beginning of the concert, they began with the Kreutzer Sonata. The familiar echoes of a large auditorium containing an attentive audience came back at him over the edge of the stage—the breathing, the surreptitious coughs, the shifting of invisible elbows and backsides against the seats. This was entirely different from doing sets at a club where only half the people were listening and none of them were all that interested. But the deep breathers out there in the dark knew the music as well as he and Gessler did, some of them perhaps even better.

He had forgotten how terrifying that could be.

Nevertheless as they began the second item on the program he felt something happening to him that was totally unexpected. He'd been afraid that his personal situation would affect his playing for the worse—but it didn't. In fact, as he adapted himself to Gessler's somewhat eccentric bowing in the Schubert he found that the music was buoying him up, comforting him, giving him a solace and strength he hadn't felt for a very, very long time. The fact was, he was doing what he knew how to do best. Here he was sure of himself, here he knew what was expected of him, what he could give. During the applause Gessler turned and leaned toward him slightly. "Ham and eggs, John," he murmured under the waves of approval that were rolling over them.

It was true. They were totally together, totally matched, and it felt beautiful. He'd forgotten how beautiful it *could* feel, when it was right. By the fifth number the audience had apparently realized something special was happening up there because they were absolutely silent. Not a cough, not a rustle, nothing.

Just the music holding them all together.

The program was not a long one, in deference to Gessler's age. When they came to the end, however, the audience would not let go. Gessler was flushed and his eyes were too bright, but he responded to the applause like a child to ice cream. Johnny sat motionless at the piano while Gessler played an encore. He stood up when the applause rushed over them because he was concerned that Gessler might push himself too far in the excitement of the moment, but Gessler waved him down again and then went toward the front edge of the platform, raising his hands for quiet. It came reluctantly, but it came.

"You have been very generous, very kind," Gessler quavered, raising his voice slightly. "But I am an old man and I am tired, now." There were murmurs of disappointment and he raised his bow and waved it at them like an admonitory schoolmaster.

"I want to give you more because you have given so much to me, but this recital's magic has not been mine alone." He turned slightly. "John, I cannot do more, but I'm sure you can." Turning back to the audience, he continued. "Accompanists are all too often overlooked, but perhaps that is because not all of them are of the caliber of John Cosatelli. I'm certain you would be pleased to have more music from him. I know I would."

Johnny stared at Gessler with a mixture of apprehension and amazement as the old man came back to the piano. The audience was applauding in agreement. He supposed none of them were eager to go back into the rainy streets. Squinting into the lights slightly, he could just make out the first couple of rows, faces smiling over the beating hands.

And then he saw her.

Dark hair in a pageboy bob, the fringe drooping over the lined face, the eyes big and brown and full of duplicity as she clapped and clapped and leaned sideways to say something to the fat man who was slumped in the seat next to her, his hands quite still and steepled together under his chin.

"You and Laynie planned this between you, you old so-and-so," he said through his teeth to Gessler as he acknowledged the applause.

"Now, John . . . you can't build an audience to order. Give them what they want and be damned grateful they want it," Gessler shot back good-humoredly. "What shall I announce?"

Johnny glanced again at Laynie. Who *was* that fat guy—he looked familiar. He knew she expected his usual encore, the Rachmaninov E Minor and G Major preludes, back to back. Suddenly he felt a surge of mischief flood through him like five-star cognac. So she wanted him to go back to this, did she? All right—he'd show her how pointless it was after all this time. Maybe that would settle the thing between them once and for all.

"Alborada del Gracioso," he told Gessler.

Gessler's smiling, wrinkled face suddenly went blank. "Don't be a fool," he hissed. The audience was waiting patiently. "All they expect is a little Chopin, Rachmaninov . . . something eas—"

"That or nothing," Johnny said firmly.

Slowly Gessler straightened from where he'd been leaning across the piano and returned to the edge of the stage. "Mr. Cosatelli will play some Ravel for you," he announced and went to stand in the wings without a backward glance.

After a few moments, Johnny lifted his hands and began the bouncing, syncopated rhythm of the opening. He heard some gasps rise like a flight of startled moths from the audience. He was right, they knew their music. And then he didn't hear anything else except the shade of old Maurice Ravel breathing over his shoulder. The bastard had always had it in for concert pianists, and the Alborada was one of his most fiendish legacies to the breed he called "circus performers."

He and Maurice kept waiting for him to blow it and

they were both disappointed. Short of actually falling off the bench, there didn't seem to be anything he could do wrong. His hands felt weightless, electric, alive. He watched them almost disinterestedly as they skittered over the keys, grabbing the notes in chunks yet keeping each one separate and distinct. Eventually they cut through the last rising phrase with razor precision and dropped into his lap. He stared at them and then at Gessler as the audience went berserk.

Jesus Christ, Laynie was right. He *could* still do it.

Gessler was applauding, too, his fiddle rammed under his armpit as if it wasn't worth sixty thousand pounds or so, his white hair lifting up and down in response to his enthusiasm. Johnny stood up and went toward him, remembering belatedly to bow and acknowledge the applause. He grabbed Gessler's wrist and pulled him back onto the stage.

"We started this thing together and we might as well finish it together," he growled.

"What do you suggest?" Gessler asked, waving his bow at the audience cheerfully. Isn't this a great party? he seemed to be saying. Aren't you glad you came?

Johnny told him what he wanted to play. Gessler looked puzzled, then horrified. "You can't be serious."

"No . . . at least, not for very long. Come on, it was bloody good when we did it the other day at your place and you know it."

"They won't like it."

"Make them like it," Johnny said. He walked to the edge of the stage and faced the audience. "Ladies and gentlemen, good melodies don't care who writes them." As he passed Gessler on the way back to the piano, he muttered, "This will teach you to ask for me."

"They won't like it," Gessler said again.

They loved it.

Backstage, Gessler couldn't stop laughing. "That went down better than all the rest put together," he chortled in amazement.

"I thought it might," Johnny said. He'd always found Lennon and McCartney's "Eleanor Rigby" a satisfying number himself, and he had to admit the rich tones of a Guarnarius del Gesu gave it something extra.

"Johnny, that was very, very naughty," said a deep, soft voice behind him. He turned and looked down into his agent's amused face.

"Wasn't it just?" he grinned at her.

"It was also showing off." This was from the fat man who'd been sitting next to Laynie out front. From behind the tinted glasses his pale eyes stared into Johnny's with what seemed like disapproval, then abruptly crinkled up into laughter. "But I suppose you earned the privilege."

"John, this is Simon Price-Temple," Laynie said with heavy emphasis. "He wants to talk to you."

He looked at the fat man again. Of course—this was "The Saint"—principal conductor of the newly formed Welsh National Philharmonic. It had been in all the papers and his parents hadn't stopped talking about it over Christmas. No wonder he looked familiar. He also looked rather rumpled and untidy to be the possessor of a reputation as the youngest musical ascetic in the business. They clamored to play for him, but they came out of the experience chastened and mute—or so he'd heard.

Gessler invited them into his dressing room and sat quietly to one side, polishing his fiddle with a soft chamois, listening and nodding occasionally, watching Johnny's face.

"The Alborada was . . . impressive," Price-Temple allowed as he settled his bulk more comfortably on a small gilt chair, overlapping it on either side. He took off his glasses and began to clean them with a rather unfortunate handkerchief that had obviously served duty as a napkin, and not recently.

"It impressed me, too," Johnny smiled. "I didn't think for a minute it would go so well."

"Then why the devil did you play it?"

"It was a kind of kamikaze run that didn't come off," Johnny said with a glance toward Laynie. "Unfortunately, I still seem to be intact."

"I *expected* the Rachmaninov Preludes," Laynie said, a little annoyed.

"I'm sure you did," he responded sharply. "But I hate it when you fall asleep in public."

"Now, now . . . children," Gessler murmured benignly.

"And as for you—" Johnny said, turning to him. Gessler grinned at him without the faintest trace of guilt.

"Darling . . ." Laynie interrupted in her sweetest voice. He braced himself. That voice was always a bad sign. He'd been right, she was after him again.

"No, Laynie," he said flatly. "No."

"Shut up and listen," she shot back. "You know about Simon and the Philharmonic."

"Yes. Congratulations," he said to Price-Temple, who waved the handkerchief negligently and then stuffed it back into his jacket pocket, replacing the glasses on his lumpy nose.

"Well, Simon wants to establish the orchestra with

something of a bang, and he's planning a Music Festival for next August, immediately following the National Eisteddfod. He wants you to serve as his musical director because the spring schedule of the WNP is so—"

"Good God, why *me?*" Johnny demanded. This was a new tack. "There must be a hundred—"

"It's an all-discipline Festival," Price-Temple interrupted abruptly. "I intend it to be educational as well as cultural. There will be a number of young people's groups taking part . . . I envisage lectures, seminars, master classes, all sorts of things in addition to the concerts. You know both sides of the street, Mr. Cosatelli."

"Even so . . ."

Price-Temple went on imperturbably. "We have provisionally booked Mr. Brubeck and Mr. Zoot Sims, and are making approaches to several leading British artists, such as Mr. Luscher and Mr. and Mrs. Dankworth. We'd want your group to play also, of course."

He couldn't knock the company they'd be keeping. "Well, thank you . . . we'd be honored. But as for the other thing—you want a full-time administrator. You *did* mean *this* August, I take it?"

Price-Temple waved a dimpled hand. "I have staff to handle all the small details. We're privately sponsored, by several large corporations. There's plenty of money."

"That makes a change," Gessler put in from the corner.

"Indeed," Price-Temple agreed. "What I want is someone with enough nous to bring some kind of logical order and balance to the thing, to get the best out of everyone concerned. I think you'd be ideal. You're Welsh-born, which will obviously go down well with the Committee. You're flexible, you can dominate, you've both the scholarship and the good sense . . ."

"But I'm booked right through—"

"We'll unbook you," Laynie snapped.

He was flattered, there was no denying it. Obviously the financial side of it was all right or Laynie wouldn't have taken it this far. And the idea was interesting—a combination of the American summer school concept with something like the Wavendon All-Music. He started to say something but Price-Temple spoke again.

"However, I've had second thoughts about you, Mr. Cosatelli."

The three of them stared at the big man, who stared back calmly.

"Simon," Laynie began in an outraged tone, "what the *hell* are you on about? We've—"

Johnny had locked eyes with the fat man. "Why?"

"You know why," Price-Temple said. "Oh, I'm still offering you the job. But on one further condition—"

"Wait just a minute, you big—" Laynie began.

Price-Temple ignored her, still staring at Johnny. "And that condition is that Mr. Cosatelli appear as a soloist with the WNP on at least two evenings, doing the Ravel and something else . . . perhaps one of the Rachmaninovs."

Johnny laughed, he couldn't help it. Laughed and choked on it. "That's bloody ridiculous."

"Oh," Laynie said in a small, mollified voice. "Oh."

"Look," Johnny said impatiently. "Just because I managed to get through the Alborada without falling on my face . . ."

Price-Temple scowled. "You say you know my reputation. If that's true, you should realize I'd hardly be stupid enough to risk such a request on the evidence of one lucky afternoon. I did not come here unprepared. I've sat in that sleazy club in which you're presently appearing for four intolerable evenings over the past month. I've listened to approximately a hundred tapes and transcriptions of your classical work and of course to that Ravel recording you did so long ago. Mr. Cosatelli, you're a fool, an idiot, a hopeless witling."

"Oh?"

"Indeed. But you are a brilliant pianist. Why you've been dissipating your gift on all this other garbage is quite beyond me. Your classical technique and interpretive ability are remarkable, quite unique in my opinion. When you're given something like that you're also given a responsibility, not only to use it but to share it."

"I've been telling him that for years," Laynie said, gratified by this unexpected and forceful ally.

"Jesus Christ!" Johnny exploded. "I'm forty-one years old. I haven't done any concentrated serious work for over fourteen years. It's too damn late for me."

"Rachmaninov started performing again at forty-five, better than ever," Gessler put in gently.

"He was an exception," Johnny snapped.

"So are you," Gessler countered. "I wouldn't have asked for you myself if you weren't."

"Dammit . . . the world is full of piano players," Johnny cried, turning his back to them and staring at the small grimy window high up in the corner of the dressing room. "Young, tough, hungry piano players. I can remember the grind, the sweat, the nerves . . . kids drop out of the circuit like flies and they've got energy, ambition, and all the rest going for them. If *they* can't handle it what the hell do you think it would do to a guy rapidly approaching the male menopause, hey? I don't *want* to go back on the concert circuit—it broke my marriage and it damn near broke me."

"It didn't break *me,*" Gessler said with some asperity. "And I'm seventy-nine. Your maturity can only work in your favor, John. You could handle the pressure, now."

"Rubbish," Johnny said flatly. "Absolute rubbish. I'm past it—who should know that better than *I* do?"

There was a silence. Price-Temple sighed deeply. "I wonder if you would be kind enough to leave us alone for a moment?" he said to the others.

"Of course," Gessler said, amused. He laid his violin in the case and offered his arm gallantly to Laynie, who took it with every evidence of not wanting to go anywhere. "Come along, dear lady, there is a coffee machine in the corridor and I will treat you to some of its ghastly contents. You may have ten percent of my sugar."

As they left, Johnny had a sudden inexplicable moment of panic at being left alone in the room with Minnesota Fats, although what he thought the big slob was capable of doing to him he didn't know. Rather than stare at Price-Temple's chubby face, Johnny went over and closed Gessler's violin case, snapping the locks.

"What are you afraid of, Mr. Cosatelli?" Price-Temple asked. "Success or failure?"

Johnny stared at the surface of the case, ran his fingertips over the battered leather. "You do psycho-analysis as a sideline, do you?"

"God forbid."

Johnny could see Price-Temple in the mirror, felt the pale eyes trying to pry his shoulder blades apart. "Perhaps I'm afraid of mediocrity," Johnny said.

"But mediocrity is what you have now," Price-Temple said blandly.

"The hell I do," Johnny retorted. "I'm one of the top session men in London and I have the bank balance to prove it. My records sell well and I was voted top keyboard man in last year's *Jazz Journal* poll."

"Yes, exactly," Price-Temple murmured. "I have the greatest respect for jazz, Mr. Cosatelli, believe me. For jazz and jazz musicians, some of whom are clearly touched by genius. You aren't."

"Bloody hell, at least I'm playing my own music!"

"Ah, but you aren't, you know. Sometimes you're Oscar Petersen, sometimes you're Teddy Wilson, sometimes you're Ellis Larkins, sometimes George Shearing, sometimes Herbie Hancock. You are consistently *listenable* but rarely innovative. You never chance your arm and your music sounds like what it is—easy. Not easy for others to do perhaps, but easy for you."

"Thank you very much, Whitney Balliett," Johnny sneered, awarding Price-Temple the mantle of one of America's senior jazz critics.

Price-Temple pressed his lips together, looked down at the floor, up at the ceiling, rotated his thumbs in his lap and clicked his tongue at them. A virtuoso performance of a fat man, thinking things over. "You've been doing retirement work, Cosatelli. Throwing out bits of yourself here and there, echoes of what you were, hints of what you could have been. Retirement work, that's all. There's your mediocrity, boyo."

"I see. Whereas busting my head playing against a brick wall is better, is it? Art for art's sake? God, I've had a bellyfull of that from Laynie. You're bigger than she is, but you still don't impress me." He sat down in Gessler's chair, surprised to find he was shaking too much to stand up any longer under Price-Temple's attack.

"You know what they call me, I suppose?" Price-Temple asked.

"Sure . . . 'The Saint.' Simon Temple, Simon Templar . . ."

"I don't mean the media—I mean musicians."

Johnny half-smiled. "I know *some* of the things they call you."

"I wouldn't *let* you be bad, John," Price-Temple said, so softly that Johnny wouldn't have caught it if he hadn't been able to see the thick lips moving in the mirror over the dressing table. "I know what happened to you in Bristol . . . *and* what had been happening from the beginning. Laynie trotted out all the accolades and praise as if she was proud of them. As bright as she is she didn't see them for what they were—indulgent, undemanding mush. I think *you* knew what they were doing to you, though—they were making it too easy for you to impress them. They weren't making you get better, weren't pushing you any closer to what you knew it should be, what it *could* be. Am I right?"

"Oh, for God's sake, we're only talking about playing the bloody piano, not metaphysical concepts," Johnny growled. But something in him was hurting—probably that baked potato he'd had for lunch. The cheese had been a mistake. He shifted his weight on the chair, caught Price-Temple's eyes in the mirror, tried to look away, could not.

"You weren't born to be comfortable," Price-Temple said. "You weren't born to be 'cozy.' It will be hard work, of course, but it's hardly a major event—just a summer festival. It will probably take you five years or more to reestablish yourself as a concert pianist, even if this goes well. The real test will be how you do *after* the Festival, how much critical attack and ridicule you're prepared to put up with. They'll be waiting with the knives out, of course. They'll put you on the defensive, make you run the gauntlet every damn time you appear. You'll hate them, but then, you always did. If you worked with me you'd come to hate me, too, but not for the reasons you despised the others. You'd hate me because I would *always* know when you weren't trying to get it right. It may well be I could break you. I've broken others. I don't particularly care whether you break or not. The only real question is whether *you* care. Failure is no shame—but not making the attempt is despicable. I'm offering you a golden chance to get back where you *belong*. Turn away from it and every time you take a breath, every time you write an advertising jingle or paraphrase somebody else's jazz chops, you'll remember that somewhere in the world there's a man who knows you were afraid to be anything but a cheap juggler in a tinsel suit."

"You?"

"Me."

"Anybody ever tell you you're an insufferable, smug, pompous fat bag of guts?"

"Frequently."

"That you should be out selling refrigerators to Eskimos and booze to the Apache?"

"That, too. Your range of insult is about equivalent to your range of aspiration, you cocked-up little Welsh shitshoveler," Price-Temple said in a calm, conversational tone.

Johnny gritted his teeth, turned, crossed his arms. "Which Rachmaninov—the Second?"

"Oh, no, that would make them love you. You've had quite enough of that. If it's to be Rachmaninov at all it must be the Fourth. Or perhaps a Bartok would be better."

"When do you want my decision?"

Price-Temple regarded him for a moment, then heaved himself out of the chair, which creaked alarmingly. "As soon as possible, time is short. I can always offer the concerts to Danny Barenboim."

"Oh, yeah . . . he *needs* the work," Johnny muttered.

"Laynie has all the details. Come and see me in a couple of weeks—we'll start work then."

"You bastard," Johnny said.

Price-Temple paused at the door. "Tsk. You'll have to do better than that. The gentle Ashkenazy once called me an impotent, bloated hyena. Not much in English, but in Russian I assure you it's enough to give one considerable pause. Good evening."

# 6

The rain was working itself into sleet, and it stung Johnny's face as he strode along the dark streets, his hands jammed into his overcoat pockets and his new shoes letting in the wet.

After Price-Temple left, Johnny had just made it to the men's room before losing his lunch and probably part of his breakfast, too. Then he'd walked past Gessler's open dressing room door, aware of Laynie turning to call after him, aware of Gessler's mocking yet sympathetic smile. But he'd grabbed his coat from the hook and left, not wanting any more talk.

Goddamn him to hell, he pleaded silently. Please, God, do it *now*.

But God was apparently tied up somewhere else, and the sleet continued to slide down the back of his neck. Johnny cannoned into another hurrying figure in the dark, mumbled an apology over his shoulder, continued to belt along the pavement as if someone were trying to catch him.

And, of course, somebody was.

In fact, it seemed like everybody was, one way or another.

He counted them off in his mind.

Laynie wanted the rising star she'd signed years ago.

Gessler wanted his act of faith justified.

Price-Temple wanted fresh meat in the bear pit.

Baz wanted someone to lean on.

Moosh wanted to go on eating regularly.

Claverton wanted his blood.

Gates wanted him for murder.

He realized he was nearly running, forced himself to slow down, and felt a stitch sink its teeth into his side. The concert had started at three and it was now nearly eight o'clock. He'd taken a bus partway but found he was suffocating in its steamy warmth. The trees beyond the iron fence of Newington Green were twisting and clacking their bare black branches in the wind. He stalked past the new and already dingy rectangles of housing projects, the old and crumbling masonry façades of the once-desirable residences that now housed second-rate solicitors, dentists, and accountants, past the occasional muddy patches and gaping ill-guarded holes of road repairs that never seemed to get finished, down narrower and narrower streets. Occasional lights glowed behind curtains that didn't quite meet, occasional bursts of gunfire and music filtered from invisible television sets, occasional voices were heard, basso profundo fathers and contralto mothers, against high piping soprano solos from children who didn't *want* to go to bed.

He had a momentary image of John Garfield standing next to some Hollywood version of a tenement window, staring out at a painted backdrop of Manhattan, and saying, "It's my City Symphony, the music of the millions . . ."

It was balls.

The bookie, the baker, the gravestone maker—what the hell did *they* want with Bartok?

Price-Temple was wrong, *wrong.* John Owen Cosatelli was born to be Captain Birdseye, not the Magic Piano Man. All he wanted was a nice life, a bit of peace and quiet, and some milk for his coffee. He was wet, he was cold, he was tired, he was *old,* goddammit. Too old to play games, much less—

He stopped and stared down the long empty street.

"You son of a bitch," he said aloud. "You want to do it, don't you?" He stood there a moment, shuddered with the cold, and went on again. Now he was talking to himself. What next?

He rounded the corner and saw the glow from Rosa's shop spilling out over the broken, glistening pavement. Milk for his coffee was available, at least. There was some comfort somewhere. He jerked open the door and saw Gino behind the counter, counting up the change and stacking it next to the scale. He looked up, his long dark hair flopping as usual over his forehead.

"Hey, Johnny . . . you want the money, take it. Take it."

"What?" He stood there, dripping onto the linoleum.

Gino grinned. "You look mad enough to steal."

"Do I?" Johnny asked, stupid with cold.

"Yeah, you do. Here—" he pushed a steaming mug across the counter. "I haven't touched it . . . it's still hot."

"No, thanks . . . I—" It was a shock, coming out of the lonely darkness into this bright fragrant haven. He stared at Gino. "He wants me to play the goddamn Rachmaninov Fourth," he blurted out, unable to stop himself.

"No kidding," Gino said. "Who?"

"Simon Price-Temple." He grabbed the mug of tea and gulped it convulsively as Gino watched.

"The Saint himself?"

Johnny nodded, feeling suddenly foolish, and put the mug back down on the counter next to the heaps of coins. He hadn't expected to see Gino there, just Rosa, smiling and unquestioningly familiar. But Gino knew all about it. The boy was a music nut, a fanatic listener. Over the past few months he'd got into the habit of talking to Johnny about this composer and that, this interpretation against that, had even come around to the flat a few times to listen to Johnny's stereo and discuss music. He was a bright, bright boy and he worshiped Bach. Gino was an unlikely son for Rosa and out of place in this neighborhood. He'd won a place at some fancy school in Hampstead and was planning to be a barrister, or perhaps a physicist. Johnny and Rosa might differ on the subject of vegetarianism, but as far as Gino was concerned, they were in complete accord. The boy was special.

"Where's your mother?" he asked, determined to cover up his outburst. "You should be studying."

Gino flushed. "She's not feeling so good, so I said I'd close up tonight. You mean he wants you to do a concert with him?"

"Not that tooth again?" Johnny asked going along to the dairy cooler and taking out a carton of milk and another of cottage cheese.

"Or does he mean a recording?" Gino asked, ignoring Johnny's question.

"No, a concert," Johnny said, digging into his pocket for the money. "How much is that?"

"That's terrific," Gino said.

Johnny paused with his hand still in his pocket. "How much is 'terrific' in English money?"

"Forty pence." Gino took the money and rang it up on the cash register, dropping the coins negligently into the drawer and closing it. Johnny picked up his purchases and started to go toward the door. "Hey, wait a minute . . . you can't come in here and make an announcement like that, drink my damn tea, and then bugger off again," Gino protested. "Come *on.*"

Johnny stopped, sighed, put the milk and cottage cheese back onto the counter. "I'm a little tense, that's all."

"I can see *that,*" Gino said. "Let it out, you'll feel better, right?"

Johnny looked at the young, interested, intelligent face and found himself letting it out, the anger and the indecision, horrified at himself for behaving like an idiot in front of a sixteen-year-old, unable to hold it back, unable to stop himself. And he knew why. Because there was no one else to tell. Only Gino. Half a friend was better than none, and he was so damn sick of everyone else, so damn tired of them all. He dug into his pocket for more change and bought a pack of cigarettes, hardly pausing in his monologue to light one and cough.

Gino heard him out. He had to give him that, the kid stood there—or leaned there against the counter—and heard him out, watched him pacing around the small space between the boxes of vegetables and the glassed-in olives and salamis, a serious and surprising maturity in his eyes. Suddenly Johnny stopped in midsentence and looked at him.

"Sorry," he said, feeling like nine kinds of fool.

Gino shrugged. "I don't know what you're sorry about. Seems to me there's no problem at all. He wants you to play, he thinks you can play . . . you should play. So?"

Johnny felt something inside let go, and he started to laugh, at himself, at the scene, at the whole situation. "Just like that? One, two, three . . . no trouble?"

"Too easy, huh?" Gino grinned. "You think complications make it more important?"

Johnny stopped laughing and stared at him. He realized that was exactly what he thought and he'd needed a kid to tell him.

"Of course," Gino went on, apparently reading his mind, "I'm only sixteen so what do I know about it? Don't pay any attention to *me*, I'm only one of the Great Unwashed."

"You know what you can do with *that* little act," Johnny said.

"It's only one of my many," Gino said with false modesty. "I've got a dutiful-son act, a tough-guy act, a brilliant-student act, a yes-sir, no-sir, three-bags-full act specially for headmasters, a—"

"Get stuffed," Johnny grinned.

"I'm still working on that one."

"Let me know when—" Johnny was saying when he heard someone clattering down the steps at the back of the shop that led to the flat above. The curtains were pushed aside and the Lady with the Briefcase appeared, looking angry.

"Gino, you've got to talk her into it, this can't go—" she trailed off, seeing Johnny standing there.

"This is Johnny Cosatelli, you know I was telling

you . . ." Gino said awkwardly, suddenly looking only sixteen and very embarrassed.

"Oh, yes. How do you do," she said hurriedly, pulling her gloves on with a brief and abstracted smile in Johnny's direction. "I have to go now, Gino, but I'll be back in the morning. Don't let her get up, the shop can stay closed for one day, no matter what she says. But it can't go on like this, it simply can't."

"Is there anything I can do?" Johnny asked, looking from one to the other.

"Nothing, thank you," the woman said abruptly. She obviously wanted to go on talking to Gino and Johnny realized he was in the way.

As he went out he thought he heard Gino call after him, but the woman's voice drowned him out. Johnny closed the door and left them to it. Whatever the problem was, it was obviously private and none of his business. He glanced back through the misted window and saw the woman virtually pounding the countertop with one small gloved fist. Next to it he also saw his milk and cottage cheese, but didn't think he should go back for it. He could use powdered milk in his coffee, after all. He wished there were something he *could* do because Gino looked worried and defenseless standing there listening to her tirade. Who the hell was she that she could charge around giving orders? He didn't doubt her concern, it had been very apparent in her tone and her expression, but Gino had gone from mature man to helpless boy in about thirty seconds flat, once she'd appeared.

Dammit, he liked Gino, and Rosa, too. They were nice people, they were neighbors as well as everything else, he didn't like to see them hassled. The wind whipped at his overcoat and the sleet trickled down his face as he walked down the street, paused, started to turn back, hesitated in the darkness. A car went past him, slowly. Maybe she was a *doctor,* maybe that was it. Maybe Rosa was sicker than Gino had made out. Maybe that swollen face hadn't been toothache at all. And there had been those blotches on her arms, too. Maybe she needed some special treatment they couldn't get on the National Health, maybe he could—

As he stood there in the shadows he saw the woman come out of the shop and disappear down the street, her briefcase banging against her shapely legs, her head down against the wind that tugged at her mop of dark hair. Before he could start back Gino had locked the door of the shop and drawn down the blind.

He sighed and grimaced. Here he'd gone on and on about his own stupid problems when the kid was burdened with God knew what. Some friend and neighbor *he* was proving to be. Reluctantly he continued toward his flat. As he pulled his keys out he noticed that one of the big double doors of the warehouse was slightly ajar, probably pried open by the wind. Gage must have forgotten to lock it again. He went over and reached out to grab the handle.

Something grabbed him instead.

Darker shadows in the gap, two of them, big and dressed for action. Iron fingers wrapped themselves around his wrist, and though he jerked back instinctively, he was dragged into the darkness. They didn't say a word—just began beating him with what felt like lengths of pipe.

Terrified, he kicked out reflexively. He connected with a shin and twisted against the grasp of the one who held him by the forearm. The hold broke and he stumbled against a stack of cardboard cartons, feeling them start to slide backward away from his outstretched hands like a toppling pile of giant children's bricks. His two attackers had pulled the door shut as they dragged him in, and the cavernous space was completely dark. He slid along the surface of other stacked cartons, moving to one side as quickly as he could, feeling for a gap to hide in before they could find the lights or use their flashlights if they had them.

The two men were as blind as he was, but they could hear him. He could hear them, too. They sounded as asthmatic as beached whales and he caught the smell of stale beer. Who the hell were they? He didn't think burglars favored baked beans and canned tomatoes as a fenceable commodity these days—rationing had been over for decades. Were they after Gage's van, parked in the center of the floor?

No—they were after him. And they kept after him, through the stacks of cartons, around the walls, across the gap and along the side of the paneled van, following his movements, swinging their lengths of pipe and feeling for him in the dark. He realized they weren't using flashlights for fear of attracting the attention of some passerby.

His thick sodden overcoat had absorbed a lot of the initial blows, but he could feel dull pain across his shoulder blades. One ear was bleeding, too, but it had been a glancing blow—he'd pulled away just in time. He could hear their shuffling steps, hear the malevolent swishing whisper of the moving lengths of pipe. If he could get back to the door . . .

Sliding along the van's side, he felt its open window just at shoulder height. Grabbing hold of the frame, he kept his legs together and swung them up, catching one of the men somewhere between chest and gut. Still hanging onto the doorframe, he followed through, straightened his legs

with a quick thrust, and felt the heavy body give way. A
second later there was an almighty crash as the man hit a
stack of what must have been cartons of squash bottles. A
thick sweet smell of concentrated orange filled the darkness, mingling with the acrid fumes of gasoline from the
van and his own bitter sweat. He crashed back against the
van like the clapper of a bell, but kept his hold and tensed
his thighs to kick again. He heard the second man moving
farther to his right but missed with his next kick, crashing
awkwardly back against the van. In that moment the man
moved in, grabbing his coat sleeve.

The gusting wind had caught the edge of the double
doors and parted them slightly. Johnny could just make
out the upraised line of the thug's free arm made twice its
length by the pipe or whatever it was he was using as a
weapon. He wrenched free and heard the pipe or crowbar
whistle past his shoulder and hit the van with a metallic
clang. The impact knocked it from the man's hand. It
dropped and skittered across the floor with the pinging
rasp of metal on concrete. From the blackness in the rear
of the warehouse he could hear cursing and a crunching of
glass as the first man scrambled to his feet to try again.
The smell of orange was getting stronger as the smashed
bottles drooled their sticky contents out through the split
cartons.

Johnny made a break for the door but the one who'd
dropped his weapon leaped after him and caught him
around the throat, pulling him back. A fist started to
hammer at the side of his head and he started to go down.
The pale yellowish glow of the streetlights outside began
to shimmer and waver, making the line between the
slightly open doors seem to leak like the squash bottles. As
he began to sag he made one last attempt and reached back

with one foot to hook his attacker's knees. Off-balance, they swayed together and then hit the floor together, with Johnny underneath.

Dizzy from the head blows and the sudden loss of all the air from his chest, Johnny felt his brain begin to play a roaring descending organ chorale. He tried to drag himself out from under and toward the doors but the man grabbed his legs and then his hips, pushing him flat. Then the first man joined them and they both had him, one by the legs and one by the hair.

"Get his hands. He told us to get his hands," one of them growled, and Johnny felt himself rolled over, felt a foot planted on his left arm, felt another crash down onto his left hand. He'd instinctively doubled up the hand but the impact was brutal and pain shot through his knuckles and up his arm like a red-hot bolt from a crossbow.

He screamed.

Suddenly the big double doors were thrown fully open and the light from the streetlights outside showed up the big shapes of the two men who stood over him. He could see their upside down faces, twisted with implacable intent, lips back and eyes wide.

"Hey!" somebody shouted from the doorway. "Hey . . . stop that!"

The two men looked toward the door, cursed, gave him a last barrage of kicks and then ran out. He could hear, very clearly, the diminishing staccato of their running feet, and the thin piercing screech of a police whistle.

Johnny closed his eyes. His hand was a balloon of agony pierced by white-hot needles, exploding and contracting continuously, throbbing in perfect synchrony with the pulse that beat in his head and behind his eyes. There was the gritty sound of footsteps approaching, and then somebody knelt beside him. Forcing his eyes open he squinted up into the faint yellowish light and saw Gino's face hanging over his own.

"Johnny? Jesu . . . Johnny . . ." Abruptly Gino jumped up and Johnny could only see the legs of his jeans marked by two dark patches where the orange squash had soaked in. Gino was shouting. "In here . . . call an ambulance . . . hey . . ."

Yeah, thought Johnny, closing his eyes again.

Somebody'd better call an ambulance.

Please.

# 7

Gates appeared while the X rays were being developed, pushing aside the curtains of the casualty ward cubicle and staring at Johnny, who was hunched over on a chair, cradling his hand in his lap. They'd managed to get his overcoat off by cutting the sleeve away first. His face was smeared with oil and dirt, his hair stuck up in spikes on one side where he'd rolled into the spreading pool of orange squash, and the legs of his black trousers were wrinkled to the knee from his long walk in the rain. By contrast the upper half of his body, still in the formal clothes he'd worn for the concert, was immaculate. Even his bow tie was still in place.

He glanced up at Gates, his face drawn with pain, and he spoke in a dead, flat voice. "Where were you when I needed you?"

"In bed. Sorry."

"Early night? How pleasant."

"Considering it was the first time I'd been in bed in the past forty-eight hours, I *was* enjoying it," Gates said, and pulled over a chair to sit down. "They give you anything for the pain yet?"

"They said they did. I haven't noticed any improvement."

Gates lit a cigarette and passed it over, then lit another for himself, ignoring the No Smoking signs like the law-abiding officer he was. After a moment he spoke apologetically. "I'm afraid they got away."

"Oh."

"Did you get a clear look at them?"

"Not really—and only upside down, anyway."

"We can turn the mug shots around for you, it might help."

"I doubt it. Didn't your pet guardians of public safety who are so carefully following me every goddamn place I go get a look at them? And what the hell were *they* doing while—"

Gates was looking around for a place to put his ash. He leaned over and took a stainless-steel kidney dish from a trolley and tapped his cigarette on the edge. "They saw you go toward your door, getting your keys out of your pocket. Then their relief signaled them so they drove on down the street to report and hand over. The relief men drove back, parked, and assumed you'd gone up to your flat."

"Didn't they get suspicious when the lights didn't go on? Didn't they *hear* anything?"

Gates shrugged. "You don't always put on your lights, they said." Johnny sighed and nodded slightly as Gates continued. "They didn't *hear* anything because the warehouse doors were closed, the wind was howling, the rain was drumming on the roof of the car, and they were radioing in that they'd taken up the surveillance. They didn't figure on anything but a long boring night in the cold until that kid came along with your milk and pulled open the doors. They moved after that."

"But not fast enough."

"No," Gates allowed. "Not fast enough. There was a car waiting around the corner for your two 'friends' with the motor running."

"And let me guess—the registration plate was covered with mud?" Johnny asked. "I mean, *I* always do that myself when I go around to beat the hell out of somebody. Regular thing with me . . . I'm the cautious ty—" He swayed slightly in the chair and Gates reached out to push him back.

"Maybe you'd better lie down on the table over there," he suggested in a worried voice. Johnny shook his head, then shook it again, harder, as if to clear it.

"I'm okay."

"The car was a stolen Granada. They found it abandoned about a mile away. They'd chased it but there was another waiting for a changeover. No prints in the Granada, and all the officer saw of the other car was that it was big . . . might even have been a van, he said."

Johnny turned slightly in the chair to face him. "It was an old Rolls Silver Cloud. Claverton sent them."

"Did they say so?"

"They said, 'Get his hands . . . he told us to get his hands.' Who else would want to do something like that to me?"

"I don't know. You pay your union dues regularly?"

"Like clockwork. I'm not in debt to any loanshark and I haven't been trying to take over anybody's rackets. Those are the usual reasons in all the books, aren't they? It was Claverton, dammit."

"Take it easy," Gates said, alarmed at the way the blood seemed to come and go in Johnny's face, making him flushed with anger one moment and death's head gray the next. "If he did send them, we'll take care of it."

"Like you took care of me, I suppose," Johnny said bitterly. He looked down at his hand, which was wrapped loosely in gauze. A few spots of blood were spreading over the knuckles, staining the bandage. He didn't think he wanted to see what was underneath.

"We were—"

"I know, I know, keeping me under surveillance, not acting as bodyguards. Even so—"

"Even so, we didn't do our job," Gates agreed. "I said I was sorry."

"Maybe you'd better go and do it now, then," Johnny said. "Thanks for bothering to come down . . . or did you come to arrest me?"

"No, I didn't come to arrest you," Gates said, a little defensively. "I came to see how you were and if there was anything I could do."

"You should have left it in the jar by the door," Johnny said.

"Left what?"

"Your heart . . . there's no need for you to break it over me."

"Do I look like it's breaking?"

Johnny glanced over at him and narrowed his eyes. Gates' long, bony face was lined with exhaustion and his cheeks were rough with a day's growth of blond beard. There were dark smudges under his green eyes.

"It looks like it's breaking over something," Johnny finally said.

"The size of my paycheck, probably." Gates stood up. "One of my men will take your statement and drive you home. Come in when you feel up to it and we can look at some pictures."

"Upside down," Johnny reminded him.

"If it helps." Gates went out without a backward glance, stepping aside as a doctor came in with a large manila envelope marked "X Ray" in black letters along the back. The doctor nodded at Johnny, then went over and turned on a light box against the wall, taking the films out of the envelope and sliding them under the clips at the top. He stood there a long time looking at them, whistling softly between his teeth.

"Will I be able to play the piano when it heals?" Johnny asked.

"Ha, ha, ha," the doctor said, not turning around. He looked about nineteen, and wore wrinkled green khakis under his white coat.

Johnny swallowed as despair filled him—was it that bad, then? "You find that funny?"

The young doctor sighed and pulled the X rays out of the clips, switching off the light box and sitting down on a stool to put the films back into the envelope. "I did the first ten times it was pulled on me . . . not anymore."

"I don't understand." His face felt hot and tight where they'd stitched the reopened cut Claverton's ring had made, plus two new ones.

The young doctor scowled. "You say 'will I be able to play the piano?' and like a dimwit I say 'yes' and then you say 'that's wonderful, I could never play it before.' Big laugh." He didn't look particularly amused.

"I'm a musician—I earn my living playing the piano," Johnny said. "It was a perfectly serious question—will I be able to play again or do I have to learn to be a computer programmer?"

"Oh." The boy—he really seemed like a boy—wasn't sure, even then. "You meant it."

"I meant it."

"That explains something, then. Sorry." He leaned back on the stool, prepared to practice being a consultant surgeon. "There are no breaks. The synovial sac of the knuckle and first joint of the index finger were ruptured—you may develop arthritis there one day, but it can be treated. The main reason there were no bones broken—sorry, there *was* one tiny carpal cracked in the back of the hand but it's not a working bone in the sense you mean—was the fact that your fingers are so heavily muscled. The tendons took most of the impact and damage and they're going to show it, but I think you'll find they'll heal up all right." He took the films out and put them on the light box again. He and Johnny stared at Johnny's bones together. Then he leaned forward and peered intently at the film. "You use the little finger a lot?"

"I use them *all*," Johnny said pointedly.

"Mmmmm." He indicated one of the pictures. "Kind of difficult to assess soft tissue on this, but you might have trouble there. There's a man in Harley Street . . ."

"Pattinson."

The doctor turned. "You already go to him?"

"No, I never had to, but most pianists know the name. I'll make an appointment tomorrow. Can you give me the X rays?"

"No, sorry." He clicked off the light box. "He'll want to take his own, anyway. If you've got the money for it, he's your best bet."

"That's it?"

The doctor smiled and reached for his clipboard. "That's it as far as we're concerned. I'll strap the hand properly now we know there's no need for plaster. Oh . . ." he picked up an envelope the nurse had brought in and held it out. "You'll be wanting these in a few hours. That hand is going to start hurting like hell."

"It already does. I've got plenty of aspirin at home."

"They'll be about as much use as Smarties unless you want to risk killing yourself by swallowing fifty. Have you any idea how many nerves there are in the human hand? Take the pills, Mr. Cosatelli."

"Just keep taking the tablets?" Johnny asked, pocketing the envelope awkwardly.

"Until your eyes stop watering, yes. Pattinson will give you more if you need them. I'll write you a note for him." He pulled out a drawer and scrabbled in it, found some paper and wrote a note, then sealed it into another envelope and handed it over. "Protocol."

"Sounds like a wonder drug," Johnny said. "Ha, ha, ha."

"Ha, ha, ha," the doctor echoed, unsmiling. "Good luck."

The two detectives who had been watching without seeing anything took him home. They seemed slightly embarrassed by having had a sixteen-year-old boy do their work for them. It seemed to Johnny that not many students in Gino's fancy Hampstead school would have had the guts to open those doors and make a rush at the two monsters who'd been laying into him. As soon as he could, he was going to buy Gino the biggest damn stereo set he could find. Or a motorbike. Or a statue with "Hero" on the base. *Something.* But it wouldn't be enough—not nearly enough.

*

Gates slammed open the door to his office and saw Dunhill waiting. He looked at the clock on the wall—nearly midnight. "You didn't have to come down," he snapped.

"Neither did you," Dunhill said with a crooked grin. "Guilt doth not a soft mattress make."

"Who the hell said that?"

"Me. How is he?"

"His left hand is smashed," Gates growled, tugging off his damp raincoat and throwing it onto the table. "There were two of them, and they had specific instructions to go for the hands, according to him. If that kid hadn't come along and heard the noise . . ." he shrugged. "The music man won't be making music for a while—if ever."

"It's not really your fault," Dunhill said.

"No? I think it is." Gates rubbed at his eyes, trying to get the sand out and the sight in. "I should have seen it coming. I knew Claverton was getting pissed off because we haven't charged Cosatelli yet. He's the kind of man who wants things done and if they aren't, *he* does them."

"It didn't *have* to be Claverton," Dunhill protested.

"Oh, really? Who do you have in mind—the Islington branch of the Kumquat Tong? It was Claverton, and Cosatelli knows it. I don't think I've ever seen a man that angry and not screaming. It was a little scary, looking at him. If we can't locate the men, or make a solid connection with Claverton . . . *he's* going to start getting impatient, too."

"You'd better issue instructions, then. Make sure—"

"I am sick and goddamn tired of 'issuing instructions,'" Gates ground out between his teeth. "I am sick and tired of being told to sit back on my duff and watch those two go round in circles. I am sick of not getting any sleep, I am sick of walking around up to my armpits in garbage, I am sick of being a bloody cop!"

"So take the job in Brussels," Dunhill said quietly.

Gates looked at him sharply. "How did you know about that?"

Dunhill smiled. "Everybody knows about it, Dave. We're all detectives, remember? We pick up clues."

"It seems to me you'd be more use picking up a few clues on who killed the Kendrick girl instead of who's offering me a cushy job," Gates muttered.

"I'd be happy to," Dunhill said. "As soon as you tell me where to look."

Gates told him where to look but Dunhill said he didn't think there would be many clues there, beside which he was no contortionist and hadn't brought a mirror with him.

*

"Laynie? This is Johnny."

"Good morning, love—you're up early."

He was up early for the simple reason that he'd never been down. An hour after getting back from the hospital the hand had started to ache, then throb, then burn . . .

and the pills the doctor had given him didn't seem to do much but make it difficult to speak clearly.

"You'd better start rebooking my dates from today."

"Johnny! You're going to do it . . . that's wonderful!"

"No, it's not." Tersely he explained what had happened, and when she spoke again her elation had changed to outrage. He wished he had enough strength to match it.

"I'll be there in twenty minutes," she said, and hung up. Three hours later they were sitting in deep leather chairs in an office on Harley Street listening to Pattinson tell Johnny he was a lucky man.

"You'll have the use of that hand in a couple of weeks."

Laynie sighed deeply in relief. "Then you'll be able to do the concerts, love. Thank God."

Pattinson was a gaunt, narrow-headed man with a thick line of eyebrows that he now drew into a frown. "When I said the use of his hand I meant just that. He'll be able to hold a knife to cut his food, *not* play the piano. It could be months before he has sufficient flexibility . . ."

"Why months?" Johnny asked as Laynie groaned and closed her eyes.

Pattinson swiveled in his chair to look at him. "Simply because it will hurt, Mr. Cosatelli. It will hurt and it will be very, very stiff. There is deep bruising there. There may also be some nerve damage . . . I hope not, I pray not, but we won't be able to tell even that until the swelling has gone down."

"Swelling" was a medical euphemism. When Pattinson had carefully removed the hospital strapping, Laynie had turned away, white-faced. Johnny's left hand resembled a distended cow's udder, black, purple, and grotesque.

"It will be some time before you can even attempt a little light Chopin, I'm afraid."

"You make it sound like an invalid's breakfast," Laynie mumbled.

"I don't care if it hurts," Johnny said. The pills were still thickening his speech, but his mind was clear. Clear enough to make him realize how desperately he wanted to take up Price-Temple's challenge. "If I push it . . . work hard . . . will I damage it?"

"No . . . assuming there are no complications," Pattinson said slowly. "Not if you go carefully in the beginning and don't aggravate anything. Hands are really very satisfactory things to treat, even though they look perhaps the worst of all to begin with." Pattinson stared at his own hands, locked together over his flat midriff. "There are some who might want to go in and stitch that ligament in the little finger . . . but in my opinion it's best left alone. If you're prepared to work closely with one of my therapists and put up with a lot of pain—and I *mean* a lot of pain, Mr. Cosatelli—then I suppose we might manage a few minor miracles. I take it you have some pressing reason for all this?"

"He has an opportunity to appear with Price-Temple," Laynie said, and Pattinson raised an eyebrow. "In August . . . late August."

"I see." Pattinson specialized in hands, and there were many pianists and other musicians who had cause to thank him for an extended career. She didn't have to say any more. "I see. Well, the next two weeks are critical," he went on, leaning forward to draw a prescription pad toward him. He brought his swivel chair down with a thump. "We'll give it heat and wax baths . . . come and see me next Monday morning, Mr. Cosatelli. Until then, give it all the rest you can, and get plenty yourself. Don't try to flex it at all, keep it elevated as much as possible. I'll write you up a prescription for more painkillers so you can sleep. Do you like oranges?"

"Oranges?" Johnny asked dully.

"Some people think vitamin C is a help in these things. I'll write you up for some of that, too . . . there's no harm in it and it might make a difference."

"Oranges, yet. My God," Laynie grumbled.

"Shut up, Laynie," Pattinson said amiably. "You come in here and disrupt my entire morning list, upset my nurses and my schedule, threaten to have your clients boycott my practice unless I see Mr. Cosatelli immediately . . . the very least you can do is accept my verdict without any snide remarks."

"May your sutures never snap, Patrick," Laynie said meekly.

"Amen," Pattinson murmured. "And may *your* tendons remain intact when you get my bill."


Laynie bustled around the flat like the mother hen she wasn't, cooking him a meal, putting clean sheets on the bed, and in general doing the things she always paid other people to do for her. She was not, as she often pointed out with asperity, one of nature's housekeepers. It wasn't until he noticed she kept slamming down every object she dusted that Johnny understood. Anger was keeping her on the move, simple, general rage.

He winced as she finished restacking a pile of scores and whapped them back onto the piano. "For pete's sake, Laynie, give it a rest, will you?"

"What?" She picked up her cigarette from the ashtray, took a deep drag, replaced it.

"The cleaning, the rearranging, the crashing—it's not

going to help and it's giving me a bloody headache trying to keep you in focus," he complained.

"Dammit, John, you've got to get yourself organized," she said. "All this coming and going, this in-ing and out-ing, no wonder you never get down to any serious work."

"I'm perfectly well organized and you know it," he said. "Sit *down*."

She stared at him for a minute, sighed, plunked herself down on the chair in the curve of the piano, and crossed her feet at the ankles, very demure, very much the lady.

"All right, then, tell me about this son of a bitch Claverton," she ordered. "I guess I'm calm enough now to listen."

"He thinks I killed Lisa, that's all."

"Stupid as well as sadistic. Go on."

"I guess he thought I should be punished, so he sent a couple of heavies around to take care of it."

"Is that what the police say? What this what's his name . . . Gates says?"

"No. It's what I say. Claverton took a swing at me the other night, and when Gates didn't arrest me on his say-so, I guess he got impatient. End of story."

"Hardly. Who is he, what does he do for a living?"

"He's an antique dealer, very rich, very big deal."

"*I've* never heard of him," she said, as if that placed him. Maybe it did, Johnny acknowledged, she knew practically everybody in the whole damn world, or so it sometimes seemed. In the beginning he'd always felt as if he were her only client because every time he called she always made him feel that way. It was only little by little that he learned about some of the *other* musicians she handled, names that made him look very small indeed. Even so, she always had time. Always. And it was only when he heard a New York agent over on a visit describe her as a tiger that he began to realize just how lucky he was. "Sweet and smiling until it comes time to make a deal," the fellow agent said. "Then watch out. It isn't until it's all over they realize they've been begging her to take everything she went in there to get in the first place. Plus whatever popped into her mind as they went along."

"It doesn't matter," Johnny said. He hadn't been lying about the headache.

"Of course it matters," she snapped. "I intend to sue him for every bloody Dresden shepherdess he's got in stock."

"Gates doesn't seem to think we can connect him with it."

"As far as I can see this Gates doesn't seem to think at all," she said crossly.

"I'm sure he's very good at his job," Johnny sighed.

"Has it occurred to him that maybe Claverton had Lisa killed the way she was and when she was in order to make you look guilty? Two birds with one kick—or one bird and one rooster."

"Why should he do that?"

"You tell me."

"I don't know. I don't care. Where did you put those pills?"

She looked at her watch. "He said every four—"

"It *hurts*, Laynie!" he shouted.

"All right, all right." She brought him the pills and some orange juice to wash them down. "You'd better get some sleep," she said gruffly, looking down at him. "I stacked some extra pillows on the bed so you could keep your hand elevated."

"You want to undress me and put me into my little jimmy-jams, too?" he asked sarcastically.

"If I'd been interested I'd have done it years ago. Musicians turn me off, frankly."

"Then why are you a musicians' agent?"

"That's why. No confusion of business and pleasure. Come on, Sunny Jim, move that tight little Welsh ass of yours off that couch and into bed so I can get back to the office."

"Well, who asked you to hang around, anyway?"

"Pattinson—he said you might get some delayed shock."

"Oh." He stood up. "Glad to know it wasn't natural sympathy—it might have ruined your image," he muttered, staggering slightly as he went toward the bedroom.

She turned away quickly. "Damn right," she whispered, then tugged her sweater down over her hips and put on her coat. "You said antique dealer, didn't you?"

There was a silence and then he appeared in the bedroom door half out of his shirt, his hair in his eyes and his face sweaty. "Why?" he asked suspiciously.

"Ilsa is into antiques." Ilsa was her partner in the agency. "We split the world down the middle, I know half and she knows the other half."

"Why?" he asked again.

She buttoned up her coat. "Because I won't know how much to sue him for until I know how much he's worth. Also I want to find out where he lives so I can send somebody around to step on *his* hands—or anything else they find dangling."

He came a few steps into the room. "I don't want you to get mixed up in all this. Leave it alone."

She gazed at him for a moment, then waved her hand

vaguely. "Darling, I'm all talk and no action, you know that."

He didn't know that at all.

"Go to bed," she ordered. "I'll ring you tonight."

He listened to her going down the stairs, not knowing whether to believe she'd only been talking or not. Something else that New York agent had said came back to him:

"The welfare offices are full of people who tried to cross Laynie Black or one of her clients."

Maybe he should stop feeling sorry for himself and start pitying Mark Claverton.

# 8

Sleep wouldn't come. The pain wouldn't go.

Although he thought of himself as right-handed, he found his left hand played a major part in his life, and every time he moved it, the point was made. Eventually he took a morbid interest in counting the times he reached for something, started to scratch his left ear, touched the edge of a piece of furniture for balance, and found the boxing glove of gauze in direct and painful contact with solid and immovable objects. When he got to a hundred he gave it up, especially as he found it made him cry.

Not a lot—just enough to be humiliating.

Getting dressed again was no more fun than getting undressed had been, and he had to get his old electric razor out of the cupboard in order to handle the beard that refused to stop growing no matter how he tried to reason with it. He hated the electric razor, never felt shaved unless he'd got soap up his nose and into his ears.

And when he tried to call for a cab he spent at least five minutes trying to keep the phone from sliding across the table, eventually steadying it with his foot. The inelegant posture reminded him that he had other bruises as souvenirs of the attack.

He did not arrive at the club a happy man.

It was neither the best club they'd played nor the worst. With the lights full on to facilitate setting the tables, its rather shabby carpet revealed the sad history of a hundred drinks spilled, a thousand cigarettes dropped, a million feet scuffed and dragged between the tables.

Moosh was sitting at the piano, idly poking a fat black finger among the keys to pick out an "Over the Rainbow" Garland would never have recognized. He heard Johnny's footsteps crossing the small dance floor and looked up, started to smile, then stopped both the music and the greeting in one. He stared at Johnny's newly decorated face and at the white boxing glove in the sling.

"Jesus . . ." he whispered. Johnny tried to smile and felt the stitches pull. After a moment, Moosh swallowed and tried again. "I told you it wouldn't get better if you picked at it." When Johnny tried to step up onto the stand he lost his balance slightly and Moosh knocked over the piano bench getting to him. They swayed for a second, then Moosh stepped back and pulled him onto solid ground. Grunting, he retrieved the bench and pushed Johnny onto it. "Why the hell didn't you call?"

"No point. I'll be all right."

"The hell you will. What happened?"

"I thought you'd never ask," Johnny said wearily. "A funny thing happened to me on the way to . . ." he trailed off. "I got beaten up by a couple of Claverton's boys."

"Claverton's 'boys'? I thought he was some kind of antique dealer, not Public Enemy Number One."

"No . . . *I'm* Public Enemy Number One, as far as he's

concerned, anyway. They were *told* to smash my hands. Only managed one."

"One's enough."

Johnny shrugged. "One's enough to play, too. Baz will just have to fill in the spaces."

Moosh leaned over to snag a chair from one of the tables near the rear edge of the stand, turned it around and straddled it, his dark, moon-shaped face balancing on his crossed arms. "You mean you're going to *play* like that?"

"Sure, why not?"

"Because it will sound crappy, that's why not. In addition to which, Masuto will try to pay you half-rate since you'll only be playing half-assed. Plus if you'd called me earlier we could have got somebody to sit in. You're crazy, John, I always knew it, now you've proved it. Anyway, it's not just the hand . . . you look like you've been harled through a knothole backwards."

"Harl" was one of the words they'd discovered many years ago while killing time on long train trips by playing word games with a dictionary. It meant to be dragged around by the hair, among other things.

"I'd have been disappointed if you hadn't said that," Johnny said, turning to face the piano. After a moment he began to play, helplessly compelled, as always, by the stretch of the keys and the silence before him. He found he had to sit well back on the bench in order to give his right arm a full reach, but managed a respectable unadorned version of "Last Night When We Were Young."

Moosh heard him out. "We can't play ballads all night, John," he said, gently.

"I'm not asking you to . . . I'll keep up."

"But why? *Why?* We've only got the week to finish out, then no more live gigs until July. You can rest up . . ."

"Call it a farewell performance," Johnny said, moving into an up-tempo version of "But Not for Me." It sounded pathetic, but he kept on, searching for the compensations and makeshifts he'd use to cover.

"It's that bad?" Moosh asked, horrified.

Johnny shook his head. "Nope . . . it'll heal. Not goodbye, music, just goodbye jazz." He let his right hand drop into his lap, shifted around on the bench and told Moosh about Price-Temple. When he'd finished he went back to his game of trying to sound like a whole man on half-power. It was starting to come out a little like the insistent treble of the Modern Jazz Quartet.

Moosh sat, watching Johnny's right hand move methodically, rhythmically, disguising as he went. He'd always been fascinated by Johnny's hands, never known a man who could keep his hands so clean without making a fuss about it. Square carpenter's hands, thick-fingered, broadpalmed, always graceful without effeminacy. No, whatever else Johnny was, he wasn't effeminate. They'd always kidded him about looking like a chartered surveyor pretending to be a musician, but Cosatelli had never made any concession to a jazz "image," often appearing in a dark three-piece suit to play the raunchiest gigs. He played strong, masculine jazz but very laid-back, with sudden and surprisingly tender passages that caught audiences unaware. Those passages had never startled Moosh or Baz—when Johnny played Debussy or Satie you'd think he had butterflies growing from those muscular wrists. Moosh wondered how Johnny would look pinned like a butterfly on a board. Finally he spoke through clenched teeth.

"Thank you, John."

Johnny glanced up, intending to smile, but was stopped

by the malevolence in Moosh's face. He stared at him as the big black man went on in a small black voice.

"I was sitting here looking forward to telling you that on today's new chart 'Samba Break' was at number forty-eight and climbing. To saying that we'd had an offer from Ronnie Scott for a couple of weeks in September. To telling you how Sam Dorking has said he can take over again on drums when Buster pisses off next week—Sam was always the best we ever had, shouldn't have lost him in the first place. And now you tell me it's all over, just like that. *Damn* you."

"Laynie never said anything about Scott's."

"No, I guess she wouldn't, what with one thing and another," Moosh snapped. "Like her blue-eyed boy going 'legit' again the way she's been plugging for years. I can imagine that bitch keeping her mouth shut on *that* score, all right."

"Hey, Moosh . . . come on—" Johnny began, but Moosh cut him off.

"Don't you 'Hey, Moosh' me, white-ass. Don't you blink those big blues at me and expect me to send flowers to you onstage when you finish making a bloody fool of yourself. You're walking out on big money and big-time for some kind of fairy tale, dammit. You won't make it, dumbo, you'll *never* make it back."

"Price-Temple thinks—"

Moosh stood up and made an ugly sucking sound with his thick lips.

"Price-Temple isn't God. If you ask me he's got his eye on all the publicity he's going to get out of it. Rachmaninov, Bartok? Like hell. You'll see—you'll end up playing Gershwin, or some young dude's idea of a jazz concerto . . . oh, yeah. You're a freak, Johnny . . . that festival is a circus and you're the Main Attraction, you'll see."

"You're wrong, Moosh. You don't understand . . ." Johnny protested feebly, wondering if maybe Moosh didn't have something.

"Damn *right* I don't understand!" Moosh shouted, hitting the piano a blow that set the strings thrumming and caused a couple of the waiters to stop what they were doing and watch the unscheduled floor show. "I don't understand how a man who's supposed to be sensible can turn his back on something he's built up for so long. Listen, I *know* you don't need the money we make, everything *you* touch pays off. But we scrabblin', man, we diggin' for every cent!" In his temper Moosh was falling back on his Poor Black Boy Act, something that was totally foreign to him and usually put on only for a laugh, seeing as his upbringing had been as middle-class and grammar school as Johnny's own.

"I've got a right to do what *I* want to do, dammit!" Johnny flared back.

"That's just it—you ain't got *no* right, not anymore. We got a name, we got a reputation, we got a *chance* here. You traipse off to play fancy-pants and we're left in the shit, all on our owney-oh. You know what happens when groups bust up . . . you *know* what happens." He hit the piano again in his fury.

"I know what happens when people start breaking up pianos in *my* place," came a voice from the side of the stage. "They pay for them." Charley Masuto stepped up onto the stand and glared at Moosh. "You two have a problem, settle it in the alley, not in my club."

"No problem, Charley," Johnny said wearily. "Just a difference of opinion, that's all."

"Sounded a little more than that—I could hear you all the way down the hall. If I want to put on fights I'll set up a ring—you guys are here to play music. Unless you feel like quitting right now." He'd crossed to the piano and caught sight of Johnny's bandaged hand for the first time. "What the hell's the matter with your hand?"

"Hangnail," Johnny said.

"Somebody stepped on it," Moosh said loudly. "Shame they didn't step on his *haid* when they had the chance."

Masuto's eyes narrowed. "That right?" he asked Johnny.

"More or less. No problem . . . I can play."

"Let me hear something . . ." Masuto challenged.

Johnny obliged with a few bars of Liszt's Hungarian Rhapsody. Seeing Masuto's expression, he switched over to "Night and Day" and Masuto's face cleared a little, but not much.

"Not exactly your best, but I guess you can play, at that," he grudged. "What's this about somebody stepping on your hand?"

"Nothing."

"I don't want any trouble here," Masuto said cautiously. "I've got my liquor license coming up for renewal. I already stretched a point with this murder business . . . you being a suspect and all . . ."

"I'm not a suspect," Johnny lied.

"You got cops *following* you . . . doesn't do a hell of a lot for my business having the place watched when you're here . . ."

"They're protecting me," Johnny said.

Masuto's eyes went to his bandaged hand. "So I see. My customers don't know that . . . cops are cops and bad news for a lot of them. I don't like my name in the papers in connection with any goddamn murder, Cosatelli. Rubs off, you know?"

"You've had your name in the papers before, Charley," Johnny said softly. Masuto's reputation was hardly savory. They'd only taken the gig here on Moosh's insistence. Glancing at Moosh he wondered if Masuto was the one who had a lock on his finances. When Moosh began to play a peace overture, his suspicion was confirmed.

"Hey, Charley, we was just arguing about music, man," Moosh said with an abrupt alteration of tone. "No problem. Johnny plays better with one hand than most guys with three, you know that."

Masuto glanced at Moosh with contempt. "I'd rather he used two, like everyone else."

"Yeah, well, it's only temporary . . . be okay in a few days," Moosh said with an attempted laugh. "Don't make no never-mind."

Masuto's lizard-black eyes shifted back to Johnny. "I don't want any trouble," he said again. "That clear?"

"As crystal," Johnny said. "There won't be any trouble from me."

"You," Masuto said to Moosh. "*You* I want to talk to in my office, presto. That bracelet you brought me—"

Moosh raised a cautionary hand, then turned the gesture into one of smoothing back his nappy hair. Masuto glanced at Johnny and saw his puzzled expression.

"You get on with your practicing, Cosatelli—you need all you can get," he growled, then jerked his head at Moosh, stepped down from the stand and started for his office. Moosh hesitated for a moment before following him.

"John . . . sorry I—" he paused. "You got to do it, then I guess you got to do it. Just—a shame, that's all."

"Yes, it's a shame," Johnny said heavily. "Hate to see you go back to pickin' cotton, Tom. Seeing as you can call your own shots as to who you go with next, as you damn well know. You *and* Baz, for that matter. You don't need me."

"*I* don't . . . no," Moosh said carefully. "Not *me* you got to worry for, is it?" And he followed Masuto down the hall.

For a while it looked like there *was* going to be trouble after all, because Baz was late arriving, and only skidded in at the last possible moment, looking like death warmed over. He stared at Johnny's hand but had no chance to ask questions before the first set. It went well enough, considering the undercurrents between Moosh and Johnny. Johnny made a joke out of the situation to the audience and they went along with it amiably enough, accepting that any man dumb enough to get caught in a revolving door couldn't be expected to sound like a genius with what was left. He didn't know how long their patience would continue, and he wasn't at all sure how long his stamina would last, either. Masuto was scowling when he finished the last number, standing in the entrance to the dressing rooms with his arms folded across his chest, but he let him pass by without comment.

Johnny was in the toilet, struggling with the realization that zippers were also a two-handed proposition, when the door flew back to hit the wall and Baz came in.

"You're out of your mind!" he shouted.

Johnny jerked around, startled. "I'll be out of my pants and into court on indecent exposure unless you pull up this goddamn zip for me," he said helplessly.

Baz walked over and did up the zip as if Johnny were his

three-year-old son, then turned away. "You should have gone before you left the house," he muttered automatically. Johnny started to laugh, but Baz whirled around again and he was surprised to see how angry he was. "Am I supposed to *believe* what Moosh just told me?" he demanded.

"I don't know—what did he tell you?" Now he was having a struggle with the roller towel. He gave it a yank and succeeded in pulling it right out of the holder. "Damn."

"That you've got delusions of grandeur about going back to classical work and leaving us . . ."

Johnny was peering up into the towel holder, trying to see what he could do to repair the damage. Nothing, as far as he could tell. He'd just qualified for a rating as Amateur Vandal, with one hand tied in front of him. "It's not really settled . . ."

"*Are* you going to do it?"

"If my hand heals up properly—maybe." He felt in his jacket pocket for his pills.

"And what's going to happen to *me?*" Baz wanted to know. His face was taut and pale, and he kept licking his lips.

Johnny was genuinely puzzled. "To you? Jesus, Baz . . . you're one of the best front men around. You could bring in another piano player and form your own group, or pick up with somebody else . . "

"No," Baz said.

"What do you mean, 'no'?" Johnny said, feeling pain and irritation finally getting the better of him. He was trying his best, wasn't he? "They'll line up to get you . . ."

"No," Baz said again. "I can't play jazz with anyone else, you know that, Johnny. You *know* that."

"Balls," Johnny snapped. "You play with other people all the time, for crying out loud. You do as much session work as I do, you—"

"Session work, sure. But not jazz, Johnny, not off the top."

He realized now what Baz was on about, and refused to go along with it. This was an old problem that never seemed to get any better, no matter how hard he tried. Baz persisted in the delusion that he could only play jazz with Johnny, that he was no good without him. It wasn't true, but it might as well have been because Baz believed it. That's all it took. Baz leaned on Johnny for support, he leaned on the bottle for support, he leaned on all kinds of things, convinced he couldn't stand alone. It was true that most of Baz's work in the quartet was carefully blocked out in advance, that he needed to know where he was going at all times, and couldn't blow a solo without preparation. In that, he was not and had never been a true jazz musician. On the other hand, his facility with so many instruments made him a gift to any group prepared to take that extra time he needed. Johnny said as much while Baz paced back and forth in the small tiled room, his face reflected in cubistic sections by the broken mirror over the washbasin.

"I can't, I can't," he kept saying.

"Then why not go back to symphony work," Johnny suggested. "I'm sure Laynie could get you—"

"Bloody Berlioz!" Baz shouted. "You know I can't stand that, I *need* jazz, Johnny, it keeps me sane, keeps me . . . free."

"Then accept jazz and do it, dammit. You can't have it

both ways, Baz. You'll be fine if you just—" He swallowed the pills with water from a paper cup. "Trust yourself," he finished.

"Don't leave me, Johnny," Baz pleaded, clutching at the sling and causing the bandaged hand to bang against Johnny's chest. Johnny could smell the liquor on his breath, and frowned. In between binges Baz usually stayed off the stuff. "We have the new album to cut in November . . . we've got a contract . . ." Baz said.

"We can still do the album . . . but it's the last one in the deal and I don't want to sign for any more . . ." Johnny said, trying to pull away.

"Don't leave, Johnny . . . not *now* . . ." Baz's voice was thinning and rising, growing shrill with desperation.

It had to be the booze. Baz had never come right out and said it in so many words before, he'd always been careful not to risk it. Bewildered and fuddled by the combination of pain, drugs, and exhaustion, Johnny tried to recall what he'd read about alcoholism. Wasn't irrationality one of the signs of advanced—

"You guys want to neck, do it on your own time, not mine," came Masuto's voice from the doorway. "Take your hands off him, Bennett," he continued levelly, stepping over and disengaging Johnny from Baz's grasp with surprising gentleness. He leaned Johnny against the wall as if he were a broomstick, then turned to Baz and spoke with venom. "I don't know what *your* complaint is, but I've got customers out there waiting to be entertained. That's what I'm paying you for, remember? I signed a nice straight quartet and all I've got tonight is arguments and lousy jazz. The man's got trouble, Bennett, he's sick and—"

"I'm sick of being yelled at," Johnny acknowledged

fuzzily. Here he was, just going along trying to do his best, and everybody was getting mad at him. He'd showed up to play, hadn't he? He hadn't let them down. Masuto, at least, saw that. But Baz and Moosh . . . they were supposed to be his friends. He's always *thought* they were his friends, anyway. He'd always been *their* friend, always tried to—

Things looked different from the floor, he discovered. The bottom of one of the urinals was cracked and discolored, there was a heap of dust in each corner of the room where the mops of the cleaners had pushed it and left it. Masuto wore socks with clocks up the side. Baz had a stain on the cuff of his trousers. They were arguing somewhere in the distance above him. He wanted to go home. He'd had enough. Or maybe he'd just go to sleep right here, if nobody minded. He'd stay well out of the way, if they wanted to use the john they could just sort of step over him. . . .

He woke up in his own bed and saw a strange man kneeling in his closet, doing something with a box.

"Uhnnnnnuah," Johnny mumbled, and the man turned around. It wasn't a strange man, it was Detective Inspector Gates, and he had a gold-buckled black moccasin in one hand.

"Good morning," Gates said, standing up and tossing the shoe into the closet. "You look like a raccoon."

"You look like a shoe salesman," Johnny grunted and tried to sit up, then yelped as a stab of pain went through his bandaged hand. "How did you get in?" For that matter how had *he* got in?

"My sergeant let me in," Gates said, coming over to stand by the bed. "They drove you home from the club— you collapsed in the john. They called a doctor but he said it was just exhaustion so they brought you home and put you to bed. Your shoes are innocent, by the way."

"Wonderful." He wondered if Gates was going to start charging him taxi fares, his men seemed to spend most of their time transporting his battered body from one place to another.

"You haven't come down to look at those pictures," Gates said.

"How careless of me." He thought about getting up, then thought about staying right where he was for the next fifteen years or so. "Why don't you just ask Claverton who they were?"

"I did," Gates told him. "He said he didn't know. He asked which hospital you were in so he could send some flowers. I told him you were at home but receiving no more visitors."

"I bet that disappointed him."

"He did seem a little downcast," Gates admitted cheerfully.

Johnny squinted at the clock beside the bed. Almost ten. He seemed to remember they'd been scheduled to do a session date somewhere this morning, and wondered if Moosh and Baz had found someone to sit in for him. That brought back the scenes in the club the night before, and he gave no thanks for the memory. He wondered if Masuto had fired them or not.

Probably.

The conclusion filled him with an immense relief, and he felt encouraged enough to try swinging his legs over the side of the bed. Nothing fell off. He knew nothing fell off because everything was still hurting, but it was a kind of reassuring torture he was learning to live with. Shivering, he discovered he was wearing his underpants and nothing else. Large discolored blotches had appeared on his body, making him look like a modern painting done by a chimpanzee with only blue, green, and purple on his palette. He staggered around the bed, past Gates, through the living room and into the kitchen, hefting the kettle to see if there was enough water in it and then plugging it in awkwardly.

Gates had followed him and leaned against the breakfast bar. "What are you going to do today?" he asked in an interested tone.

"Ache," Johnny said, going past him again to get his robe out of the bathroom and struggle into it.

"No plans for a recital at the Albert Hall or cutting a Number One pop single?"

Johnny glowered at him on the way back to the kitchen. "Go away."

"You're very grouchy in the morning," Gates observed.

Johnny looked at him across the counter. "Why don't you go arrest somebody for parking illegally?" he said.

"It's my day off," Gates said. "I'm going to a funeral."

"Oh?"

"Lisa Kendrick's funeral," Gates went on quietly.

"Oh." Oh hell, oh damn, oh blast.

"Thought maybe you'd like to come along," Gates said.

"Why?" He shouldn't have got up after all, he felt lousy.

Gates raised one shoulder slightly. "Pay your last respects . . . you did love her, once, or so you said."

"Did I?"

"Did you love her or did you say it?" Gates countered.

"Go to hell," Johnny snapped, jerking his good arm back as the kettle suddenly hissed steam against it. What did the man want from him? Tears and protestations? Anger? A confession? Of course, that was it. More pressure. More bloody pressure.

"Do you want to go with me?" Gates asked.

"To hell?"

"To the funeral."

"No. Yes. I don't *know* . . . I just woke up, dammit."

"It isn't until twelve-thirty," Gates said. "You don't have to decide this minute."

"Are you going to stand there until I *do* decide?" Johnny wanted to know. "If so, you might as well be useful and do some toast."

"Fair enough," Gates said, taking off his coat. Johnny watched him cut the bread and put it into the toaster.

"I *have* to go, is that it?" he asked, after a minute.

"It's entirely up to you," Gates said, getting the butter out of the refrigerator. Next, Johnny decided, he'd be moving into the place.

"I don't like funerals," he said sulkily.

"Neither do I," Gates agreed. "But you just can't leave dead bodies lying around all over the place without—"

"Shut up!" Johnny heard himself shout suddenly. Where had that come from?

"Sorry," Gates said, softly, watching him.

He walked out of the kitchen and sat down at the piano, shaking. He could hear Gates pottering about, clunking down cups and knives, could almost hear him breathing, waiting, like a cat at a mousehole.

"I didn't kill her," he whispered to the keyboard.

"What?" Gates asked, from right behind him.

"I said I didn't kill her," he repeated, more loudly, without turning around.

"As long as you're sure." Out of the corner of his eye he saw that Gates had put everything onto a tray and was carrying it across to the coffee table. The smell of the buttered toast made his stomach turn over. Abruptly he began to play, attacking the piano as if it had accused him, forcing the sound up to clear his head and drive the anger out, lunging from right to left trying to get everything in and missing most of it.

Gates, on the settee with a cup halfway to his mouth, watched the stocky figure at the piano. The top of the toweling robe had fallen open, exposing the play of the muscles beneath it. He could see that Cosatelli's chest development was similar to that of a tennis player's, which made sense, he supposed. The bare thigh was well-muscled, too, pelted with a thick growth of hair that flexed as the skin stretched over the pumping leg, pedal down, pedal up, pedal down. The music was ragged, and though it was not familiar he instinctively sensed gaps and emptiness that should have been filled. Despite that, he was stunned with the display of both expertise and passion. Perhaps he'd been wrong about Cosatelli. Perhaps he *could* kill, after all.

Johnny hit the final chord so hard he jarred his wrist and sat back, rubbing it against his leg.

The silence was almost louder than the music. "That was Bach," Gates said, in some awe.

Johnny nodded. "Not quite as Bach intended, of course." Lightly, he ran over a phrase or two again, listening, correcting.

Suddenly Gates understood something about Cosatelli. He saw the music had done something to him, changed him, and he recognized the signs. Cosatelli was an addict. Not to drugs or drink, but to his instrument. He didn't work all the hours God sent because he was ambitious or liked to keep his bank balance sweet—he worked because he couldn't let it alone. And he saw how much destruction Claverton had achieved—because he was as certain as Cosatelli that it had been Claverton's doing—by smashing even one hand, even temporarily.

It had been a stupid move—as stupid as wounding a tiger and leaving it alive.

"Your coffee's getting cold," he said quietly, carefully.

Johnny sighed and got up to come over. "Thanks," he said, settling into one of the chairs opposite Gates.

"I thought you were strictly a jazz man," Gates said after a while.

"No," Johnny said.

"What's the difference—technically?" Gates asked idly.

Johnny squinted at him. He'd been right the first time, Gates *was* a strange man. A minute before he'd been after a murderer, now he wanted music lessons.

"Technically—a lot less than most people think," Johnny said quietly. "Rhythm and phrasing, for the most part. Structurally a tune is a tune, no matter who composed it. As a matter of fact, there always used to be an improvisatory section in sonatas and concertos, when the performer was allowed to do his own thing with the composer's material. And that's all a jazz musician does with a standard popular tune. He knocks the phrasing around against different rhythms, of course."

"And that's it?"

Johnny nodded. "If he's playing solo, that's it. It's sort of like—" he paused, considering. "Have you ever seen a slalom course?"

"Skiing, you mean?"

"Uh-huh. Jazz is like that. But instead of those sticks with flags on them, you have what's called a chord chart—a set sequence of chords arising from the melody. When you play, you have to follow the course, go around all the flags in precisely the right order and at exactly the right time—but what you do in between is entirely up to you. And what you do in between is jazz. Instant composition off the top of your head. When you play in a group, it gets a little more complicated, because you not only have to follow the chord chart and do your own thing, you also have to blend with what the *others* are doing at the same time. That's why a musician needs two good ears as well as two good hands." He stared down at his white gauze boxing glove. "You have to know *exactly* what the others are doing and *exactly* where they're going—otherwise you can get yourselves into one hell of a crash." He smiled, slightly. "Sticks and skis and broken legs all over the place."

"I'm afraid that's what it sounds like to me, sometimes," Gates said.

Johnny nodded. "Me, too. Generally you're supposed to avoid it, for the sake of the audience. Although sometimes you get the feeling they come on the off-chance you'll draw blood, the way people go to car races or boxing matches. When it's absolutely perfect, the thrill is gone."

"Is that why a lot of jazz musicians die young?"

Dying again, Johnny thought. It wasn't far away, after all.

"They don't, not anymore. Music is a business, now. A few use drugs or booze to dull the strain of performing, but not so many. If you have two good ears and two good hands you still need one other thing. Like any worker, you've got to show up to get paid. Because studio time is expensive, and because the few clubs there are run on a very narrow profit margin, you've got to be reliable and produce according to contract. The guys who pay you don't have a lot of sympathy with hangovers, artistic tantrums, and sloppy work, and they don't have to put up with it because there's always somebody waiting to step into your blue suede shoes. Take a look at the top jazz men today and you'll see a very tough, very healthy, very practical bunch of geniuses who've got their dates booked two, sometimes three years in advance. In that they're exactly like classical musicians."

"You make it sound like a grind."

"*That's* a grind, but the music doesn't need to be. When you sit down to play—when they flip their switches or turn the lights down—then you're free. When you're actually playing, nobody can get at you. It's the only time you're safe." He drank a little of his coffee. "The only time," he whispered, half to himself.

Gates saw the shaking had stopped, now. Cosatelli still hadn't eaten anything, but he seemed to have been nourished, and no longer had to rest his coffee mug on the belt of his robe to keep from spilling it. That had been Gates' intention, but he almost hated himself in that moment, knowing he was simply manipulating Cosatelli for his own ends. Pushing him around, over, and perhaps even through the hurdles of an altogether different obstacle course. One that was as strange to a musician as it was familiar to a detective who *was* waiting for the crash. Cosatelli's business was music, his was murder, and they were both experts. But they didn't belong in the same room together, and he regretted it. On the other hand, he didn't think Cosatelli was a fool. He was perfectly capable of recognizing danger—when he could see it coming his way.

Johnny closed his eyes, leaned his head against the back of his chair, and addressed the ceiling. "Where are they burying her?" he asked.

It seemed a perfectly straightforward question, but to Gates it almost sounded like surrender.

# 9

The weather cooperated with the occasion, pouring down in a steady mistlike drizzle that permeated everything with damp misery. Having performed all *their* forensic rituals on Lisa Mary Kendrick, Gates realized she was now having her last slow dance with society. Apparently the morticians could not undo what the murderer had done, for the coffin was closed.

The service had been brief, the words mere incantation by a stranger, and attendance was minimal. The bulk of the cortege was made up of Claverton's friends and business associates, and among all the vicuna overcoats and cashmere suits, Johnny's was the only black armband. He'd had to ask Rosa to sew it on for him. She seemed to have recovered from her illness and had done the sewing with quick stitches and nods of approval as he stood next to the slicing machine waiting for Gates to come back for him. Not a funeral lover, but a lover nonetheless, it seemed the least Johnny could do. A final, empty caress.

At the cemetery the leafless trees bowed their heads more heavily than the mourners, long slow drips of moisture sliding down their branches to spatter and blot the shoulders beneath. The open spaces stretched on all sides. Only trees and gravestones, hazing together in the gray shrouds of rain that billowed occasionally in the fitful gusts of wind, broke the illusion of infinite expanses of grass and endless graveled paths. In the invisible distance, the circling traffic played a single-chord requiem that only Johnny and the robin perched on a nearby marble angel seemed to appreciate. For one mad and maudlin moment Johnny eyed the robin, wondering if Lisa had been reincarnated into its cheerful guise and had come to watch. It would have been like her to wear red to her own funeral. Toujours gai, Lisa.

Flanked by Gates and buttressed by two more plain-clothes detectives who blended into the background and seemed more interested in distant figures than those around them, Johnny had been unnoticed by Claverton at first. But now, as the earth fell onto the coffin between them, he lifted his eyes and met Johnny's gaze. It didn't register at first.

He stared into Johnny's face blankly, and then recognition drew his lips back slightly from the perfect teeth. Johnny gazed back at him steadily, watching anger grow in the red-rimmed eyes. Claverton looked older than he had outside the police station the other night. Deep gullies now ran through his cheeks from temple to jaw, and his mustache was badly trimmed, giving a slightly askew look to his face. The rain had beaten his thick graying hair into a flat mat that overhung his forehead, and what might have been tears or just more rain glistened in the shadows under his eyes.

When his gaze dropped to Johnny's bandaged hand and

then returned to his face, there was a kind of dull and malicious satisfaction in them. And Johnny knew that he'd been right—his attackers had come from Claverton, and Claverton only regretted they'd not had time to complete the work.

The final moments over, the mourners turned to walk back down the puddled paths to the gate and the cars. When the grab came at Johnny's arm in its sling, Gates intercepted it as if he'd been waiting for it. Johnny certainly had. They stood on the path, the other people filing past them with incurious glances, impatient for the dry caves of the limousines and a stiff brandy at the nearest pub.

"How dare you come here?" Claverton hissed.

"That's enough, Mr. Claverton," Gates said. Claverton ignored him, his entire attention fixed on Johnny, whose lack of response seemed to further infuriate him.

"You killed her, you took her away from me, and you have the gall to come here and gloat . . ."

"You took her from *me*," Johnny corrected him quietly. "She was yours when she died, and she wanted to be yours. You made her happy, Claverton . . . or didn't you know that? *I* never made her happy." It was perfectly true, he realized, he never had.

His words seemed to startle Claverton, they blanked his eyes for a moment—then the anger returned. "But she kept going back to you, more than once. I had her—"

"Had her what, Mr. Claverton?" Gates asked. "Had her followed?" Claverton ignored him.

"Didn't she?" he demanded, still staring at Johnny.

"She got lonely sometimes. You left her alone too much, she needed somebody she could talk to, that's all," Johnny lied. He didn't know why he was trying to placate a man who had possibly destroyed his career with his vindictiveness. Perhaps it was because Claverton was so obviously wretched over Lisa's death while he was not. Guilt spoke the lie, not he—guilt over his own shallowness.

Lewis Manvers gave a bark of empty amusement. "*Talk?* Are we supposed to believe that? Lisa wasn't the talking kind . . . she was—"

Johnny and Mark Claverton stared at one another, both knowing what she had been, both at a loss to deny it. Johnny tried again.

"Maybe she liked to throw it back in my face, did you ever think of that? You, your fancy life, the way you could give her things I couldn't . . . maybe she just liked making me feel small."

Claverton eyed him maliciously. "It wouldn't take much, would it?" he sneered.

All right, he'd gone as far as he could, he'd had it. "Listen, you toffee-nosed creep, just get off my back, will you? First you make false accusations, then you send some goons around to break my hands . . . maybe you think all that so-called class of yours is some kind of free ticket to everything. It isn't. I told her what I thought and I don't mind telling you. She wasn't perfect but she was okay until you touched her with your dirty hands and your dirty money. I don't care if you look good and sound good and all the rest of it . . . you're dirt and we both know it."

"I loved her," Claverton said, white-faced.

"Then why wouldn't you marry her? She was carrying your kid in her belly and you knew it. Or was that it? What's the matter, did you think the baby was *mine?* She said you were a little nuts, cockeyed with jealousy, always accusing her of seeing other men. All right, yes, she came to me and slept with me but I've had a vasectomy. Now, wouldn't *that* be a laugh? You had her killed because you thought she was having my baby when all the time it was yours—you killed them both and they *both* belonged to you." He was shaking again, and Gates could feel it as they stood shoulder to shoulder. "Some mastermind you are, Claverton, some big deal, all right. You couldn't even work *that* out. All it would have taken was a goddamn blood test."

Tall, smooth, thin-lipped, Manvers glowered at Johnny with sudden suspicion but the look was objective, almost clinical.

"Come along, Mark, there's no point in listening to any more of this," he urged, touching Claverton's sleeve with a proprietary air, almost father to son, although Claverton was clearly ten or fifteen years his senior.

"It was mine," Claverton said to him dully.

"Of course it was yours, you pathetic bugger," Johnny snapped, before Manvers could speak again. "And *she* was yours, whether you believed it or not. She actually loved you." Why was he bothering? he kept asking himself. What the hell did it matter? She was dead, already starting to rot and shrivel, a nothing, a husk, gone. And here they stood, still arguing ownership, as if she had been a chair or a table instead of a woman who really only belonged to herself. Not even that, now.

Claverton started to speak, choked, began to cry. Manvers put an arm around his shoulders and glared at Johnny. "Haven't you done enough? Can't you leave it alone . . . must you go on talking about her?"

"I—" Johnny began, staring at Claverton, who was making no attempt to stifle his grief, sobbing as openly as a child.

"Come along, Mark . . . it's time to go home," Manvers said, and with a final infuriated glance at Johnny he led Claverton away down the path. Gates stared after them, unmoving.

"So you knew about the baby," he finally said.

"Yes, I knew about it. Who else could she tell? She was so damn pleased, so . . . oh, hell, what does it matter now?"

"I thought it might be yours, too," Gates said. "Why didn't you say you'd had a vasectomy?"

"You didn't ask," Johnny growled. "What do you suggest, I wear a sign around my neck?"

"I can think of more appropriate locations for it," Gates said, starting down the path. "Don't you like kids?"

Johnny walked past him, his unbandaged hand in a fist. "I love kids, but I left one without a father and I didn't want to get into the habit. It's not important."

Gates fell into step beside him. "Oh, I think it is, you know. You go on like this and I'll run out of motives for you altogether." They crunched along the wet gravel companionably. "Was that just your smashed hand talking, or do you really think he might have had her killed for those reasons?"

Johnny glanced at him. "Don't you?"

"It has always been a possibility. Was she afraid of him?"

Johnny wanted to say she'd been terrified, but it wasn't so. "More of making him angry than anything else. She really did want to be Mrs. Mark Claverton . . . but it didn't look like it was going to happen."

"It couldn't, at least not before the baby was born. He's married. He and his wife have been separated for a long time, but she's a Catholic and she also controls his business, through her brother."

"That smooth type who's always got his hand on Claverton's elbow?" Johnny asked. "I wondered who he was."

"Lewis Manvers, Claverton's brother-in-law," Gates said.

"Oh . . . so *that's* Manvers . . . I remember her mentioning him." He looked at Gates speculatively. "He kept putting her down to Claverton, feeding his jealousy."

"Oh?"

"She said Manvers offered to arrange for an abortion, really pushed the idea. She got upset about that . . . but the thought of having a kid that was a bastard bothered her even more."

"Kind of an old-fashioned attitude these days, isn't it?"

Johnny looked at Gates resentfully. "You live by the new morality, do you? Well, the world is full of people who still think the old kind is better. Lisa was only a swinger on the outside—inside she was still a conventional middle-class girl. To her having a bastard was wrong. To me, too, as it happens. There was even a moment or two when she'd start crying about it that I considered marrying her just to give the kid a name, because she really wanted to have it. I happen to be one of those corny dinosaurs called a nice man, remember us? There are still a few about."

"My wife says I'm a nice man, too," Gates protested mildly.

"Maybe we should form a club," Johnny muttered, stalking off down the path. Gates let him go, then followed slowly. You poor sod, he thought. Don't you know what they say about nice guys?

# 10

The following Monday Johnny went back to Pattinson's office.

The ordeal was even worse than he'd expected, and although the therapist was gentle he sensed reserves of sadism hidden behind her demure uniform. The swelling had diminished quite a bit, but he still had to look away when she removed the bandages. He tried to think of the hand as being temporarily separated from the rest of his body, but the pain made the connection perfectly clear. After the treatment she bandaged it, reducing the protective padding a little. He went home feeling vulnerable, weak and childish.

A few hours' sleep helped, but not much. Without the discipline of having to perform with the quartet or make any session dates he felt as if he were in a hazy limbo, rootless and without purpose. There was just one job outstanding, a theme for a new television series for children about mathematics and science, and he was trying to concentrate on that when there was a knock at the door. He was expecting almost anyone but the Lady of

The Legs. But there she stood. He looked down—yes, she'd brought them with her.

"Mr. Cosatelli?"

"Yes."

"I'm Elizabeth Fisher, Department of Social Services."

"I gave at the office."

She didn't smile. In fact, the expression on her pleasant face took a lot of pleasantness out of it. She had a knitted cap pulled over her dark curly hair and held her briefcase tightly under one arm. "I'd like to talk to you about Gino Pantoni, please."

"Oh." He stepped back a little. "Come in." He gestured toward the settee and scooped up the scatter of music he'd left there. "Sit down. Would you like some coffee or something?"

"No, thank you." She perched on the edge of the easy chair as if she needed to be ready to make a run for it, and propped her briefcase on the floor beside her legs. They really were good legs—delicate ankles, a rich full curve of calf, the promise of more fullness above the knee. She'd called it exactly when she'd compared them to the various makes of pianos, and he'd been as much startled by her knowledge as her momentarily spirited response to his rather heavyhanded challenge. Now it was there again, the strange and slightly exhilarating tension between them. He knew exactly what it was, but it still puzzled him. He usually went for skinny blondes. She pulled her voluminous wool cape around her and covered them slightly, as if conscious of his gaze and annoyed that he had even noticed she was female. She'd certainly done everything she could to disguise the fact, he decided as he sat down. No makeup, the all-concealing cape, the sensible shoes. But they couldn't take the elegant line away from these legs—they were the nicest thing that had happened to him all week, although that wasn't saying much.

"About Gino, you said?"

"Yes. You've become quite friendly with him recently." It sounded like an accusation and he immediately resented it.

"Why not? He's a bright boy, he likes music and I'm a musician."

"I know that."

"So. . . ?"

"I've just come from there, Mr. Cosatelli. I saw the stereo system you sent him. Quite an expensive present for a boy you don't know all that well, isn't it?"

So it had been delivered, that was quick. "He saved my life—is there a law against saying thank you, now?" he snapped.

"No, but—"

"Look, Miss Fisher—"

"Mrs. Fisher," she interrupted. He glanced at her hand but saw no ring there. "I'm divorced," she added and then looked even more angry, apparently at herself.

"All right, Mrs. Fisher. I don't exactly see what business it is of yours whether I give Gino a present or—" he stopped, tilted his head to one side, and then began to laugh softly. "You don't by any chance think I'm trying to seduce him, do you?"

She flushed. "No, of course not," she said, too quickly.

He leaned back and regarded her with genuine amusement. This was getting better and better. "I think you did. Rosa told you I was a middle-aged musician who lived alone and you've dropped around to see if I'm gay or not, isn't that so? What would you suggest I do to prove I'm not—make a pass at you?"

"There's no need to be offensive."

"Would you find it offensive? If I made a pass, I mean?"

"No. I mean, yes. Stop that!"

"Stop what?" he asked innocently.

"You know perfectly well what," she said angrily. He started to laugh again, and she felt her color rising. Whatever Beth Fisher had expected, it was not the man sitting opposite her. He wasn't handsome, and certainly with his pale shadowed face and bandaged hand he wasn't a picture of male virility. She looked at his nose—long and irregular—he probably got at least two head colds a year. She looked at his mouth—small for the jaw but well-shaped and with more than a touch of sensuality in the lower lip. Two lines between his eyebrows indicated he was probably shortsighted and too vain to wear glasses. His straight hair was medium brown with some gray in it. Good, square body, good, square face, soft steady voice.

There was absolutely no reason for him to affect her this way.

"I'm afraid there's far more to the situation than you realize, Mr. Cosatelli," she heard herself saying primly.

He raised an eyebrow. "Oh? What situation, Mrs. Fisher?"

"With Gino."

He could see she was getting flustered, although he didn't understand exactly why. "All right," he said gently. "I'm *not* gay, I'm a normal man, I'm divorced like you are, and I have a kid of my own, a girl about the age of Gino's sister. I felt sorry for the boy, not having a father and—"

"Oh, he has a father, all right. You should be glad it's

me who's come around to see you and not Mr. Pantoni," she said.

"My mistake. I've never seen him in the shop so I assumed—"

"No, you wouldn't have seen him in the shop because he's been in jail for the past three years. He got out a few weeks ago. Have you seen Mrs. Pantoni lately?"

"Sure . . . I saw her this morning when I went to buy the papers."

"You saw her face?"

"Yes, we compared black eyes. I told her she shouldn't argue with large cartons of baked beans—" he stopped. "It wasn't a carton of baked beans."

"No, it wasn't. Her husband did that, Mr. Cosatelli. He's done it regularly since getting out of jail and because she won't lodge a complaint against him he'll probably go on doing it. He's not a very nice man."

"Apparently not," he said, feeling a surge of anger.

"No." She seemed to relax a little more, and pulled off the knitted cap, releasing the mass of dark curls which he saw were touched with gray here and there. "All right, Mr. Cosatelli, I can see you're not a moral danger to Gino, please forgive me for thinking you might be, but there *was* a reason for that."

"Oh?"

She nodded and took a deep breath. Without the cap she looked younger, but still tired and overintense. He held no brief for social workers, especially after some of the tales Lisa had told him, but this one seemed genuinely concerned. "I got to know the Pantoni family about four years ago. Gino—quite innocently—became friendly with another older man, one of his teachers. This man *was* secretly gay, and there came the inevitable moment when he tried to—" she compressed her mouth over the words. "At any rate, Gino came home in a state of shock, very distressed. Mr. Pantoni was still living at home then. He went around and literally beat the man senseless."

"I can understand his—" Johnny began.

"Certainly, yes, any father would have *felt* like doing that. Mr. Pantoni not only felt like doing it, he did it, and what's more, he *enjoyed* doing it," she said, her voice harsh. "Like you, he's a man who lets his hands speak for him . . . but the reasons and the results are a little different."

"What happened?"

"I said he beat him senseless—in fact he inflicted permanent brain damage and the man is now a vegetable. What Pantoni did was clearly criminal and he went to jail for it, naturally. Mrs. Pantoni obtained a legal separation while he was there, but that's as far as she will go. Our department had been called in before when he'd beaten her, but these family situations are never easy to deal with because with the best will in the world our hands are absolutely tied if she won't press charges against him." She sighed heavily, and brushed away a stray lock of hair with the back of her hand. "I'm not being fair."

"Oh?"

She shook her head. "Vito Pantoni isn't an evil man, he's just a man who's trapped and frustrated and confused. He came to this country after the war, determined to succeed, to become some kind of import-export baron, I suppose, and just couldn't make it. The language defeated him, the way of life, everything. Every time he and Rosa accumulated some money, he immediately threw it into some mad scheme that fell apart on him. It was Rosa who made that little shop pay and kept them from starving. I suppose you know how that might affect a man of his ethnic background, being Italian yourself."

"Only half Italian. Believe me, Italians have no corner on resenting their balls being cut out from under them," Johnny said with reluctant sympathy. "I suppose he couldn't see he was lucky to have a wife like that."

"No, he couldn't. And when the shame got too much, he'd take his resentment out on her. Physically. I think after a while she almost got used to it, began to feel guilty about causing his anger and almost *accepted* that she should be beaten. She loved the man, and couldn't bear to see him so unhappy. If hitting her helped, so be it. Some women are voluntary victims, you know."

"Did your husband beat you?" It was out before he could stop it, and she stared at him. There was an inner struggle, but she answered his question in a reasonable if slightly chilly tone.

"No. At least, not with his fists. There are all kinds of battering people can give one another. Sometimes I would have preferred a black eye to what I got."

"I'm sorry, I had no right to ask that."

"Then why did you?"

"I don't know," he muttered. "Presumably because I wanted to know. Anyway—how did you get involved in all this. With the Pantonis, I mean?"

She shifted in the chair and avoided his eyes. "I inherited the case when the criminal charges against Mr. Pantoni involved Gino having to testify. I became interested in the boy's welfare, perhaps a little more than I should have. But he *is* a bright boy, quite remarkably bright, and I hated to see that going to waste. I got in touch with the headmaster of the school he's attending now and explained the situation. He's an old friend, and he agreed to take the boy on. Gino is doing wonderfully well."

"He loves the school."

She smiled, suddenly, and it changed her entire face. Her teeth were slightly crooked and they gave a raffish, urchinlike quality to her expression. He felt himself smiling back.

"Oh, he has fun sending up their accents and their manners, but yes, he's very happy there," she said. "In fact, there's every chance he'll be going on to Cambridge if he keeps up his present standard of work. He recently sat exams for a full private grant."

"That's great."

She nodded. "Yes, I'm very proud of Gino. So you can understand that when I saw the stereo and—"

"I understand perfectly, I'm sorry I gave you a hard time about it."

"It's not just Gino who concerns me . . ." she said hesitantly. "You see, if Mr. Pantoni gets the wrong idea he might . . . you've had a bit of trouble already, and when Gino told me about your being attacked I wondered if it was—"

"There were two of them, Mrs. Fisher . . . I know who sent them and why. Would you like some coffee?"

"Oh, no, there's no—" She began to gather her things together.

"Let me put it another way. Would you mind making us both some coffee? Since you're in the social service business, maybe you could extend a little my way. I keep dropping the kettle on my foot." He gestured slightly with his bandaged hand. It was a lie, but he didn't want her to go just yet. "Just think of me as another male chauvinist pig taking advantage of our respective gender roles and playing on your sympathy."

"I'd rather think of you as thirsty, like me," she smiled, standing up and letting the cape drop onto the chair behind her. What she wore underneath was just as concealing, a heavy, slightly lumpy wool dress. Some of the lumps were nice, the rest were the result of Mrs. Fisher, divorced, letting her figure go to hell. The legs were even better standing up, though. "I'll wait on you if you'll do something for me," she said.

"Sure—what?"

She looked around and started toward the kitchen. "Tell me something about yourself."

"Why?"

"Let's just say I'm also in the nosy-parker business," she said.

He was puzzled. "What do you want to know . . . my favorite color, my inside leg measurement, my—"

"Whatever you feel like telling me," she called, making busy noises in the kitchen. First he'd had Gates making breakfast, now he had her making coffee. Maybe he'd take to wearing a bandage as a regular thing. He found himself saying far more about himself than he intended in response to occasional pointed questions from beyond the breakfast bar. She took a long time to make coffee, it seemed to him. When she finally reappeared it was with a sandwich for him as well as two cups of coffee.

"Say, when you're sympathetic you go all the way, don't you?"

"It was your pathetic careworn face that got to me."

"Ah, it gets them all in the end. I push it for all it's worth."

"I can imagine you do," she said wryly, and tucked her legs up in the chair. She'd raided his refrigerator and combined cheese, tomato, onions, peppers, and lettuce. It was delicious and he told her so.

"Ah, with you it's boyish charm, with me it's my cooking. I haven't got a whole lot else going for me these days." It seemed to him a more revealing remark than any he'd made to her.

"Why didn't you make one for yourself?" he asked.

"I've already had lunch," she said offhandedly.

He thought it was more probable she was on a diet. "Do I pass the test?" he asked.

"What test?"

"The surrogate-father test."

"You're very sharp, Mr. Cosatelli."

"Sure, I'm sharp, I'm a well-educated fellow all round. People comment on it in the street—there goes a sharp, well-educated, piano-playing bum, they say."

"Aside from a tendency to flippant and pointless humor, yes, you pass the test."

"Nice to have the official stamp of approval, I must say. Do I have to marry Rosa . . . or you?"

"Don't be ridiculous."

"Don't be so defensive." He'd never met a woman he could throw off-balance so easily. She was clearly an intelligent person, and yet he could get under her skin with a word. What was the word? Ah yes, marry. Two could play the psychoanalysis game. "You're very involved with Gino, aren't you?"

"I'm concerned for him, certainly. And for Rosa and Theresa, too."

He shook his head. "I can't believe you take this much trouble over all your cases . . . and I'm sure you have quite a few." He nodded toward her bulging briefcase. "I'm perfectly happy to take an interest in Gino, provide a role model for him—that is the current jargon, isn't it?"

She had the grace to smile. "It is."

"The kicker is Mr. Pantoni, though. I don't much fancy a life as a vegetable, Mrs. Elizabeth Fisher. Would you?"

"No, I wouldn't. Beth."

"What?"

"My name is Beth." He grinned at her and she looked away quickly, fussing with a loose thread on her cape. Damn the man, anyway. "And I hadn't visualized regular seminars, you know. It's just that Gino could use a man to talk to now and again, instead of me or someone at school. I don't always know what to say to him about . . . things."

"Like Beethoven, the economic situation, and how to give a girl an orgasm?" he asked, wanting to see her blush again. He saw it.

"Oh, I don't have any trouble with Beethoven, but the economic situation has always been beyond me," she said lightly.

"Maybe we ought to get together and discuss just what should be done . . . about Gino," he suggested.

"I don't think that's necessary."

"No, maybe not . . . but it might be fun." Now what the devil was he getting himself into here? he suddenly thought. Why should he want to spend time with a plump, inhibited social worker—he had enough problems already.

"Fun doesn't enter into it," she said firmly, standing up

and fastening her cape. It swirled around her and settled its protective folds in place. "My only concern is that Gino's life isn't upset by his father or anyone else at this stage. Next year he'll be at Cambridge . . ."

"And we won't have a common interest anymore," he said. Damn the woman, she wasn't even his type.

"Which will no doubt be a relief to you." She dug into her briefcase and produced a card. "You can get in touch with me at one of these numbers if there's a problem, but I'm sure you have enough to keep you busy at the moment."

When she talked like that she reminded him of his ex-wife, all brains, mouth, and rules of impeccable behavior. But Wendy had never blushed, and hadn't laughed all that much, either. He rather thought this one would laugh a lot if she let go. What would make her let go?

"Thanks for your time . . . and the coffee." She was leaving.

"Stop running away from me," he heard himself saying.

She glanced back from the door. "I'm not running away from you, Mr. Cosatelli. I'm running to my next case—an elderly woman with advanced phlebitis whom the council in its infinite wisdom has housed on the sixteenth floor of a high-rise building. If I don't do her shopping she won't have any dinner. Goodbye—hope your hand gets better soon."

And she was gone, with a swirl of her cape and a bump of her briefcase against the doorframe. He heard the sensible shoes clump downstairs.

He hoped his hand would get better, too. He hoped everything would get better, soon.

It certainly couldn't get much worse.

# 11

The second session with Pattinson's therapist was even more agonizing than the first. He'd had a good night's sleep, but the efforts to move even his thumb had wiped all that away.

He paid off the cab and went up the stairs to his flat, wondering if he'd ever feel like a whole human being again.

His head was down when he opened the door, so when he looked up it hit him all at once.

They'd done a more thorough job on his flat than they had on his hand.

The place was a complete wreck. The upholstered furniture was slashed to ribbons, the stuffing strewn around the room like snowdrifts. There was black paint splashed everywhere and some kind of excrement had been ground into the carpet. Every one of his records had been taken out of the sleeves and either bent, broken, or scratched heavily with something like a fork. The tape cassettes were splintered and coils of brown plastic were everywhere, drifting over heaps of torn manuscript.

And they'd taken an ax to the Bechstein.

It stood like a dead elephant canted over on one leg, its wire guts spilling out and half the keys gone. He felt that if it could have bled it would have.

After one incredulous stare around, he backed out and closed the door on the scene of devastation and hate. Sitting on the top step, he stared down at the light coming through the small pane of glass in the door below. He sat there for a long time, perfectly still and perfectly quiet. Then, getting up with an arthritic stiffness, he went slowly down the stairs and along the street to the telephone booth opposite Rosa's shop.

\*

Gates wouldn't let him back into the flat until the forensic team was through with their investigation.

He sat in the passenger seat of Gates' unmarked car smoking Gates' cigarettes until his throat was raw. After about twenty minutes Gates came down and got in behind the wheel, although he didn't start the engine. He looked at the overflowing ashtray and the empty packet on the seat, then offered one from his case. Johnny shook his head.

"It's mostly the living room," Gates said, lighting a cigarette and staring out at the darkening street. He removed the ashtray and as he emptied it out of the window the streetlights came on. "You *could* sleep there tonight, but I don't recommend it. Better stay with a friend."

"Okay," Johnny said in a faraway voice.

Gates glanced at him. "I'll give you the name of a firm

who can come around and clean up the mess—they've made quite a thing out of vandalized flats lately. I suppose your insurance will cover everything. The piano can come out in pieces—how the hell did you get it in there in the first place?"

"They knocked out the windows and swung it in with a crane," Johnny said glumly. "Then they rebuilt the windows."

"Guess they'll have to do it again. Shame."

"Not much of an improvement on 'sorry,' is it?"

"No, it isn't," Gates allowed. "You'll have to give us the names of anyone who's been here over the past few days so we can take their fingerprints and eliminate them. We might be left with one or two we can put a name to from our files."

"What files? It was Claverton again, you know that."

"If it was, and if we can pick up a print that might lead us back to him, then—"

"I'll be there ahead of you."

Gates turned in the seat to face him. "I wouldn't suggest that. Really . . . it would be a very bad move for a dozen reasons." He glanced down at Johnny's bandaged hand. "Besides, what could you do to him?"

"I could kick his bloody face in, for a start," Johnny muttered.

"I didn't hear that. Just leave it to us, please."

"So far leaving it to you has resulted in one smashed hand, one smashed flat, and no solution to Lisa's murder. How long do you suggest I go *on* leaving it to you?"

"For as long as it takes," Gates said.

Johnny stared out of the car. The street was quiet, the shops closed, traffic virtually nil. On the far side of the street he saw Gino trudging home with his schoolbag over his shoulder, late back because this was his day for some kind of club meeting, Johnny remembered.

"There is another possibility," Johnny said reluctantly. He told Gates about the visit from Beth Fisher, and about Gino's father.

Gates considered it. "He sounds like the type who'd prefer a personal confrontation, but I'll check with his parole officer."

"Can you manage that without the boy or his mother finding out? Gino doesn't know I've been told about his home situation—I'd kind of like to keep it that way for the moment."

"I'll try."

"If it *was* Pantoni at least it would mean he'd go back to jail and give them some peace for a while," Johnny mused. "They could use it."

"So could you." Gates stubbed out his cigarette. "I noticed some women's clothes in the spare bedroom," he said casually.

"Lisa's. She always meant to take them, but I guess he bought her everything she needed."

"Did she ever leave anything else with you . . . after she went to live with Claverton, I mean?"

"No—not unless you count those baby clothes."

"Baby clothes?"

"Yes. When she found out she was pregnant she went a little potty and bought a whole bunch of stuff, then got cold feet about it, I guess. She brought them around and left them with me."

"What did she buy?" Gates asked idly.

Johnny shrugged. "I don't know. I asked her to show them off but she was in a silly mood and went all coy. I figured she was embarrassed about being so mumsy all of a sudden, so I let her get on with it. She had them in a little case and left them with the rest of her things. Why?"

"Just curious."

"Well, they were still there, weren't they?"

"Little plastic case with ducks and teddy bears on it?"

"That's right."

"Yes, it was there."

Johnny looked uncomfortable. "I suppose I should give them to charity or something—her things, too."

"Be a nice gesture."

Johnny was silent for a while. "I don't want to go back up there, the way it is. Do I have to?"

Gates shook his head. "No rush. Tell me what you want and I'll have one of the men pack a case for you. You'd better call your friends to say you're coming over." He reached for the door handle.

"I'll go to a hotel. I don't want to involve anyone."

Gates looked over at his dejected figure. "Like to keep yourself to yourself, don't you?"

"I don't seem to be able to lately," Johnny said wryly. "People keep dropping in."

*

In a fit of self-pity he opted for luxurious comfort to take the stink of the flat out of his nostrils. But after hanging his one surviving suit in the cupboard and putting other things in the drawers of the bureau, he was left with nothing to do but stare out of the window. The sky was lavender as twilight spread along the river, and on the far bank the Royal Festival Hall was coming alive, its long windows glowing gold. As he stood there the floodlights on the terraces came on, and the entire building seemed to hover above the glimmering dark channel of the river. Toy people moved along the Embankment below, and the headlights of the rush hour twinkled between the naked branches and along the white span of the Waterloo Bridge.

Gates and his men had not been able to locate the one thing he'd wanted to rescue from the mess, and as he stood there he began to wonder if it had been there at all.

Going to the phone, he dialed Laynie's office and found her still there, waiting for her cab. He told her what had happened and asked her to sort out the insurance and the rest of the details because he just couldn't face it.

"Laynie . . . when you were flashing your duster around the other day, where did you put Cymru?"

"What?"

"You know, my lucky piece. I think he was on the piano, that's where I usually keep him."

"It wasn't there. Didn't he give it back to you?"

"Who?"

"Baz. You left it on the table at the benefit and I told him to get it to you right away because I know what a dimwit you are about it. He said he would."

"Oh, okay. He must have forgotten. No wonder things have been going all to hell for me."

"Oh, John, come on. Really, I wish you'd grow up."

"I can't help it, Laynie. At least it isn't a teddy bear." Cymru was a small brass dragon he'd found in the toe of his stocking one Christmas. It was his one and only superstition.

"Might as well be." There was a pause. "You didn't have it with you when you played with Gessler, John, and you did well."

So he had. "I didn't have it with me when those two bastards set on me, either," he countered.

"Which proves everything, I suppose," she said sarcastically.

"All right, all right. I want it now. I'll call Baz."

He put down the phone before she could continue the argument, then dialed Baz's number. His wife answered.

"Hi, Molly, could I have a word with Baz?"

"He . . . isn't here just now, Johnny. How are you?"

"Getting by. When will he be back . . . is he playing somewhere tonight or what?"

"No. I expect him back soon."

Suddenly, in the background, he heard Baz's voice shouting at one of the children, followed by a burst of wailing. So Molly was lying for him, now.

"Umm . . . it's about my lucky piece . . . Laynie said she asked Baz to bring it back to me but I can't find it anywhere. Would you ask him if he's still got it?"

"Sure. You can't play without it, can y—" she hesitated. "I mean—"

"The hand will get better, Molly. But I'd like to have it to help things along, you know."

"I'm sorry about . . . everything, Johnny." She seemed close to tears, and there was another burst of wailing in the distance. It sounded like the five-year-old.

"Yes, well . . . so am I," he said lamely.

"If he has it I'll tell him to bring it around to you," Molly said with what sounded like defiance. He could imagine her glaring at Baz and Baz glaring back, facing off across their big green and gold living room.

"Thanks. Oh—I'm not at the flat, I'm at a hotel." She didn't say anything. "I'm having the flat redecorated." That was true enough, or would be. "Tell him . . . tell

him just to get it to Laynie, okay?" If Baz didn't want to
see him or talk to him, he'd make it easy.

"All right." He started to put the phone down, but she
spoke again. "John? Terry Wogan played 'Samba Break 6'
this morning on the radio. He said some nice things about
it."

"Good. That's good, Molly, thanks for telling me."

"Johnny . . . I wish you—" Whatever she wished was
cut short. He heard her give a squeak of surprise and then
the phone was put down, hard. He stared at the receiver
in his hand.

"'Bye, Molly," he said softly and replaced it in the
cradle.

He went back to the window.

It was darker now and the Festival Hall looked like a
birthday present waiting to be opened. He wondered if
there would ever be anything in it for him. Raising his
bandaged hand, he tried to flex it and got a response. He
also got a cold sweat from the pain, but he did it again,
just to make sure it had moved. It had. Maybe there was a
chance. Maybe he would get back, maybe big fat Price-
Temple and Laynie were right, but neither of them was
there to reassure him on the matter. He'd never felt so
alone in his life. Suspended behind an expanse of double-
glazing that made the vista outside into a silent film of
London at night, lights and movement against the blackness, he felt like the Pretender to some unnamed throne
locked in the Tower, with no voices cheering.

Turning away, he kicked savagely at the chair in front
of the little writing desk, saw it fall to the floor and after a
beat or two, started to laugh. It sounded a little thin, the
only sound in the room.

It wasn't funny, not really. But he did wonder if Benny

Goodman would have approved of the Cosatelli version of "Stompin' at the Savoy."

Probably not.

It didn't swing.

So it didn't mean a thing.

# 12

Gates and Dunhill stared at the little blue and yellow suitcase, its ducks and teddy bears incongruous in the glare of the Forensic Laboratory.

"Why the hell would anyone steal baby clothes?" Dunhill asked.

"They wouldn't," Gates said. He looked across the table at the white-coated technician. "How much do you think you can tell us about what was in it?"

The technician looked unhopeful. "It's new—looks clean. It will need microscopic analysis, presuming we find anything at all."

"We lifted prints from it, the girl's and somebody else's. Maybe we'll get lucky," Gates said.

"Probably Cosatelli's," Dunhill said.

"No . . . not his, I checked that first. Of course, whoever took the thing or things out might have assumed he'd looked inside. It had been in his flat long enough for him to get curious."

"He said he didn't."

"I know what he *said*. But Claverton doesn't."

Dunhill moved away, scowling. "You still have a team on Cosatelli?"

"Of course."

"He might have been lying about thinking it was baby clothes, you know. He might even have taken whatever was in there out a long time ago . . . there were some smudged prints on it beside the ones we got clear."

"I know."

"Then why the hell didn't you press him on it?" Dunhill demanded.

"Because if he *didn't* know I didn't want to make him suspicious. And if he does know—"

"What?" Dunhill asked.

"I want to see what he'll do about it," Gates answered, and walked out.

*

Aside from the morning visits to Pattinson's office Johnny had stayed quietly in his room, sleeping, eating, watching television and devouring paperbacks by the dozen. He'd had them bring him in a piano and had managed to finish the theme song and send it off. But by Saturday he was ready to climb the wall and swing from the chandelier if there'd been one. And if he could have got a grip on it.

The swelling had almost completely gone, and the sharp pain had been reduced to an omnipresent ache that was almost worse. Somehow the swelling had seemed a kind of cushion, but now there was only the stiff black and green hand curled like a claw. Laynie had found carpenters and decorators to restore the flat, and there was nothing for him to do except make a life or death decision about what color he wanted them to paint the walls. The prospect of days or weeks of just sitting around and thinking was making his skin crawl. Even the splendor of the Savoy wasn't enough to make thinking a comfortable occupation, because of the things he had to think about.

He'd bought the papers on the way up from lunch and had spent a boring hour leafing through them. A great many people seemed to have problems at least as big as his, if not bigger. On the whole he felt he could have coped better with the falling pound or a faithless wife or a bogged-down peace talk than with the consideration of whether he'd been wasting the last fourteen years of his life or that somebody hated him enough to smash his hands and his furniture out of sheer bloody-mindedness. Or that he might still be arrested for a murder he hadn't committed.

In fact the only story he read completely was about a man who was bringing a suit against the police for harassment and false arrest. It had held his interest, but it hadn't cheered him up.

Irritably he shuffled through the scattered papers and found the entertainment page of the *Guardian*. Glumly he scanned the columns. Did he want to see *Snow White and the Seven Dwarfs* again? He did not. How about a little Swedish porn? No, thanks—it would only leave him all dressed up with nowhere to go. His eye caught, held. Ashkenazy and Previn were guesting with the LSO tonight. Doing the Rachmaninov Fourth. He'd given up believing in coincidences.

After a minute he reached for the phone, wondering

what the hell he thought he was up to, now. His subconscious never told him anything, these days.


Was it his imagination, the black dress, or *was* she a little thinner?

She'd been cautious on the phone, not quite sure what he was after or why he'd really called, but he'd managed to persuade her in the end. Now, seeing her across the foyer he was glad he had. She was looking around, watching the doors, and hadn't seen him yet.

It *was* a nice face, even with that apprehensive expression. The gray in her dark curls had a silvery shimmer and with makeup on her eyes were enormous against the pale skin. The Legs, in sheer black, looked simply incredible—he was glad she realized their sumptuous elegance shouldn't be hidden but paid tribute. Tentatively enchanted, he watched his stranger across the crowded room as she scanned the faces of the people arriving with blasts of cold air from outside. Laughing and talking, they passed her by—a woman in black with her coat over her arm, nervously brushing at the shoulders of her dress and surreptitiously slipping a mint into her mouth.

Something made her turn and she saw him dodging between the chattering knots of people who were lingering before committing themselves to being an audience. A few random notes sounded as the orchestra began to arrive and tune up.

"Beth?"

"Oh . . . hi," she said, trying on a smile for size. "I see your hand is better."

He raised it slightly and they inspected the elastic bandage that did not match his new dark gray suit. "Out of a sling and down to a truss," he said. "I considered a black leather glove but it looked sinister."

"I suppose it would," she said, and the smile began to fit better. "It was very nice of you to think of me . . ."

"No, it wasn't, it was pure selfishness. I wanted to see you again."

This seemed to disconcert her entirely and for a moment he thought she was going to drop her coat onto the floor. He took it from her and deposited it in the cloakroom, pocketing the plastic disc and taking her arm gently.

"We might as well find our seats . . . Previn likes to start on time."

"Oh, does he?" she asked vaguely, walking beside him. "Do you know him?"

"I played with him once, a long time ago. Why?" The floor sloped under their feet and he steadied her as a rather enthusiastic type in a beard backed into the aisle without looking.

She glanced sideways at him. "It just seems strange . . . being with someone who knows . . . I mean, they're such remote figures, conductors. Like film stars. You never expect them to be like other people, somehow. To have friends and tell jokes and—"

"And put their pants on one leg at a time?" he said easily, stopping her and indicating their seats. "Why not? They've even been known to suffer from dandruff and indigestion."

She was leafing through the program. "And Ashkenazy—do you know him, too?" It seemed to bemuse her.

"I've only met him briefly."

"What's *he* like?"

"Soft-spoken, witty, very fond of his family."

"And brilliant."

"That, too." He smiled at her and she looked down.

"I'm sorry . . . I'm acting rather like a child, aren't I? I'm not normally so . . . gauche."

"Are you normally this honest?"

She glanced up, startled. "No . . . I'm not."

"Good," he said. "I must be getting to you with that boyish charm you accused me of using."

"Ummmm. You said you wanted to hear him because *you're* going to be playing this concerto in August?"

"I might be—it isn't settled yet."

She fixed him with a suddenly bright and wicked eye, throwing him completely. He was sorry to see she was regaining her composure. "Does that mean you're brilliant, too—or just that you get dandruff and indigestion like the rest?"

"Well, I'll be playing it on a Wednesday—I'm usually pretty brilliant on a Wednesday."

"Why Wednesdays, particularly?"

The lights were starting to go down. "Because I always spend Tuesdays drinking the blood of beautiful young virgins."

Her reply came out of the darkness beside him. "You must have been pretty thirsty lately, then."

He started to reply but was overtaken by the applause as the concertmaster took his place, followed by Previn. He didn't know what he'd been going to say, but it certainly wouldn't have been worth shouting.

The program opener was the overture to *The Marriage of Figaro,* not one of his favorites. Perhaps if it had been he wouldn't have been so aware of her response to it. As it was, he began to sense something as they sat shoulder to shoulder in the darkness. Puzzled, he leaned marginally closer, pressing his arm against hers. She didn't notice. Eventually he realized what it was. Her response was so complete that her body was making minute movements that coincided precisely with the music. He could feel a flutter of her muscles as her fingers "played" along with each section of the orchestra. It was as if the music were feeding directly into her body and then escaping through these delicate movements of hand, knee, head. She was literally a music lover—she responded to it as if it were a passionate embrace. After a while her invisible perform- ance fascinated him far more than the orchestra's. He kept waiting for her to miss something, but she never did. Not once. Either she couldn't let go of it, or it wouldn't let go of her. It was even more pronounced during the Debussy Images.

"You liked that," he said, in the interval.

"Oh, yes. Didn't you?"

"I wouldn't say it grabbed me in quite the same way it did you," he said.

She frowned. "What do you mean? Don't you like Debussy?"

"Very much. But I don't think I'm as close to it as you are—what instrument do you play?"

She giggled. "I play the phonograph *extremely* well."

"You seemed very familiar with the score."

"Oh." She looked down and began to pleat a page of the program. "You mean I was twitching . . . I've been trying to give it up, I hear it stunts the growth." She seemed very embarrassed by something so minor, and he was sorry he'd mentioned it.

"I wouldn't call it twitching, exactly. More like step- ping on the clutch when somebody else is driving."

"I'm sorry if it annoyed you," she said stiffly.

"Hey . . ." he reached over and put his hand over hers. "It didn't annoy me at all—I do it all the time myself. Most musicians do, to some degree or other. Involuntary response. The only reason I mentioned it was because you knew *all* the parts, not just bits of it. You're a born conductor."

"Very funny," she snapped.

He tightened his hand. God, she was so prickly. "I meant it as a compliment, you idiot. A good conductor is aware of the total orchestra, all the time. Bernstein lets it show, most of them keep it under control so it won't distract the musicians, who are just trying to keep together without falling into their music stands. It's not a talent, as such. Just a . . . condition."

"Like asthma?"

He laughed. "If you like. It's just the way you are, that's all. That's *all.*" He felt her hand relax slightly under his, and went on, trying to make it better. "Now Gino—Gino loves music, too, but *his* response is all in his head. He likes to take it apart, analyze it, as if it were some kind of physics problem."

"Don't you?" she asked, watching as they wrestled the piano into position onstage.

"I do both . . . or I *can* do both . . . I'm trained for it, that's my work." He tugged at her hand. "Hey . . . look at me when I'm talking to you." When she wouldn't he let go of her hand and reached up to take hold of her chin and bring it around. Impulsively he leaned over and kissed her lightly on the mouth. "There. Now. Shut up, listen to the music, and twitch all you damn well like," he grinned. Somebody cleared a throat behind him and he looked up to see half the row watching their little drama while waiting patiently to get back to their seats. "Oh . . . sorry," he said, and stood up awkwardly to let them past. By the time everyone was settled the auditorium was dark again and Beth's face was invisible. He took hold of her hand again, but she was utterly still and stayed that way throughout Ashkenazy's performance, which was probably just as well. He had a lot of his own twitching to do, mostly out of envy and frustration.

He was just so bloody good.

She avoided looking at him when the concert was over, or at least never glanced at him for longer than a second or two as they crossed the foyer and went outside. The air was surprisingly warm, and he suggested they walk across the bridge instead of fighting everybody for a cab. It wasn't that far to the Savoy, where he'd booked a table in the Grille Room for supper.

They paused in the middle of the bridge and stared at what was, undeniably, the best night view in London. The dark shimmer of the river stretched away on either side, up past the Houses of Parliament and down past the Tower and to the sea. A tug went under the bridge with a throaty chug and the opalescent circle of Big Ben floated like a moon in the rigging of the Embankment. The long, glowing caterpillar of a train, most of its cars empty, rumbled over the Hungerford Bridge upriver, twinkling through the dark strands of steel web strung between the banks. Despite the traffic behind them the scene was hushed, mystic, enchanting. It was also, now that they had stopped walking, extremely chilly. The wind off the river still had an edge of winter in it, and the steamy exhalation of a passing bus hung in the air like smoke.

Beth shivered suddenly. "I guess we'd better keep moving," she said.

"Have you no romance in your soul?" he teased her. "I

had all this laid on at vast expense especially for you. The least you can do is say thank you, John."

"Thank you, John."

"That's a good start." He put an arm around her tentatively, and felt her stiffen up again. "Dammit," he said in exasperation. "Why do you keep doing that?"

"Doing what?"

"Leaping like a shot gazelle every time I touch you."

"I don't."

"You do."

"I *don't*," she protested. He didn't remove his arm, and after a while she spoke again, in an overcasual tone. "You just startled me, that's all."

"Maybe I should ring a bell or something."

She glanced at him sideways. "It might help."

He smiled at her, and then the smile went away, making room for something else. Drawing her to him firmly, he kissed her very completely and for quite a long time. Awkward at first, she gradually relaxed against him until he lost track of her elbows and knees and felt only the warm luxury of a woman in his arms, kissing back, holding on. Another train rumbled over the distant bridge and he moved his mouth to the hollow under her ear and spoke into her collar. "There's better."

"Yes," she answered, decided she couldn't improve on that, and added nothing more.

His cheek was rough and the wool of his coat smelled of after-shave, the dry cleaners, damp misty air, and him. Opening her eyes, she saw the garish neon sculpture on the roof of the Hayward Gallery turning against the sky. The last stragglers from the concert were stepping around them as they stood there against the rail of the bridge.

Hey, look at me, she wanted to shout. I'm being kissed

by a nearly famous man right here on this bridge in front of everyone, like something out of an old MGM film for heaven's sake! Isn't it worth a glance, a nod of approval, an Academy Award or two?

And then she sneezed.

She thought at first he was shivering, but it was laughter. He moved away slightly, still holding her, and looked down into her face.

"Either you're allergic to me or coming down with double pneumonia. Either way, it makes me look bad. Come on." He took her arm and marched her along the pavement, wondering if he was getting too old for romantic gestures, and also wondering what was impelling him to make them all of a sudden. It wasn't his usual style—but then, she wasn't his usual type, was she?

They had almost reached the end of the bridge when Beth suddenly said "Oh!" and stopped, putting her hand up to her cheek. She looked up at the sky and said, loudly, "Go ahead, everybody else does."

He looked at her in astonishment. "What's the matter?"

"Damn pigeons," she muttered.

"Here—let me. Penalty of living in London," he said, reaching for his handkerchief. His hand froze halfway.

There was a thin smear of blood on her cheek, and as he watched a small drop formed and glittered along a line under her eye. Just above her ear, a tiny chip of concrete was caught in her hair. He whirled around and looked back along the bridge and the line of traffic that was temporarily held up by a bus at the far end. As he turned back to her, he saw a second chip fly up from the parapet, leaving a narrow scar that showed white against the surface, and there was an odd "ping" from the metal railings.

Somebody was shooting at them.

Or more precisely, at him.

The thing was so preposterous that he couldn't speak for a moment, just stood there, staring at her in horror. A second crimson drop joined the first along the cut on her cheekbone and she took his handkerchief out of his hand and dabbed at her cheek. Before she could see what was on the square of linen, he grabbed it and then her hand, and started to run, jerking her along with him.

"Hey!" she shouted, pulling back instinctively.

"Let's run . . . it will warm us up. Come on!"

"In these shoes?" she protested, forced by his hold to keep pace with him. "John . . . *please* . . ."

"Exercise will do you good," he gasped, dodging into the opening of the stairway that went down through the bridge to the Embankment below. It was darker there. The faint stench of urine and litter made a sharp and unpleasant contrast to the freshness of the air outside. She stumbled behind him, wailing, and at the first landing he half-scooped her against him and despite the pain in his bandaged hand managed to keep her there all the way to the bottom. He stopped abruptly just inside the opening to the street and looked out.

There hadn't been anyone near them on the pavement. Had the police tailing him been caught off-guard when he'd decided to walk, and was their car stalled in the traffic jam with all the rest? There hadn't been anything to see except the chip flying up, no reason for them to think anything was wrong. Had they even noticed them running instead of walking the last few yards to the steps? Probably not, or they'd have caught up with them by now. He hadn't *heard* the shots, so maybe whoever had been doing the shooting had been in one of the cars on the bridge, too, and had used a silencer.

Unless, of course, it was someone with a rifle shooting from the catwalk of the Hungerford Bridge or the roof of Festival Hall. He'd read some rifles could cover even that distance with accuracy.

Beth was gasping and complaining beside him, but he kept hold of her, staring out into the street and the final open sweep of the stairs, unsure whether to go or stay. He stared across at the converted paddle-steamer *Caledonia* and saw the crowds moving inside the glowing windows of the various bars and restaurant. There were a few silhouettes on the deck, mostly couples ducking out for a quick kiss and grope, but it was too cold for drinking outside. Was one of those silhouettes carrying a gun? If the shots had come *up* at them from the deck that would account for the concrete chip hitting Beth on the cheek. It also meant that as soon as they stepped out onto the last unprotected flight of steps they'd be clear targets.

Suddenly the traffic signals changed, and a double-decker bus skidded to a stop with a hiss of brakes, blocking the steamer from view.

"Now!" he said, and dragging her with him, he leaped down the last stairs and started running toward the crescent curve of the Victoria Embankment Gardens. The distance wasn't great, and as the traffic began to move forward again, they gained the shadows of the trees and bushes. Beth stumbled once in front of the headquarters of the Electrical Engineers Society, giving a little cry of pain, but he refused to stop until they'd got inside the rear entrance of the Savoy, getting an astonished salute from the doorman as they ran into the small foyer. Johnny turned left and took her into the little corner lounge, where she pulled herself free of him at last and sank gasping and whimpering onto a settee.

"Are you all right?" he panted, dropping down beside her.

"I—" she choked. "I think I strained a fetlock or something going over that last fence. Did we win?"

"I think they're going to hold a Steward's Enquiry," he informed her, reaching down. "Which one?"

"The right . . . ouch!"

Fine time and place to finally get his hands on Those Legs. He ran his fingers lightly over her right ankle and felt a slight puffiness under the sheer stocking. "I'm afraid you did." He straightened up and looked at her. "What can I say . . . I'm sorry, Beth."

"I didn't know you were scared of pigeons," she said crossly, trying to wiggle her ankle and drawing in her breath sharply.

"I'm not." Just terrified of something happening to you, he thought, staring at her. I've just discovered Fat Ladies Are Beautiful. Nobody told me that before. "It was just . . . an impulse."

She wiped the perspiration from her forehead with the back of her hand. And looked at him warily. "No, it wasn't. You're shaking. What was it . . . some outraged husband you're trying to avoid?"

"No, of course not. Don't be silly."

"I'm *trying* not to be silly, John, but it's difficult."

"Oh . . . hell." He made an exasperated gesture of defeat. "Come on . . . I've got plenty of elastic bandage in my room, I'll bind that ankle for you."

"That's quite an advance on etchings," she said, raising an eyebrow.

"Don't be stupid . . . I only—" he snapped.

"I see. First I'm silly, now I'm stupid," she snapped back. "Thank you *very* much."

"J*esus*, will you listen?"

"Yes," she said, suddenly contrite. He looked so upset and strained, she wanted to pat his head and tell him it would be all right, but she couldn't think of a way to do it without making both of them look foolish. "I'll listen."

"Can I help you, sir?" It was the doorman, looking around the corner, a curious expression on his face.

"No . . . yes . . ." Johnny stammered, standing up abruptly. "I'm in 408 and 9 . . . which is the nearest lift? The lady's sprained her ankle."

The doorman's eyes flickered. He didn't know Johnny by sight, but he knew the room number, and what was charged for suites on the river side.

"The west lift is just around to the left, sir, not far. Shall I help?"

"Perhaps . . ." Johnny said, helping Beth to her feet. Or foot. She hopped unsteadily beside him, unable to put her weight on the swelling ankle.

"I can bring a wheelchair from—" the doorman began.

"No . . . it's all right," Beth said hurriedly. "Really."

"I'll call our doctor," the doorman said, as Johnny put an arm around Beth's waist. "He can be here in—"

Johnny looked at Beth. "Do you want—"

"No," Beth said, feeling totally foolish. "It's only—"

Suddenly Johnny bent down and scooped her up in his arms. She squeaked in surprise as he went unsteadily across the carpet and through the doors to the hallway. "Put me *down!*" she said furiously, as a page turned to stare at them.

"Shut up," Johnny said, his voice a little thin. "I only

do this once a year, so I'd appreciate a little respect. One more word and I'll drop you right on your ass."

She started to speak, then clutched at his shoulders as he lurched to a stop in front of the lift doors and pushed the call button with his elbow. The doors slid back and he stepped inside, plunking her down without much ceremony on the small seat at the back, then turned and punched the button for the fourth floor. He tried not to wheeze and wiped his upper lip with his sleeve. Fat Ladies might be Beautiful, but they were also an armful. He just hadn't wanted to stand there arguing any longer.

As the lift started up, she spoke in a small voice.

"John?"

"What?" He didn't turn around.

"Have you got enough elastic bandage for your hernia?"

He closed his eyes, leaned against the wood paneling, and started to laugh weakly. As the lift jolted to a stop and the doors slid back on the mercifully empty hall, he looked at her. "Will you tape it up for me?"

"No."

"Then the hell with it. Come on, Hopalong, I've done my Hercules act, the rest is up to you."

Her eyes widened as she hobbled into the living room of his suite. "My goodness . . ." she whispered, staring around at the white paneling picked out in Wedgwood blue and the graceful armchairs and sofas grouped around the room. He didn't put on the lights, but the glow from the Embankment outside was sufficient to show her the delicate polished tables and the mirrored doors reflecting the thick carpet and the arrangements of flowers on the sideboard and the piano.

"My lair," he countered caustically, and crossed to close the curtains with one swift pull of the cords.

"Oh . . . can't we have the view?" she asked, disappointed.

"Some other time."

"What makes you think I'll be by this way again?"

"Hmmmm?" He was peering out through the crack in the curtains, not really listening.

"Not that it hasn't been fun," she went on, managing to get over to the blue velvet chaise longue before collapsing. "A quiet concert, a kiss in the dark, a new world-record for the three-hundred-yard sprint . . ."

"I—" he began, but was interrupted by a knock at the outer door. "Now what?" he muttered, going out, shrugging off his coat and turning on the lights all at once. Beth looked around the room, only half-hearing the murmur of voices in the entrance hall. She'd never been in a hotel suite before, much less one as opulent as this. So this was how the rich lived . . . Fitzgerald was right, they were different, all right. Just as John was different, and probably crazy into the bargain. What had she got herself into?

He reappeared in the doorway and smiled vaguely. "That was the assistant manager making sure we didn't want a doctor. I've asked them to serve our dinner up here, if that's all right. If you're still hungry, I mean." He was holding a menu. "I said I'd call the order down. What would you like?"

"An explanation. With lots of butter, please."

He stood there for a moment, then put the menu down on the desk. "Take your pantyhose off."

"What?" she choked.

He made a face. "I said your pantyhose, not your panties. So I can bandage that ankle, dammit."

"Oh."

Scowling, he disappeared again, and she heard him banging drawers open and closed in the bedroom. She pulled up her skirt quickly.

He came back and stopped dead in the doorway, staring like an idiot. There she sat, his supposed nominee for Inhibited Social Worker of the Year—unfastening a black lace suspender belt and sliding a sheer black stocking down her long, shapely leg, looking as sexy as any centerfold. And there he stood with his hands full of ugly pink elastic bandage about to play Boy Scout.

It was the most blatant example of wasted natural resources he'd ever encountered.

She finally noticed him standing there. "Ready when you are, Dr. Welby," she said a little too brightly.

He knelt on the floor and wrapped her ankle with quick expertise, despite the encumbrance of his own bandaged hand and a slight attack of the sexual shakes. Her high-arched foot was small and fitted into his palm easily. When he'd finished, and fastened off the end with the small metal clips, he picked up her stocking, turned it right-side out, and started to slip it over her foot, stretching it to accommodate the bulk of the bandage. When he'd got it halfway up her leg, she took it gently from him.

"I can manage the rest," she said.

He looked up at her and she was startled to see a faint twinkle behind his weary eyes. "I was afraid you'd say that," he said, and stood up to retrieve the menu from the desk. When he turned back the show was over, the hem of her dress drawn neatly back over her knee. He started to hold out the menu.

"Explanation," she reminded him firmly.

He sighed and sat down on one of the chairs, holding

the menu awkwardly between his knees. "Look at yourself in the mirror," he suggested.

She turned, frowned, and leaned back over the chaise to look more closely at her reflection. Tentatively she touched the mark on her cheek. "It's blood," she said faintly.

"Somebody was shooting at us. At me," he amended. "Somebody was trying to kill me—they missed, and you got cut by a flying piece of Waterloo Bridge."

"I didn't."

"You did," he argued automatically, then just sat there.

"Call the police," she commanded with more confidence than she felt. He looked so pale, so bleak, so dismal she could scarcely bear to look at him, yet found it just as difficult to look away.

"It won't do any good," he told her. And then told her the rest, all of it, everything. In half-whispers and bursts of words, as if confessing to something shameful, a disgusting habit he couldn't break.

"Call Inspector Gates," she said when he'd finished.

"What's the point? I have no proof . . . a scratch on your face and a couple of marks on the bridge."

"But your hand, your flat . . . it's all part of the same thing."

"Probably."

"But he'll have to give you protection. He *must*." She couldn't understand why he just sat there, making no move.

"I'll take care of it," he said finally, making it clear the subject was closed. "Better than I've taken care of you, I hope. Believe me, I would never have called you if I'd thought there was the least chance Claverton was going to go on with—"

"John, you *must*—"

"Don't give me orders," he snapped, then closed his eyes and let his shoulders sag momentarily. "Unless it's for dinner, that is."

"John . . . if I'm in the way . . . if you'd rather we just—"

"I'd rather we just had dinner and tried to forget the whole damn thing," he said. "Unless you're afraid of being poisoned."

"At the *Savoy?*"

"Absolutely right," he said with forced cheer. "Let's start at the top and eat the place dry."


They tried to pretend nothing was wrong.

Tried to enjoy the meal, to make one another laugh. Told one another their life histories, argued amiably about nothing that mattered, and in general avoided the two topics that were uppermost in their minds—whether Claverton was going to succeed in killing him, and whether they were going to bed for dessert.

Beth sat at the table, crumbling a water biscuit, watching his face across the linen and silver. She wanted him to ask her to stay. This one, this one, her head kept saying, this one I could love. But I'm nearly forty, my boobs sag and so do both my chins. I haven't slept with a man for over six years and I'm probably getting desperate. I know I am. You don't fall in love like a kid at forty. You watch yourself, you know the problems, you've been there too often not to know the trouble and pain such nonsense brings. So let me be casual, let me be cool. If he asks me to stay, let me act like it happens all the time, let me do it right.

But he didn't ask.

He poured out the last of the wine and saw her hand shake as she reached for her glass. He could hardly blame her, he'd taken her out, kissed her, got her shot at and sprained her ankle, and now had her alone in his hotel suite, slightly tight on good wine and incipient hysteria.

He'd never liked the idea of shooting fish in a barrel.

But there was more to it than that, he admitted to himself.

He simply didn't want to make it like that with her. For all his experience and supposed expertise with women, this one made him feel different. This one, this one, his head kept saying, this one I could hurt. And he realized that was absolutely the last thing he wanted to do. He had a dozen numbers he could ring if sex was all he wanted. A dozen names on tap, but he couldn't remember a single one of them without looking in his diary. He realized he wanted her far too much to ask her to stay tonight. He'd foul up, he'd make a mess of it, sprain her other ankle, maybe, or her ego, certainly. And his own. He felt as unhinged as a boy and was furious with himself. At your age you know better, at your age the time is past for lollipops and roses and poetry in the goddamn dark, for crying out loud. If you want to screw the woman, say so.

But he couldn't.

Instead he found himself apologizing to her. "This mess I'm in, Beth . . . it could go on for a long time or be over tomorrow. I just have no way of knowing. I don't want you involved, but I'd like to see you again—"

"When the bullets stop flying?" she finished for him. "That would be nice, John. Just give me a ring and I'll put on my track shoes so we can have another go at the record."

He could see she thought he was just trying to get out gracefully, assumed she heard goodbye in his tone. "We can have another go at . . . everything."

"Why not?" she said briskly in her best social worker voice. "Meanwhile . . . it's late, so why don't you just summon my pumpkin and send me home so you can get some sleep? I've enjoyed tonight—"

"Don't be so goddamn polite," he heard himself say.

"You started it," she countered.

They stared at one another, knowing it could go either way right then, and the silence stretched until it simply disappeared, leaving them there, beached. Finally he got up and called down for a cab, then saw her downstairs. He walked back across the big empty lobby to the lift, aware that absolutely nobody was looking at him, five-star discretion everywhere. It was a big hotel.

It wasn't their fault he felt so small.

# 13

"Divorce?" the little man asked, pulling out a leather-covered notebook that was a duplicate of the one Gates kept producing.

"No," Johnny said, poking suspiciously at the opaque cube of ice floating on the surface of his Coke. "Somebody's trying to kill me and I'm getting tired of it."

The cheerfulness went out of R. Priddy, Private Enquiry Agent. He took a long pull at his lager, staring over the edge of the glass with sharp black eyes that seemed to have been meant for someone else's face, then put the glass down with a bump and licked his upper lip delicately. "I presume you've told the police about this?"

"Of course I've told the bloody police about it," Johnny snapped.

"And?"

"It's not all that simple." He told the story again, but without the hesitation he'd had with Beth. Priddy listened attentively but made no notes. He seemed to have rejected the job already.

"You'd be throwing your money away, Mr. Cosatelli,"

he said when Johnny had finished. "I'm a one-man operation, I can't provide the kind of protection you'd—"

"I don't want protection," Johnny interrupted.

Priddy's eyebrows drew together. "What, then?"

"I want to know why Mark Claverton is so afraid of me."

"I don't understand," Priddy said.

"No, that's just it, neither do I." He leaned back against the leather of the booth they were defending against all comers as the lunchtime crowd moved in. "He got his revenge by smashing my hand, got a little more by smashing my flat. But he's keeping it up." (And nearly killing vulnerable women with beautiful legs, he added to himself. I could take the rest of it, I can't take that.) "He tried to get the police to arrest me for Lisa's murder—"

"Why haven't they?"

"Because I didn't do it," Johnny answered evenly. Priddy nodded, but it wasn't acceptance, just judgment reserved. "Claverton thinks I did, but I think *he* did, so we're even there, because as Inspector Gates keeps repeating, there's no evidence either way. Okay?"

"So far. Go on."

"He may have reasons to hate my guts, he may have reasons for wanting to make my life hell, but he has absolutely no reason to want me dead that I can see. So, I want you to *find* the reason."

"I don't get—"

"I want you to find out everything there is to know about Mark Claverton. I want you to dig and dig until you come up with something rotten I can use for a trade."

"A trade."

Johnny had the distinct impression Priddy was humoring him. "That's right. Something I can put down on paper, deposit with my bank manager to be opened in the event of my death, and then go to Claverton and say, 'Keep off my back and I'll keep my mouth shut.' A trade."

Priddy smiled briefly and drank a little more lager. Johnny had picked his name at random out of the Yellow Pages, expecting Jim Rockford or Lew Archer to appear. Instead, he'd got a slightly podgy man in his late fifties with a bald spot in the middle of tight gray curls and a mustard stain on his tie. "You know what I spend most of my time doing?" Priddy asked. Johnny shook his head and Priddy smiled again. "Tracking down defaulters for finance companies. Repossessing cars and television sets. I used to do a lot of divorce but with the new laws most people prefer to wait the two years than catch a wife or husband in the wrong bed. I must say your case has a certain novelty value, but I still reckon you'd be wasting your money. Not only because I'd be duplicating everything the police are doing, which will annoy them, but because despite what you think this Claverton could actually be a model citizen in every way. I could poke around for weeks, months even, and come up empty-handed. Add to that the fact that what you're proposing is blackmail about which there are no new laws, just the same old ones, all against it, and if I come up with anything actually criminal I'd be obliged to tell the police about it because I want to go on doing what I'm doing. It's all I know *how* to do."

Johnny nodded and sighed. "Can you recommend anyone who'd be willing to take it on?"

"I haven't turned it down, yet, I just wanted to get all that off my chest so you'd be more sympathetic when you have to write out the checks. It will be expensive."

"I realize that."

"I charge thirty quid a day, plus expenses, double on weekends. Expenses include bribes where necessary, entertainment where necessary, and tranquilizers where necessary. I don't hit people and I don't like people to hit me, so if it looks like anyone is going to, I'll quit."

"Anything else?" Johnny asked, dryly.

"Yes. The police have a good closure rate on homicide but they date it by the year, not in weeks or months. I hope you like the wallpaper in this place because you might have to stare at it for a long time."

"You don't sound very optimistic."

"I'm not. For a start I'd like to know why the police are letting you run around loose the way they are. It seems to me you have a valid claim for some kind of protection."

"Gates doesn't seem to think so."

"Don't you find that odd?"

"I don't know—I've never had any dealings with the police before, I haven't any idea how they're supposed to act. Is it odd?"

"Yes, it is," Priddy said. "Do they know you're staying here?"

"Yes, Gates drove me here himself after my flat got done over."

"Did he, now? That's interesting."

"And I think he had a word with the hotel security man, and I think there are still policemen following me, but the faces keep changing so I'm not sure."

"Ah. That's more like it. In here, are they?"

Johnny glanced around. "They could be—I don't know. They don't wear white hats or anything."

Priddy's expression softened a little, but not much. "Look, son, I know how you feel. A little frustration can

SOLO BLUES / 189

be a dangerous thing, makes you do things you wouldn't do normally."

"Like hire private detectives?"

"Maybe."

"I just want somebody on *my* side for a change," Johnny said desperately. "And *doing* something for a change. I feel so bloody helpless."

Priddy nodded. "What they're after, of course."

"Who?"

"The police. Gates is only a cog in the big machine, but the general procedure is usually the same when they haven't got hard evidence. Keep a suspect off-balance, pressure him without making bruises, make him feel more and more hemmed in until he cracks. Using the time to gather what evidence they need, of course."

"You mean Gates still thinks I might have killed Lisa?"

"That's what it sounds like to me. If I were you I'd play by their rules instead of making up your own as you go along."

"Are you going to work for me or not?" Johnny asked abruptly.

"Sure. It beats chasing cars like some damn dog. I'll make daily reports by phone, weekly in writing, including a detailed expense sheet."

Johnny reached into his jacket for his checkbook. "Is two hundred all right for a retainer?"

"Fine." Priddy watched as Johnny steadied the checkbook awkwardly with his bandaged hand. "You're sure you can afford this? I don't mean to be rude, but if your hand doesn't heal you might need—"

"Mr. Priddy, if I never play piano again I can still earn a nice steady twenty thousand a year simply writing advertising jingles and box openers. My parents brought me up to be a concert pianist, but all the time I was playing Mozart I was actually destined to be the man who wrote a little number called 'Stick It in Your Ear' for a punk group called the Stinkspots. It's been in the charts for four weeks now, and if I hear it just one more time, I'll puke. In fact, I think that's what they did when they recorded it—made for a very distinctive sound." He put his checkbook back in his jacket pocket. "Money I've got, for all the good it's doing me."

"I should have made it fifty a day," Priddy mourned, looking at the check drawn on Coutt's Bank. He grinned, suddenly. "I'll use it to take music lessons. Always knew I was in the wrong business."

"That's where we're different . . . I never realized it until recently," Johnny said. "How about another lager before you start?"

*

"Well," Dunhill said. "Now you know what he's going to do."

"Do I?" Gates wondered. "We don't know why he's hired this Priddy character. Certainly not for protection . . . he's out and about, not lurking around the Savoy."

"We could pull Priddy in and ask him," Dunhill suggested.

Gates shook his head. "He's ex-Met, I had him checked out. He's got no reason to love us. He was asked to resign after some hassle about unauthorized activities."

Dunhill raised an eyebrow. "On the take?"

"No, on the make—evidence on a case that was up the creek. *He* went up the creek instead."

"A cowboy."

"Well, if he was he isn't anymore. From us he went to a couple of security firms, did a few years as an investigator for an insurance company, then got himself a job as head of security for some electronics firm in Slough. He got fired from *that* for being too honest—he clamped down on pilferage so tightly that the unions began to complain. The company had the choice of writing off the thefts as an unavoidable overhead or writing Priddy off as a bad investment. He got it in the neck again."

"That could make a man depressed," Dunhill said.

"It must have . . . he's been working solo ever since, using what old contacts he's got to stay off the dole but not really making all that much."

"I wonder what made Cosatelli choose him?"

"Knowing Cosatelli as I don't, I imagine the fact that Priddy's office is just down the Strand from the Savoy had something to do with it. Our musician is the type who goes from A to B in strange territory."

"That's a pretty fancy location for someone like Priddy," Dunhill said. "You sure he's not making—"

Gates smiled. "The Strand goes up and the Strand goes down. Priddy's 'office' is a ten by ten room on the top floor of a building due for demolition in the next year."

"From his history I'd say the address is right . . . Priddy sounds like a man about to be stepped on by the advance of civilization, too. How old is he?"

"Fifty-eight." Gates was plucking at the papers on his desk and suddenly grabbed one. "When did this come through?"

"I don't know . . ." Dunhill peered over his shoulder. "Must have been dumped with the rest of the stuff this morning." He whistled softly as he read the forensic report on the little suitcase Lisa Kendrick had entrusted to Johnny. "So C-11 was right about Claverton . . ."

"So it would seem," Gates said, dropping the report back onto the heap of letters and flyers. "But I'm beginning to wonder how much of this we can put down to Claverton, and how much to the man who's always around, telling him what to say and think."

Dunhill raised an eyebrow. "You mean Manvers?"

Gates nodded. "Gut feelings are supposed to be out of style these days, seeing as computers are practically walking our beats for us—but I have an old-fashioned gut feeling about the very charming Lewis Manvers."

"He's got no form, nothing in the records."

"Nothing in writing, I agree. But I've asked around and he's come close to the line a few times. Not enough to make waves . . . just ripples. I don't like the man."

"Whereas you do like Claverton. *And* Cosatelli. I don't understand you, Dave. You never used to get emotionally involved with the work like this. Left it at the door when you went out, picked it up when you came back." Gates' head came up as he caught the echo of his own remark to Cosatelli. "Worrying about people is a bad habit to get into. It can spoil your aim."

"There's nothing wrong with my aim," Gates snapped, and he glowered at his subordinate. "It's just when you've got a couple of wounded rabbits in the trap and you see the wolf creeping up on them from the other side, it's difficult to know which to shoot first."

Dunhill sighed. "It's the kids who've done it."

"Kids? What kids?"

"*Your* kids. You used to be a mean son of a bitch, but lately I see you hurting when you should be hating, wondering when you should be moving your ass toward a quick conviction with no complications. Cosatelli and Claverton aren't wounded rabbits, for crying out loud, they're suspects. End of story, no pictures for slow readers."

"I think you and I are reading different books," Gates said, locking his hands behind his head and staring at the ceiling. "I see a lot of pictures in mine. One of them is you and me running in all the wrong directions while Manvers and some others I could mention are laughing their heads off in the background."

"Go home and get some sleep, Dave," Dunhill said. "You're beginning to get silly with it."

"I wonder," Gates murmured.

# 14

He'd taken the suite at the Savoy initially because it was something he'd always wanted to do. For the first, and undoubtedly the only time he would be living the way most people thought successful musicians always lived. He didn't think it was the way they *should* live, however, because he'd always had a sneaking suspicion that the true experience of making music professionally— an erratic and bewildering succession of airports, bus terminals, bland or even grotty hotel rooms whose numbers he invariably got wrong because he was always at least one key behind, badly tuned instruments, missing scores, and mounting piles of dirty laundry that eventually entailed making furtive visits to all-night launderettes instead of getting desperately needed sleep—created a background of nervous static that only the music could allay. It meant that you were always grateful for the music because it healed you.

In this particular instance, even if it meant sending all his capital down the elegant Savoy drains, he was glad he'd followed his sentimental impulse because he'd come to roost in a place he'd never have to leave from one day to the next.

The Savoy, fully accustomed to protecting major film stars and minor oriental potentates, had no difficulty in coping with the care, feeding, and total isolation of one medium-sized eccentric musician. He'd arranged for the therapist to come to him each morning, and no other visitors arrived without being announced and described. He specified that the same waiters bring all his meals to the room, and didn't open the door unless he knew the voice outside.

He found that being waited on hand and foot had a drawback, however, in that it left you without even the distraction of buying an egg and boiling it. Even so, voluntary self-imprisonment on this level was infinitely preferable to an abrupt and unscheduled release from all earthly cares.

Moosh dropped by twice to try to talk him out of leaving jazz. Laynie dropped by and made sure she'd talked him into it. Baz would neither come to the hotel or the telephone. Apparently he was still taking Johnny's decision as a personal betrayal. Moosh said he was drinking a lot and was pretty sure he'd knocked Molly around once or twice. Johnny felt guilty about it, but there wasn't a thing he could do.

He'd sent a page out to buy him an electric kettle because he was damned if he was going to have waiters hotfooting back and forth to supply him with the coffee he needed, night and day. He felt cheap each time he plugged it in, but it meant he was able to offer Priddy a cup the minute he arrived, three days later.

Priddy watched him open the wardrobe and extract the

kettle, the jar of instant coffee, and the can of powdered milk.

"Secret drinker, I see," the old man commented.

"If I'd known you were coming I'd have baked a cake," Johnny said, jabbing the plug into the wall outlet by the writing desk. "I thought you were going to report by phone."

Priddy sighed. He saw his client was no longer making concessions to his surroundings, but was walking around barefoot wearing jeans and a wrinkled sweatshirt. The elegance of the room was overlaid with an odor of tobacco smoke and orange peels were heaped on the top of the piano. There was a cassette recorder on one of the tables, playing away. Priddy didn't know much about classical music—whatever it was sounded nervous and in a hurry. He took off his hat, put it onto the floor, and accepted the mug of coffee Johnny held out on his way to the piano. "Look here," he said, gesturing at his bald spot as Johnny sat down. "See the bruise?"

Johnny looked but saw nothing except shiny pink skin. "You mean Claverton had—"

"No. I mean I've been hitting it against a brick wall, that's all." He sipped his coffee and made a face. "You got any sugar?" he asked, standing up and looking at the wardrobe.

"Sugar is bad for you," Johnny said severely, and Priddy sat back down.

"What do you put on your cornflakes?"

"Raisins. Sometimes bananas," Johnny told him. "What brick wall?"

Priddy was tapping some saccharin pellets into his mug from a plastic container he'd dug out of his coat pocket. "The very high, very wide, very complete brick wall that's gone up around the activities of Mark Claverton and Associates, courtesy of the police, Claverton himself, and somebody else I can't identify."

"How do you mean?"

"I mean when I ask for business records at Companies House they 'aren't available' or can't be located. I mean when I ask people who should know about Claverton they get tight-lipped or downright rude and tell me to get the hell out. I've even had informants turn down good money. I'm just not getting anywhere."

"Nothing?"

"Nothing that's any use to you. Claverton has a gallery in Bond Street and another in Hampstead from which he sells very high-priced antiques and paintings. He has a big house just outside Maidenhead in a place called Dorney Reach. Ernie Wise also lives in the area, but I didn't drop in to ask him about Claverton. Maybe I should have, I might have got a laugh or two to break up the day. He'd at least have been civil, which is more than I can say for any other neighbor of Claverton's."

Johnny sipped at his coffee for a while, staring at the carpet. "What about their servants?"

"You mean my accent is wrong?" Priddy shook his head. "I'm not the best in the business by a long shot, but I've been doing it long enough to know which roles to play on which doorsteps. By this time even *I* should have been able to get an edge on the bastard . . ."

Johnny looked up suddenly. "You don't like him either."

"I don't like brick walls. I'll tell you one thing, they don't build brick walls around people with nothing to hide. There's something in there, all right, Claverton is as bent as a blue-balled babboon, but I don't know how."

"Any hunches?"

Priddy snorted. "Kojak gets hunches, I get bunions. At a guess I'd say he's either into fakes and forgeries or he's got another line of business that doesn't need a fancy place in Bond Street to make money."

"Such as?"

"There are seven deadly sins—pick a number." Priddy stirred his coffee with a ball-point pen, then drank some. "It could be a lot more complicated than that, of course. Could be some kind of business fraud or con, in which case you'd better sign me up for a year. There are more ways of making fast-deal setups than there are laws about them to break. I don't care how much money you've got in the bank, Mr. Cosatelli, Claverton can sink you with his petty cash. You've picked yourself a bad enemy."

"I didn't pick him," Johnny pointed out. "We'd never have walked down the same street if it hadn't been for Lisa."

"I guess she was someone pretty special to snag you and then somebody like Claverton," Priddy said cautiously.

"She was. Very beautiful, very smart, very sexy . . . but with no illusions about herself. She was—honest. It was almost a kind of innocence, I suppose." For some reason Beth came into his mind. "I can see that combination appealing to a man like Claverton. It appealed to me for a while, too."

"But only for a while."

Johnny considered it. "She didn't really need me," he finally said. "I suppose that sounds kind of adolescent."

"Did it feel adolescent?"

"No. I didn't need her either. I suppose you could say we had a business arrangement, the business being bed and someone to have dinner with every night."

"And is that how she felt about Claverton?"

"No. I think she really loved him. She really wanted to have his kid. Not just any kid—*his*."

"I thought you said she was smart."

"Have you ever been in love?"

"Sure."

"And were you 'smart' about it?"

"Not very," Priddy admitted ruefully. "And I've got the divorce papers to prove it."

"Snap," Johnny said. "I think Claverton was more than she could handle, though. Toward the end, she was getting a little frantic, a little desperate to get him to marry her. Maybe she pushed too hard, maybe she—" he trailed off and stared at Priddy without seeing him. "She didn't *say* baby clothes . . . what she said was 'a little insurance for the future' . . ."

"What?" Priddy asked, leaning forward a little.

Johnny told Priddy about the suitcase Lisa had left with him. "Gates said it was still there, though."

"Didn't you see it?"

"No . . . I said I didn't want to go back up there and he said okay. They packed my things for me and he brought them down."

"They always want the victim to make a list of anything that's missing . . . didn't you do that?"

"He said there was no rush . . . I figured he felt sorry for me."

"CID men *don't* feel sorry for people, especially murder suspects," Priddy said firmly. "He said the case was there—contents intact?"

"He didn't say anything about the contents."

"*They* went over the flat, *they* packed your things, *they* are letting you run around without protection, and the first time you go out at night somebody takes a shot at you," Priddy said slowly. "Where's your suitcase, show me what they put in it."

"It's under the bed," Johnny said in a puzzled voice. "All they put in it was what I asked for—the clothes that hadn't been ripped to pieces, my electric razor . . . I had to buy everything else, like toothpaste—"

Priddy dragged out the suitcase and went over everything, particularly the case itself. And came up with nothing.

"What did you expect to find?" Johnny asked.

"I don't know. Something. If we just knew what the hell she had there . . . what they went looking for . . . what Gates went looking for . . . or found . . ."

"Well, we don't," Johnny said, slamming the wardrobe door shut after hanging up his things.

"No need to get huffy about it," Priddy said defensively. "You still want me to go on with this dumb stunt of yours?"

"Yes, I still want you to go on with this dumb stunt of mine," Johnny growled. "I want to go *home,* when I've got a home again, I want to get on with my life, not sit on my ass in some fancy hotel counting my goddamn toes!"

"Okay, okay," Priddy said, picking his hat up and jamming it on his head. "It certainly isn't doing much for your personality.

"Not a lot, no."

"I'll ring you tomorrow," Priddy said.

"Thank you."

"You're paying for it."

"In every possible way there is," Johnny said, and shut the door, hard.

He'd been trying to ring Beth for the past few days

without success. Finally, at just after eleven that night, she answered the phone. Having had plenty of time to rehearse the smooth things he was going to say, he managed to start totally wrong.

"Where the hell have you been?" was what came out.

There was a moment of silence from the other end. "John?"

"No, Gunga Din. Do you realize I've called you about fifty times a day since Saturday? I thought you said you led a quiet life?"

"I do. It's just been kind of . . . hectic lately. How are you?"

"Fine." Now that was a dumb thing to say, wasn't it?

"I tried to call you on Monday morning," she told him.

"I must have been at the doctor's," he said, pleased she'd called, sorry he'd missed her. "What's the problem?"

"Problem?" She sounded tense and wary.

"Yes . . . why did you call?"

"Oh . . it doesn't matter. It was . . . I don't need you, now."

"You sure know how to make a man feel good," he said sarcastically.

"Oh, I didn't mean . . . that is—" Now she was getting flustered. Good. "I just meant the thing . . . the reason I called . . . sorted itself out, in a way. That's all."

"I see." He didn't, but obviously he wasn't going to get much more out of her on the subject. What the hell was the matter with her, anyway? "Well, I'm calling *you* to ask if you'd like to come over and have dinner with me tomorrow."

"Oh. Have the bullets stopped flying already?"

"I don't know. I haven't stuck my nose out the door to see.

But we'd be perfectly safe here . . . really. How about it?"

"I . . . not tomorrow, I'm afraid."

"The day after?"

"No, that's not any good either."

He didn't blame her, he supposed. "All right, Beth. Sorry to ring you so late . . ."

"There's no need to sulk. I really *can't* . . ."

"I'm not sulking," he said. "I just wanted to see you again, that's all. No big deal."

"Of course you want to see me again," she snapped, startling him. "Who wouldn't? It's hardly *my* fault you have to stand in line . . ."

*Now* what?

"Don't jump down my throat. You're worth queueing up for, if I have to stand in line then I damn well will stand in line, all right?"

"All right."

"Fine. How about Friday?"

"I don't know . . ."

Even he could get the message, eventually. He'd been wrong about her, she wasn't interested, too bad, tough luck, say goodbye.

"Goodbye, Beth."

"John . . . it's not that I—"

"No need to make a symphony out of it. I won't bother you again."

"But I *want* you to bother me."

"Maybe next week, then." Next year, never.

"Fine. I'll look forward to that." She hung up abruptly.

He stared at the phone for a long time, put it down, looked at the walls, the ceiling, the floor, his own puzzled face in the mirror.

She answered on the sixth ring, giving her number in a muffled voice.

"What's the matter, Beth?"

She burst into a wail, nearly shattering his eardrum. "Oh, Johnny, I'm so scared . . ."

He felt his insides slip, leaving an icy void. They'd seen her with him on Saturday night, could have waited and followed her cab home later, found out her name and who she was . . .

"Has anybody tried to hurt you?" he asked savagely.

"No, no . . . not *me* . . . it's Gino. I tried to call you . . . I thought maybe you could rea—son . . . help . . . me . . ." She was coming apart on him. He'd never felt so useless in his life.

"Is he sick . . . hurt . . . *what*, Beth?"

"It's not . . . that will mend . . ."

What would mend?

"It's what he's been . . . saying . . ." she babbled on, almost totally incoherent. "I can't . . . that man . . . nobody will—"

This was hopeless, a woman in that much pain needed holding. But they were watching the hotel, waiting for him to come out into the open again. If he led them to her . . . or worse, if they were also watching *her* place on the chance he might visit her . . .

"Beth, listen . . . you live in a block of flats, don't you?"

Sniff. "Yes."

"Is there a back entrance . . . a side entrance?"

"A back entrance. Why?" Sniff, sniff.

"I'm coming over to see you."

Sniff, sniff, gulp, gulp. "See me?"

She'd *seemed* intelligent the other night. "Just tell me

how I can get into your building without being seen, if I can. Tell me *now.*"

"But you don't have to—"

"Dammit, *tell* me!"

He went to the window, parted the curtain a crack, and looked out. It was a long way down. He didn't think the Savoy would appreciate his knotting together their Irish linen sheets and rapelling down the rear face of the building. Claverton was sure to have someone watching his window, as well as the front and rear entrances. He'd make a splendid target, hanging there.

He could always borrow a doorman's uniform and call himself a cab. "Congratulations, Cosatelli, you're a cab." What else?

Hotel Security? He could just picture the look on their faces. Somebody trying to kill you, Mr. Cosatelli, why didn't you tell us sooner?

He probably should have, but it was too late, now.

It was, he saw by his watch, well past midnight. He opened the window a little and took a breath of fresh air to clear his head. From far below he heard faint music. Opening the window a little more, he frowned in concentration, then smiled. Good night, ladies, milkman's on his way.

The River Room was crowded with what looked like and apparently was a wiggle of starlets and a pinch of producers, interspersed with a freeload of drunks, all awaiting the verdicts of a shrivel of critics. Or, as the notice outside said, Premiere Party for *The Bitch Meets the Stud.* He slipped inside, wondering who'd come out on top in *that* little cinematic encounter, and sidled around the perimeter of the room until he reached the edge of the bandstand. When the number they were playing finished, he poked the trumpet player in the back, and he turned around with a start.

"Hey, Johnny, how are you?"

"In a bind, Harry. What time do you pack up?"

The trumpeter glanced at the clock on the wall. "Any time, now. Why?"

"There's somebody waiting outside I'm trying to avoid. Any chance of carrying your trumpet case, mister?"

Harry's face took on a knowing expression. "You never change," he laughed. "Pick the wrong bird again?"

Johnny grimaced. "She was fine . . . it's her husband I don't fancy."

"Big, is he?"

"About twenty stone in his socks. I'll need to borrow somebody's gear to get through the lobby."

Harry nodded toward the other members of the group. "No problem . . . if you're not proud."

Johnny took a good look at the band for the first time, and choked. "What the hell are you guys supposed to *be?*"

"What does it look like?"

"It looks like somebody raided the closet in a Turkish bordello with his eyes closed."

Harry grunted. "You should have seen us *last* night. We played a dinner dance for the Sons of the Purple Plains in Wimbledon. You ever tried to play 'Goodbye Old Paint' as a bossa nova while wearing a six-gun?"

"Not lately."

"You have not lived, my friend. You have not lived."


Twenty minutes later Johnny was taking off the last of the beads and the purple sequined bolero he'd borrowed from the saxophonist. As the VW minibus went around

Marble Arch, the scimitar the guitarist was still wearing jabbed him in the ribs.

"Aren't you going to take that off?" he asked him.

"Hell, no—I'm going to use it to prune the roses tomorrow."

"Where do you want me to drop you?" Harry asked from the driver's seat, as Johnny put on his own jacket.

"Here's fine. When they arrest you guys I don't want to have to explain why I'm the only one not wearing earrings," Johnny said. As he stepped down onto the pavement, he turned to look at Harry. "Thanks."

"Tomorrow night we're wearing ordinary blue suits," Harry grinned. "I probably won't be able to play a goddamned note. See you, Sunshine."

Johnny watched the minibus move back into the stream of traffic, then hailed a passing taxi. The cabby pulled over and gave him an old-fashioned look. *"Love* your hair," he said.

Johnny glared after the minibus and reached up to remove the curly blond wig he'd forgotten he was wearing. Somehow, some day, he'd pay Harry back for *that* one.


He barked a shin on some timber in the builder's yard he had to cut through in the dark, and nearly lost a shoe going over the fence into the narrow patch of overgrown greenery that served the little block of flats as some kind of garden in summer but was still a jungle in early March. There was a network of rusty scaffolding erected up the back of the building—apparently the roof was being repaired. She'd promised to come down and unlock the door for him. He ducked under the scaffolding, opened the door, then locked it behind him. He went as quietly as he could up all the flights of carpeted stairs to her door, feeling about as unlike Romeo as it was possible to feel.

She'd gone to some effort with her makeup, but the sight of him standing there was apparently very sad. The tears came again, anyway. He held her close, kicking the door shut behind him. The way she clung should have made him feel about nine feet tall and very necessary. Mostly it exasperated him. Glancing around the small entrance hall of the flat, he decided the living room was through the door on the left and managed to maneuver her in and onto the couch that sat just in front of a bank of crowded bookshelves. By the time he'd accomplished that, she was regaining control. Grabbing a handful of tissues from a box on a sidetable, she began to blot her face and apologize all at once, each activity impeding the other. He tossed his jacket on the end of the couch, then sat down next to her and counted to one hundred and nine.

She'd drawn the curtains as he'd instructed her. The room wasn't big, and it was cluttered, but he liked it. It was like Beth, a bit muddled, a bit frayed, but basically sound. He couldn't decide who was winning the battle of the shelves—the books, the records, or the houseplants.

"Okay, now tell me about it," he said when the mopping-up seemed to have been completed. Syncopated with a few sniffs and hiccups, the story came out.

Gino's father had shown up on Sunday evening, drunk and mean. He'd taken all the money from the till, then had stormed through the little flat over the shop looking for more. He'd discovered the stereo equipment Johnny had given Gino and had smashed it to pieces, then started in on Mrs. Pantoni, accusing her of letting Gino get into "dirty company" again. When Gino had tried to intervene, he'd been pretty badly beaten. The daughter had been out with a boy, and this was also a crime for which Mrs. Pantoni had to be punished, to the tune of one broken cheekbone and two front teeth. Finally he'd left, falling down the stairs to the shop but unfortunately doing himself no damage.

As far as Beth was concerned, that wasn't the worst part.

The worst part was that Gino had now left school to work in the shop full-time. He didn't want to leave his mother alone there, and he was all she had. End of story, end of Gino.

She was so stiff with regenerated rage that there was no point in trying to comfort her, so he got up and began to walk around the room, wishing it were his own place so he could throw a few things at the wall.

"Has she made a complaint to the police *now?*" he asked.

"Yes, we've managed to get a court order denying him access or contact, but he has to break it to be arrested."

"Terrific."

"Gino mustn't leave school, John . . . he has such ability, such potential . . ."

"Such a goddamn rotten father."

"Oh . . . it's such a mess." He looked over at her—so was her face. She caught his glance and put a hand up, using the tissue as a kind of mask, pretending to wipe her eyes. "You shouldn't have come . . . if anything had happened to you . . . just because I couldn't . . . control myself . . ."

"I'll make some coffee," he said, and went to find the kitchen. She ran past him into the bedroom, to put on some makeup, he supposed. He didn't stop her—she needed to hide and he needed to simmer down.

Beth despaired at herself in the bathroom mirror. She hadn't meant to tell John a word about it. When she had tried to call him Monday morning it had been in a weak moment, and she was almost relieved not to find him in. He had enough problems of his own. This was hers and she'd been trained to handle it. Trained to be objective, too, and not break down. The activity necessary to getting the legal details of the Pantoni case into some kind of order had helped her to get over that weak moment. She hadn't tried to call him again, she didn't want him to think she was chasing him, after all, didn't want to reveal how much she cared about him, already.

If only he hadn't rung back a second time. If only his voice hadn't been so warm, so gentle. If only he hadn't come rushing over like this . . . then she wouldn't be standing here with a swollen face and a red nose. Was he destined to always see her with a red nose? She could hear him pacing around the sitting room like an animal in a cage too small to contain him, back and forth, back and forth. What on earth was she going to do with him, now that he was here?

When she got back to the living room she found her coffee waiting on the table. He was carrying his with him as he peered at her record collection. She liked the way the dark blue sweater fitted his shoulders. She liked the square set of him, the big head, the way he balanced himself, moving more slowly now. She'd hoped her memory of their one evening together had made him seem more marvelous than he really was, but it hadn't.

"As you can see, I have pretty bad taste in music," she tried, sitting down on the couch again and picking up her coffee.

"Odd, not bad. Odd." She had classics jumbled against

film scores, jazz mixed with pop, Balinese gamelan (Balinese gamelan?) music with folk collections and more classics. Lots of Bach and Mozart, then a big chronological gap until the Impressionists, stopping short of the true moderns. He turned to face her.

"What are we going to do about Gino?" he asked quietly. She bit her lip, made a face, balanced her coffee mug on her knee.

"Well, when you get right down to it, there isn't much more we *can* do," she admitted. "Perhaps when he's had a little time to think . . . maybe it would be better not to push him just now . . . I don't know. I'm sorry I started crying on the phone and made you come all the way over here . . . compared to what you're going through, what does it matter about Gino . . ."

"It *doesn't* matter about Gino," he said brusquely. "Oh . . . of course it matters about Gino . . . I didn't mean—" He came across and sat beside her, putting his coffee mug on the floor. "I guess I meant he was as good an excuse as any." She didn't say anything. "So . . ." He brought his hands down with a slap onto his thighs and stood up, walking over to the shelves of records. "So—since I'm here—maybe you can explain why you like Balinese gamelan music. I don't think I've ever heard any, to tell you the truth." He pulled the record out of its sleeve and put it on the turntable, bending down slightly to figure out the controls and get it started. After listening to the first track, he turned to look at her. "Does it get any better?"

She wouldn't or couldn't meet his eyes. "It doesn't change much, if that's what you mean. It's an acquired taste, like coffee. I'll make some more . . . put something else on." Collecting his mug from the floor, she fled to the kitchen. The oriental music stopped, some Mozart began.

She was rinsing out the mugs in the sink when he came up behind her.

"I'm really sorry about Gino. Maybe he'll see sense if you let him work it through." He watched her rinsing the mugs over and over again, and felt like an idiot for making such a big thing about this. He'd done his noble Romeo act only to be left standing on one foot plucking thorns out of his damned doublet. Or was she this twitchy with everyone? "I guess you want me to go, since there's noth—"

"No . . ." She got her voice under control. "No, of course I don't want you to go. You *know* I don't."

"Then why do you keep running out of the room every two minutes? I'm not going to leap on you if you don't want me to." He saw her hands double up into fists on the edge of the drainboard, her knuckles white. When she finally spoke her voice was strained and angry.

"I keep running out of the room to stop myself from leaping on *you.*"

He closed his eyes and felt his body suddenly relax. "Who's stopping you?" he said softly. "I promise not to scream."

He got her up to the bedroom on laughter, suggesting that since she was so hot for him maybe *she* should do the carrying over the threshold bit, and then got her onto the bed by the simple expedient of putting her there.

He could tell she was ashamed of her body by the way she moved against him. There was absolutely nothing wrong with her figure that a couple of weeks on a diet wouldn't cure, if it meant so damn much to her. Her breasts were full and still firm, her hips wide and deep.

He began gently, for him, discovering to his own surprise that what he wanted most was simply to make her happy. No big erotic scene, no athletics—he felt only tenderness for her need and patience for his own. When he lifted his mouth from hers for a moment, caught a glimpse of her face in the faint light from the hall with her eyes closed and a moan starting in her throat, he recognized the sight and sound. Astonishment. Not at him, but at herself.

That she could feel this way, this much, still.

Her total response to the music at the concert should have told him, her awkward self-consciousness should have told him, *something* should have been fair warning that what she was really afraid of was herself. And no wonder. She was totally sensual when released, blind and wild in his arms, crying out, turning and twisting beneath him, unable to control or contain her own passion. Only he could do so, and did. At last, breathing unevenly, still a little damp with sweat but trusting him to protect her through the night, she slept.

He found he was a little astonished, too. Not at her, but at himself, and what had happened to him there in that jumbled, stormy bed.

He stroked her breasts, saw the lines of stretch marks making silvery tracks from the wide aureoles of the nipples and across the rounded slope of her belly. She'd borne two children who were now at university, far away, leaving her empty and alone. That insensitive ex-husband of hers had certainly done a number on her, convincing her she was nothing when she was just about everything a sane man could want in a woman. She had a brain, she had wit, she had humor. But stripped of her concealing clothes, her official briefcase, her sensible shoes, her excuses and her defenses, she was a vulnerable and precious thing.

What she needed was someone to tell her so, and often.

He had the distinct feeling he was about to volunteer.

When he woke up the first thing that he saw was the sun through yellow curtains making a rainbow on the wall. Then her face on the pillow, lax and pale in sleep, her hair curling into the back of her neck, her nose shiny, and a streak of eye makeup across one cheek. Because he didn't want to give her a chance to get awkward and embarrassed all over again, he began to caress her until she came awake halfway to heat, and there was no time for polite conversation.

After that they had breakfast in bed, sharing the toast and morning paper like any old married couple. Eventually she put the papers down, however, and got out of bed.

"What's the matter?" he asked lazily, enjoying the sight of her dimpled backside as she stalked purposefully toward the closet. He didn't think he would ever fancy a skinny woman again.

"I have to go to work," she said, sounding cross.

"Call them up and say you've got leprosy or something."

She turned with an armful of dress clutched up against her nakedness, the hanger digging into her shoulder. "I can't—we have a staff meeting on the tenth of every month and I have to make a report." She sat down on the edge of the bed and started to unbutton the dress.

"Oh."

"And while I prefer meeting *your* staff to the one at the

office, they really are expecting me," she said firmly. "I'll get back as soon as I can."

"Will you?"

Something in the tone of his voice made her look up. He had rolled onto one elbow and was looking at her oddly. "Well, I *could* be, if you . . . that is . . ."

"I take it you're assuming you'd be so fantastic in bed that I'd never be able to tear myself away? That I think you're altogether irresistible and want to spend the rest of my life with you, after one *night?*" he said, mockingly.

"No . . . *no* . . ." she said, flushing.

"Go ahead and assume," he relented, reaching for her. "You'd be absolutely right." He proceeded to clarify his position. Afterward, she mumbled into his neck that this was all very well but she still had to go to work. He heaved himself up and scowled down. "You know your trouble? You're unromantic."

She reached up and ran her fingertips over his cheekbones. "I am not. I'm *very* romantic. You do know your face is very beautiful, I suppose?"

"Oh, sure . . . it has all the gnarled majesty of an old sycamore."

She prodded the lines around his eyes and mouth. "A *very* old sycamore."

"Mmmmmmm." He rolled over and they contemplated the ceiling. It needed painting. "Since you seem determined to ignore my earlier statement, I wish to have a brief discussion before you leave."

Beth felt cold, without his body between her and the room. She'd ignored what he'd said because he couldn't *possibly* have said what she'd thought she'd heard. "A discussion?"

"Yes. You know—I say something and then you say

something and then I tell you to shut up. A discussion. Ready?"

"I guess so."

"Good." He'd been working this out for most of the night, but still felt unsure. He took a deep breath. "There are some who might say that my feelings about you have been caused by the fact that my life is in a complete state of balls-up at the moment. They might be right, but I don't think so, because I know me better than they do. It's still a possibility we have to face, isn't it?"

"I—"

"Shut up. That being the case, perhaps we shouldn't give too much importance to it, and maybe we'd better stop it right here, but I don't want to. I want to go on, probably for quite a while, maybe forever, although that's a commitment I'm not fully prepared to make at this time since I may discover you have disgusting personal habits I can't tolerate, such as putting tomato sauce on chocolate ice cream, and you may object to my playing with battleships in the bath. We have to face that, too, don't we?"

"We—"

"Shut up. I told you the other night about going back to serious work. If I do I'll probably turn back into the nervous, self-centered, obsessive bastard I really am, and if my first wife couldn't stand it there's no reason why you should be able to. Maybe you're made of sterner stuff, but you do seem to cry a lot and if you persist in the habit my shoulders will get waterlogged, I'll get rheumatism and won't be able to play Bach. I play Bach very well, you must hear me sometime, I'm a goddamn whiz."

"You—"

"Shut up. The only reason I'm bothering to say all this

on such short acquaintance is because one, I'm not used to feeling like this, and two, you seem to spend all your time with me worrying about making a good impression and not wanting to seem possessive and I don't like to see you worried. I think you need me and I think I need you. I don't see why it's got to be coy and silly when really it's quite straightforward, isn't it?"

"John—"

"Wait a minute . . . I'm trying to think if I've left anything out." He stared at the ceiling for a few more seconds. "I'll do it the other way if you prefer—flowers and candy and meeting you under the clock at eight—but I'd really rather not. I'm not saying I don't know *how* to do all that stuff, and I'm not saying I might not buy you the odd daffodil now and again, but I'd really just rather go on from here. Your turn."

"I love you." She couldn't stop it—out it came.

Silence.

"No, you don't," he said quietly. "But you may in time as I'm entirely lovable in every way. So are you. God knows how two such fantastic people happened to go unclaimed for all this time, but we did and here we are. Your turn again."

"I love you."

Suddenly he was above her, hands braced on either side of her shoulders, looking down. "Then why don't you go to work and let me get some sleep so I'll be ready for you when you come home? I'm an old man and you're wearing me out."

"Is the discussion over?"

"The discussion is over. Nothing else—just the discussion."

"And *you're* assuming I've agreed to all this, are you?"

"Not at all. Let's hear your arguments against it."

She sighed, raised her hands and started to count off on her fingers. "One—" He waited. "I haven't any."

He collapsed, suddenly, and held her against him, saying nothing, just holding on tight, until she realized with amazement and a great tenderness that he'd babbled on like that because he'd been afraid. He'd actually been *afraid* she'd say no.

When she came out of the bathroom dressed, made up, and full of specious dedication to the cause of righting social injustice, she saw he had dozed off. He looked so vulnerable lying there only half-covered by the duvet, his unbandaged hand open palm up like a child's beside his head and his hair all ruffled. It was an illusion, of course. If he opened his eyes she knew she'd see no child behind them, and shivered with remembered sensations. Incredible enough that she suddenly had a man in her bed again—the *kind* of man he was made it simply astounding. He was demanding, he was funny, he was gifted, he was attractive, and, dammit, he was still *there*. Snoring just a little through his open mouth, and with a brown mole next to his navel, but she *had* him, he was *hers*.

The only trouble was, somebody was trying to kill him.

"John?" His eyes flew open. She'd been right, no child there.

"Hmmm?" He squinted at her.

"I'm going to double-lock the door from outside when I leave. It will mean you can't get out, but it will also stop anyone getting in. All right?" She *had* to go, if only to get some time and distance between her and this amazing thing that had happened.

"Stay with me," he mumbled, closing his eyes again and curling up on his side.

"Did you hear what I said about the lock?"

"Sounds wonderful. Nicest jail in town," he whispered, squashing her pillow up and holding it against his chest with a beatific smile. She looked at him for a moment longer, sighed, then resolutely started out.

"I'm going to go to work. Goodbye."

"Goodbye, Fat Lady."

She wavered, then went on before she could change her mind.

"I'll try to get home early."

"I'll be here," he called after her.

But he wasn't.

# 15

He'd spent the morning feeling happy and temporarily secure, wandering around Beth's flat being unashamedly nosy, trying to discover more about this woman with whom he'd suddenly and inexplicably fallen in love. All her clothes were plain, all her underthings incredibly lacy. She wore a five-and-a-half shoe, used fluoride toothpaste, and seemed to spend a lot of time in the bath, if the array of oils and essences were anything to go by. She kept a bottle of white wine in the ice compartment of the fridge next to the frozen carrots and peas, ate a lot of fruit-flavored yogurt, and apparently baked her own bread because there was a block of fresh yeast in the vegetable crisper next to half a green pepper that had seen better days. That had probably been the moment he'd decided he couldn't let her get away— somebody had to break her of the habit of freezing decent wine. He'd been looking at the pictures of her children on the bureau, trying to imagine what they'd think of him (not much, he decided, they didn't have her eyes or mouth), when the telephone rang.

It was Priddy.

"Why the hell did you leave the hotel . . . what's this number they gave me?" Priddy demanded, over a background of some child squalling outside his phone booth.

"A friend's. Where are *you?*"

"Maidenhead Shopping Precinct. Listen, Claverton's taken off for parts unknown."

"How do you know?" He stretched the phone cord to its limit and turned down the stereo.

Priddy sighed in direct-dial exasperation. "Because while I was pretending to be a sewer inspector in the street outside his place he came out with his partner and that ox of a chauffeur of his put two suitcases into the trunk of the Rolls before driving off. I also spoke to the milkman, who said they'd stopped the milk until next Monday, and a little later I saw the housekeeper leave with *her* suitcase and take a cab into town. Being possessed of a razor-sharp mind, I figured it was holiday time, folks."

"I wonder if Gates knows about this?"

"Who? Gates? Probably—why?"

"Is anybody else watching Claverton's place besides you?"

"Nobody as far as I can see. *Why?*" Priddy repeated.

The pips went and he heard Priddy cursing as he searched for more change. "Tell me your number and I'll ring you back." While he looked up the Maidenhead dialing code he was also consulting his subconscious, which seemed to be up to something again.

Priddy picked up the phone on the first ring. The child was still whining and shrieking behind him and Johnny visualized Priddy beseiged in the phone booth, irate mothers piling up like driftwood outside.

"Has he got any other servants, guards, anything like

that?" Johnny asked before Priddy could do more than
grunt. He had no idea how big Claverton's place actually
was.

"Gardener comes twice a week, came yesterday. Nothing else." Priddy breathed heavily into the receiver for a
minute. "You're not thinking—"

But he was.

*

First of all, he had to find wheels.

His driver's license was somewhere in the chaos at the
flat, probably under layers of painter's dropcloths, so he
couldn't rent a car. Laynie didn't drive. He rang Moosh's
place only to be told by a somewhat worried Mrs. Moosh
that her husband had left for somewhere or other that
morning, saying that he'd call later. He hadn't called yet.

"Well—he will," Johnny said encouragingly.

"I suppose so," she said slowly. "Mr. Masuto wants
him—*he's* called twice already. Something about the fence
at the club."

"*Charley* Masuto?" Fences in a cellar club?

"Uh-huh. He sounded angry when I said Maurice
wasn't here."

"Charley always sounds angry. How are you—isn't the
baby due pretty soon?" No sense in worrying her.

She laughed—it was a nice laugh he'd always enjoyed
hearing. "The doctor says yesterday."

"What do *you* say?"

"Next week—just doesn't feel *done* yet."

He grinned. "Let me know when it pops—you know I
always like to be first across the wire with roses."

"Okay. You take care, John, hear?"

"I hear. You too." And Moosh—if Charley was mad at him.

He hung up slowly. He could always go back to the hotel and get them to hire him a car, but it would take hours and he didn't have hours. Which left him with only one alternative.

Even so—as he walked up the neatly manicured Hampstead drive some forty minutes later—he wished there'd been time to find another way. Something short of facing World War Three.

"Oh, Johnny . . . thank God . . . maybe you can talk some sense into him," Molly said when she opened the door. She grabbed his arm and pulled him into the hall, her fingers tight.

"See sense about what?"

There was a crash from the kitchen and he heard Baz's voice rising in a crescendo of foul language. Their youngest boy came running down the hall, took one wild-eyed look at his mother, then darted up the stairs on his chubby legs, howling. Molly wavered between going after him and making sure Johnny wouldn't dash off, too.

"About going to an audition when he's like—"

"When he's like what?" Baz asked from the kitchen doorway. Johnny peered into the shadows, trying to make out the expression on Baz's face, but it was too dark in the hall. Only when he took a few steps closer could he see the big gray eyes weren't functioning together, and had a glazed glow, like ice burning from underneath. "Well, if it isn't Judas himself," Baz said maliciously. "What the hell are you doing here—hoping I was out so you could add my old lady to your list?"

"No," Johnny said evenly. "I came to see if I could borrow your car."

"My *car?* Why, so you can drive up to those dizzy heights of brilliance Laynie is always crapping on about? Fat chance." Baz swayed slightly and put out a hand, steadying himself against the wall. "*I* need it myself, so bug off. Steal one, why don't you?"

Johnny glanced at Molly. She was staring at her husband with genuine fear in her eyes, and still had hold of Johnny's arm.

"And stop pawing him, you slut!" Baz said, taking a step forward and raising a hand as if to strike her. Johnny slapped the hand away and Baz staggered back.

"Let me talk to him, Molly . . . you go look after Davey," Johnny said, pushing her gently toward the stairs. "Go on . . ."

With one last fearful glance, Molly hastened up the stairs. Baz kept his eyes on Johnny's face, and Johnny felt as well as saw the hate in them.

"Well, you're doing just fine, aren't you?" Johnny said angrily. "Really beautiful . . . the Head of the House, or should I say louse? You bastard . . . you said you'd never bring it home with you."

"Get out."

"No."

"It's my bloody house . . . get *out!*" Baz came at him and Johnny slapped him in the face, hard, one side then the other. Baz stared at him for a minute, open-mouthed, the marks blazing on his pale skin. Then, suddenly, he began to cry. Johnny sighed, and pushed Baz roughly into the living room, closing the door behind him. He watched as Baz tottered over to the sideboard and picked up a bottle of whiskey and a glass, spilling a little as he poured.

"That's not going to help anything," Johnny said.

"What do you know about it, Judas?" Baz mumbled.

"I know *all* about it, Baz. We've stood and talked like this before, and I *do* remember where and when. All of them," Johnny said impatiently.

Baz went over and curled up into a corner of the settee, cradling the bottle of scotch like a teddy bear. He sat down on the other end of the settee and Baz eyed him slyly.

"Got a new one, yet, Johnny-boy?"

"A new what?"

"A new bird. Put one in the ground, pick up another, no trouble for you. Never has been."

"It's never easy and you know it," Johnny said, puzzled.

"Oh, yes, oh, yes. They fall into your lap, just like that. Guess they know what's waiting for them there, huh?"

"Oh, for Christ's sake, you're a little old for penis envy, aren't you? What the hell's the *matter* with you? What's my track record with women got to do with anything . . . it never bothered you before."

"Did. Did, too. Always did."

"I'm sorry, Baz. I can't help you, I never could. You know that."

Baz's eyes filled again with whiskey tears. "You bastard."

There was no point in going on with this. He watched Baz in despair, terrified Molly might be listening outside the door. It was bad enough that her husband was an alcoholic. He'd gone past the point of hiding that anymore. It was the rest of what he was hiding that worried Johnny. That Baz's alcoholism was a cover for, or perhaps a result of Baz's other, deeper need to go to bed with truck drivers.

Johnny had only discovered it by accident—a bloody and terrifying accident.

Bristol, many years ago. A concert appearance blown to hell. Nothing terrible, just going straight from the second to the fourth movement of a Brahms concerto, leaving the orchestra and conductor stalled behind their music racks, staring at him. Because he was tired, because he wanted it over with, because of a lot of things he was finding it more and more difficult to face. He'd stopped after five bars, made a burlesque gesture of shooting himself in the head, everyone had laughed and he'd backtracked to the third movement. A warm and human moment that no doubt had made the audience love him. It hadn't made him love himself, but then nothing much did at that time.

And so, afterward, he'd gone on a drunken spree, something he'd been doing with increasing frequency as the pressures had escalated. Except that time, being in a strange city, he'd unwittingly staggered into a gay bar, and been approached by an aggressive closet queen. It was neither his scene nor his nature and he'd overreacted. The spurned would-be suitor had gone for him with a broken bottle and Baz had appeared from the shadows, got between them, and had taken the slashing blow on his own back. Somehow, in the shrill chaos that had followed they'd managed to get one another out and to the nearest hospital. Johnny had passed out in Casualty from acute alcoholic poisoning, and it wasn't until a couple of days later that Baz had come to see him. They'd known one another before, but only as nodding acquaintances. Now they knew one another a little too well for Baz's comfort.

The stupid thing was that Johnny couldn't have cared

less whether Baz or anyone else swung on both sides of the bed, as long as it wasn't his bed.

But Baz cared.

He didn't want Johnny to get the wrong idea, he'd said. He didn't make a *habit* of going to places like that, it was just that his marriage was going through a bad patch and sometimes . . . sometimes . . . but he was fighting it, he'd get over it, it was only a phase. He adored his wife, he couldn't bear to hurt her, he'd never, never do it again if only Johnny wouldn't tell. Johnny had never had any intention of telling. He was just grateful that his face still had its components in their original order.

As far as he could see, he and Baz had both been in a pit, then. Johnny because he no longer could accept the burden of his own impossibly high standards, Baz because he was trying to fight something in himself that filled him with disgust and shame. Out of that original encounter had grown their friendship, and even a kind of love, Johnny supposed. Bomb-shelter love. There were times when he wondered if Baz wanted it to be more, but it never had been, because Baz realized that even the tiniest move in Johnny's direction would be the end of their friendship.

So they'd gone on. As far as he knew Baz *had* beaten it, but there were times when it was a close-run thing, when only a long drunken night of Johnny listening to things he didn't want to hear helped Baz talk himself out of it. He wondered, now, if that had been wrong. If those confessional torments had only made Baz's dependence on him run more and more deeply. Baz saw his defection from the quartet as a personal rejection — divorce from a one-sided marriage.

"Who's this audition with, then?" Johnny asked.

Baz looked away. "No audition—just told Molly that to get out. Had to get out. Had to . . . it's bad, this time, Johnny . . . so bad."

Johnny glanced surreptitiously at his watch. There wasn't time to go through the ritual again, Priddy was waiting. He reached across, took the bottle of whiskey from Baz's grasp, poured him a stiff shot and pushed it into his hand. "Get yourself stinking and go to bed, Baz. Later . . . later, we'll talk if you have to."

"No . . . don't understand . . . he wants money, Johnny. He says he'll tell . . . I didn't mean it to happen, God, I didn't really want it . . . but you didn't—"

"Don't make me your conscience and don't make me your goddamn excuse," Johnny snapped before he could stop himself. "I've got a life of my own to live, I can't go on propping you up while you sort yourself out . . . if you haven't grown out of it by now, you never will. Why don't you face up to it . . ."

"Don't . . . don't say that . . ."

"What else do you expect me to say?" He got up and walked to the far end of the room. Through the long window he could see the children's swing moving gently in the late afternoon sunlight, pushed by a breeze that wanted someone to play with.

"It's your fault . . . if you hadn't . . . if you—"

"*My* fault?" Johnny exploded and turned to stare at him. "How on God's green earth could it be *my* fault?"

"You don't understand," Baz moaned, trying to get up and falling back in a jumble of knees and cushions.

"No, that's right, I don't understand and I probably never will. You've got to get help, Baz, talk to somebody who knows *how* to help, not me. Don't you see . . . I just can't take care of you anymore . . . you've got to—"

"Shut up . . . just *shut up!*" Baz shouted, making it to his feet this time. He lurched down the room toward him, waving the bottle and spilling a spiral of whiskey across the carpet. "I only did it . . . because you left . . . and she said I couldn't do it then . . ."

"Of course you can do it. Molly loves you, Baz. If only you'd stop making such a big deal out of playing jazz without me, and be honest with Molly and yourself about this other thing, maybe together you could—"

"Too late . . . don't you see that? It's too *late!*" The maudlin tears of self-pity had given way once more, this time to frantic desperation. "You've got to help me, Johnny, you've got to . . . got to . . ." He dropped the bottle and took hold of Johnny's jacket, shaking him. "I've got to pay him to keep quiet, I've got to . . ."

Johnny pulled away. "If you need money, I'll give you money, Baz." Now he was buying his way out of his obligations, he thought, hating himself.

"You don't care, do you? Let me go down the toilet, what the hell, as long as I don't mess up your goddamn career, your big chance . . ." Baz's voice was rising, he was going out of control.

Suddenly the living room door opened and Molly stood there. "Baz . . . stop it . . . stop it . . . let him go . . ." she said, terrified at what she saw. Baz turned on her.

"Get out . . . none of your business . . . get out, you damn bitch . . . leave us alone . . ."

He was going for Molly now, his rage unfocused and wild. Johnny did the only thing he could do—he picked up the fallen bottle of whiskey and knocked Baz cold with it. Baz went down like an empty sack and lay still and white between them.

With a little cry Molly ran over and knelt beside him.

Johnny dropped the bottle. "I'm sorry, Molly . . . God, I'm sorry . . ."

"It's all right . . . you couldn't do anything else," she said in a low, strange voice. "Nobody can do anything . . . it's just getting worse and worse every day."

"How long has he been like this?" Johnny asked, kneeling beside her and trying to get a hand under Baz's shoulders. They couldn't just leave him lying there like that.

"Drunk or angry?" she asked, still in that distant voice.

"I don't know. Both, I guess." She'd always been such a pretty girl, soft and warm, like Beth. Now her face was tight with shame and pain.

"He can't sleep . . . the nightmares . . . horrible nightmares about you . . . running away . . . people chasing you, dragons and monsters . . . I guess pink elephants are out of season . . . he wakes up screaming for you to stop. He seems to think you hate him, that it's because of *him* you're running away . . ."

"I'm not running away, I'm right here," Johnny said irritably. She started to cry, then, and he felt like a heel, reached for her hand and held it. "I'm right here, Molly. I always will be, if you need me. If either of you need me."

She shook her head. "No . . . you can't spend your life protecting him . . . protecting me . . . you've got your own problems, Johnny."

He did, too, that was the damnable part of it. "Let's get him upstairs," he said quickly. "With all the booze he's got in him I don't expect he'll wake up until tomorrow. I didn't hit him all that hard—he was about to pass out anyway." He didn't want her to go on, didn't want to hear what she knew or suspected. Together they managed to get Baz into bed. Johnny stood looking down at the white sweaty face on the pillow, the dark circles under the closed eyes, the long bony fingers lying limp on the blanket.

"*Is* it my fault, Molly? If I stayed with the quartet, if I didn't leave, do you think it would make any difference?"

"I don't know, Johnny. I only know he's changed since—" She looked over at him. "But you can't do that . . . you have this chance . . ."

He lifted his bandaged hand. The elastic binding was a little grimy around the edges, now. "There aren't many classical pieces written for one hand . . . I may have a very limited repertoire."

"But Baz said your doctor told you it would heal, that it would be good enough—"

"It's my hand," he said quickly. "I ought to know."

\*

After unloading Baz's two saxes, trumpet, oboe, flute and trombone from the space behind the seats, he got into the Spitfire and stared out of the open doors of the garage that framed the flowers along the edge of the drive. Baz had said it was "too late." Well, maybe he was right, maybe it was too late for all of them. Dreams were for people who drove sports cars—maybe it was time they all settled down to sensible lives and sensible cars and sensible expectations. He reached down to adjust the seat. Baz's long legs always needed the maximum. He felt for the gearshift and hunched the seat forward until it wouldn't go any farther, but found he still wasn't comfortable. He'd driven the car before when they had gigs out of town, he was even listed on Baz's insurance, and it had always been all right for him. He pushed and pushed, but it wouldn't go any farther. Muttering, he got out and knelt beside the car, poking underneath the driver's seat. Something was blocking the track. After a moment he got it free . . . oh, great. By repeatedly trying to force the seat he'd managed to bugger up what looked like part of one of Baz's instruments. The mangled lump of brass glinted like gold in his palm—just another thing he'd managed to ruin. Maybe his genius wasn't for music at all, but for destruction. He got back in. The seat slid up all the way, now. He shoved the crumpled bit of bright metal into the glove compartment along with the road maps and unpaid parking tickets. At least by taking the car he'd ensured that Baz wouldn't drive it while he was pissed out of his mind and would maybe kill someone.

That was some consolation.

# 16

Skindles did not specialize in vegetarian cuisine.

Still, it was the only place in Maidenhead that Johnny knew, so they'd agreed to meet there. When he came through the archway into the restaurant he saw Priddy had managed to get a table next to the windows overlooking the river. Early Wednesday evening was not exactly the rush hour, he supposed. His hand ached abominably from constantly having to shift gears in the Spitfire, and as he sidled between the tables he was aware that he hadn't got a very good shave with Beth's little razor and that his clothes hadn't exactly been improved by lying scattered over her bedroom floor all night and half the day. At least he was clean. Some people spent a fortune trying to achieve the casual look, didn't they? Could he help it if his wrinkles weren't as symmetrical as Gucci's?

He pulled out a chair and glanced around at the few other diners as he sat down. "This wasn't such a good idea," he grumbled to Priddy as he unfolded his napkin. "We should have met in the parking lot outside and gone on from there."

Priddy gazed at him over the top of his wineglass. "Listen, son, I want one decent meal before they toss me in the slammer." He put his glass down. "Anyway, when it comes to bad ideas, you take the prize, not me."

The waiter appeared, took Johnny's order for Perrier with a twist of lemon, thrust a menu at him and went off in a huff. Either Perrier lacked style or a good profit margin. "Have you ordered?" Johnny asked, looking with dismay at the long list of steaks, chops, and roasts.

"No, I've just been sitting here getting quietly stoned," Priddy said, pouring some wine into Johnny's glass before he could cover it. "I suggest you do the same. Maybe if I get you drunk I can talk you out of this."

"I don't drink much," Johnny grinned. "Try logic."

"I'm not strong on logic."

"Good. Neither am I."

"I noticed," Priddy said heavily.

The waiter reappeared, pencil at the ready, and they had to order. Priddy took a New York cut sirloin, Johnny said to bring him a plateful of all the vegetables that were on tonight, plus a couple of jacket potatoes. He and the waiter had quite a conversation about this, which did nothing to ease Priddy's conviction that he was sitting opposite a nut case. Johnny smiled when the waiter admitted defeat and wandered off, shaking his head. "There goes a victim of organized thinking," he said, then caught Priddy's expression. "Look, you don't *have* to go with me, you know. Just give me the stuff and I'll—"

"Be in trouble before you even cross the lawn," Priddy predicted in a sour voice.

Outside, the last light was going and the water that rippled out from under the arches of the bridge twinkled with the reflections from the opposite shore. The long sloping lawn that ran down to the water's edge on this side was still uncut, but there was a stack of white tables and folded umbrellas leaning against the wall of the hotel patio, ready to be set out at the first sign of warm weather. A long line of rush-hour stragglers still made a continuous chain of lights across the bridge and along the road on the far side. The silhouettes of the trees were furred with buds. Perhaps one summer day he'd bring Beth here and they could sit on the lawn at one of those tables watching the boats on the river waiting to go through the lock downstream. Was she back at the flat, now? Had she found his note? Had she found all the notes?

"You're sure no one's left at the house?"

Priddy nodded, wiping a dribble of juice from his lower lip.

Johnny spooned sour cream into his jacket potato. "Where do you suppose he's gone?"

"There's a big antiques fair in Bristol over the weekend, probably there, playing ring around the Rosettis with his cronies."

"Around the what?"

"He specializes in late-Victorian paintings, didn't you know? Also South American primitive art, alongside the usual carved George the Second what-nots, bracket clocks, and Delft posset pots."

Johnny stared at him. "Where the hell did you pick up all that?"

"You pick up a lot of useless information working for an insurance company. I was an investigator for one of the big ones before I went out on my own."

Johnny detected an overcasual note in Priddy's answer and wondered if he'd been fired from the job. It wasn't any of his business one way or the other, but it put Priddy's capitulation to his suggestion that they burglarize Claverton's house into clearer perspective. He supposed he was lucky, in a way, to have hit on this old sneak out of all those others. His ignorance of this side of life was becoming more apparent to him all the time. How the devil did "nice" people find their way to thieves, contract killers, fences and all the rest of it when they wanted something criminal done? You can hardly look *them* up in the Yellow Pages.

"When are we going to do it?" he asked edgily.

Priddy scowled. "Later. When all the neighbors are asleep. When everybody's busy screwing somebody else's wife."

*

Beth was staring at the note she'd found on the table in the living room. Across the top he'd printed in large letters: DO YOU REALIZE HOW MUCH A LOCK-SMITH CHARGES TO LET SOMEBODY *OUT*?

Underneath that he'd scribbled:

Something has come up that can't wait. I'll call you as soon as I can. With luck this whole thing will be over by tomorrow and we can get back to where we were this morning. I don't understand how all this has happened between us so quickly, but I do know it's good, and we're too old to waste the time we've got ahead. *Don't worry.*

Love<br>John

PS—Beth, you is my woman, now.

Don't worry?

She worried.

She worried while she put away the food she'd bought

to feed him and perhaps would never cook, now. She worried while she undressed, soaked in the bath, and put on something loose and comfortable that should have made her relax but didn't. She worried when she turned back the neatly made bed and discovered her vibrator with the batteries removed and a very rude note attached to the effect that she wouldn't be needing *this* damn thing anymore. She worried when she opened the cupboard to get herself some biscuits and was showered with a booby trap of dry rice he'd rigged somehow with paper and tape. The note with that said, "Just practicing." She worried when she opened the medicine cabinet in the bathroom to get some aspirin and found a silly drawing of an enormously fat nude lady with the words "A little wobble is a wonderful thing" printed underneath. These foolish things . . .

The flat was full of him, and yet it had never felt so empty. She was still worrying when the buzzer to the downstairs door went, nearly sending her out of her skin with a combination of shock and relief. Running to the hall, she pressed the intercom button. "John?"

But a woman's voice answered from the grille, an American voice. "It's Laynie Black, Mrs. Fisher. John asked me to drop something off here on my way home."

Beth stared at the grille. Who? Oh, of course, John's agent.

"Mrs. Fisher?" the grille said. "May I come up?"

"Oh, I'm sorry, yes, of course." She pressed the release for the downstairs door and then went out onto the landing. Presently a foreshortened figure appeared, toiling up the stairs. As Laynie rounded the last bend she looked up and took a deep breath.

"My God, I hope they supply oxygen as part of your lease."

So this was John's high-powered agent. Beth saw a pair of enormous eyes and a brief wide smile. She had expected soignée chic and found instead a simply dressed woman in a plain cloth coat. She didn't even wear any makeup. Could this really be the woman who made entrepreneurs tremble and second violinists believe they could challenge Menuhin and win?

"Tell John he'll have to carry me up the last flight."

"He isn't here," Beth said, and to her utter horror burst into tears. Laynie Black reacted to this with what Beth was to learn was a typical response to emotional displays.

"Oh, shit. Where do you keep the gin?"

"In the . . . cupboard over . . . the sink," Beth sniveled into her sleeve while searching unsuccessfully in her caftan pockets for a shred of Kleenex to hide behind. "I'm sorry . . ."

"Oh, let it out, I don't mind," Laynie said, going into the flat and looking around for the kitchen. "I might join you once I've had a stiff drink or three. Go sit down someplace, you're beginning to drip onto the carpet." She dropped her briefcase and disappeared into the kitchen. After a while she appeared in the living room and thrust a glass into Beth's hand.

"Here—it may help." Her voice was deep and husky, with sympathetic amusement behind it. "I don't ordinarily make alcoholic demands before saying hello, but it's just been one of those goddamn days," she rasped, dropping into the chair opposite the settee and fumbling in her handbag. She finally found her cigarettes and lighter and Beth watched as she flicked irritably for a flame with no result. How old was this woman—fifty—thirty—ninety?

There was a little gray in the thick pageboy bob and some arthritis in the knuckles of the hand that gripped the glass of gin. When she got her cigarette lit at last, Laynie stretched out her legs with an aggrieved sigh and stared at the ankles, which looked slightly swollen above her neat pumps. "Jesus, it feels so good when it stops," she said, and swallowed a good third of her drink. That accomplished, she looked over at Beth and again that brief wide smile came and went. "Hello, Beth Fisher."

"Hello," Beth answered, feeling a complete fool but not minding all that much because the other woman didn't seem bothered by it.

"Giving you a hard time already, is he?" Laynie smiled.

"No . . . no . . . he's wonderful . . . it's just that I don't know where he *is* and that man is trying to kill him and I'm afraid he's gone to have it out with him and he might get hurt even more and—"

"Whoa . . . slow down," Laynie directed. "One word at a time with as many deep breaths as you need in between. One, two, three, go." When Beth had finished explaining, Laynie looked older than she had a few minutes before. "A perfect end to a perfect day," she said angrily. "I should have known something was wrong . . . he sounded too happy on the phone. Never trust him when he's happy, it always means he's really miserable."

"Does it?" Beth said, miserable herself. "I don't know him all that well."

"I see—he's going to marry you first and then let you find out about him the hard way. Typical."

"Marry me?" Beth gasped.

"That's what he said on the phone," Laynie said, then raised her eyes to the ceiling when Beth burst into fresh tears. "Jesus, stop that, will you? It makes me want to do the same thing and somebody told me the other day it's fattening."

"He calls me . . . Fat Lady." Beth hiccuped.

"My God, he's gotten the terminal cutes already," Laynie said in disgust. *"Stop that,"* she added fiercely.

Beth stopped crying instantly, to her own amazement. She stared at Laynie, who stared back with lively curiosity. "Does he really call you Fat Lady?"

Beth nodded and blew her nose.

"Has he started playing practical jokes on you?"

"Yes . . . how did you know?"

"Always does to people he likes. Used to make my life hell before I put my foot down. Nothing nasty, mind you. He once sneaked into my office when I was out to lunch and glued down every single thing on my desk. I could have killed him. You aren't what I expected, at all."

"I'm not?"

"No, thank God. I couldn't imagine what kind of woman could turn John Cosatelli around from the coldest fish in town to the idiot who called me this morning, babbling about cottages in the country. Made my blood run cold, but now I see you . . . I guess it will be all right. You look sensible enough when you aren't bawling your head off. He's not as easy a man to handle as he seems at first, you know. He's a complicated bastard."

"No, he's not," Beth said. "He just needs to be in charge, that's all. He wants to know who you are and what you are, and once he's sure, then he wants you to stay that way and let him look after everything else."

Laynie was startled. It had taken her years to find that out, and this girl had done it practically overnight. "How old are you?" she asked.

"Thirty-nine. Most of the time, anyway."

Laynie nodded and looked at Beth as she scrubbed at her face with the tattered tissue, trying to visualize Johnny with her. She was no raving beauty, certainly, but there was a warmth there she'd never seen in his other women. Particularly not in his first wife, who'd been so stiff-assed she'd probably creaked when she put on her pantyhose. This one was actually a little like John, himself. A tough outer shell carefully maintained to protect a soft vulnerable interior—an interior that contained, in turn, the steel spine found only in geniuses and natural survivors. Well, Beth Fisher's outer shell was gone, and she'd lay odds that Johnny's was gone, too. At last. "You'll do," she concluded. "Now . . . where do you suppose he's gone?"

"I don't *know*." Beth looked at Laynie. "You said he asked you to bring something over here—would that tell us anything?"

Laynie gave a short bark of laughter. "Hardly." She got up with a groan and went into the hall to retrieve her briefcase. After sitting down again and thrashing around inside it she produced two objects. "He wanted this because he said you both needed a little luck at the moment." She tossed Beth the small brass figure of a dragon. It was cold and lay in her palm, looking up at her with heavy-lidded and secret eyes. "It's his lucky piece. And this . . . this he said would either make you laugh or blush." Leaning down, she slid an LP across the carpet. Beth stared at it. She'd told him over their dinner at the Savoy that her late husband had the happy habit of breaking up her favorite possessions in front of her during arguments. One of them had been the best recording of the Ravel G Major Piano Concerto she'd ever heard, but when she'd tried to replace it, she'd found it was out of print and had to settle for the Michelangeli. She said she couldn't remember who it was by, but the cover had had a picture of trees and a sunset on it. He'd looked at her oddly and said he thought he knew the one she meant— and might be able to get her a copy.

"He never said," Beth whispered, looking down.

The words across the top were in white. "Ravel Piano Concerto in G Major, Rachmaninov Piano Concerto No. 4 in G Minor. Philharmonia Orchestra, Luigi Fermi, Conductor. John Owen Cosatelli, soloist." "He must have thought I was putting him on. The smug little bastard."

Laynie almost choked on the last of her drink.

Beth picked up the record and turned it over. On the back she saw the photograph that accompanied the sleeve notes. John looked back at her with longer hair and no lines in his face, John in white tie and tails, with one elbow leaning on the piano, looking very serious and very, very young. "He never said," she whispered again. "Even when I went on about it."

Laynie shrugged. "He hits two real stinkers in the Rachmaninov but the Ravel is okay. He'd signed with that junk label before I started handling him. It folded, of course, and by the time the bankruptcy court got finished, he'd gone into jazz and nobody would sign him for serious work anymore. I suppose he's told you about Price-Temple?"

Beth nodded. "A little. I don't quite under—" she began, then stiffened as the buzzer in the hall went again. She leaped to her feet, her face shining. "That must be him . . ."

Laynie heard her talking into the intercom for quite a while. When she came back she looked both disappointed and puzzled.

"Is it—?"

Beth shook her head and half-turned as footsteps came up the stairs outside the door. "No . . . it's only Gino," she said sadly.

"Gino?" Laynie asked. "Who the hell is *Gino?*"

# 17

It was very dark and quiet by the river. It was also damp and cold. They had left the cars some distance away, at the other end of the cul-de-sac that led to Claverton's place. They'd been forced to enter the grounds of "Chippendale" by the front gate, there being, according to Priddy, no other way in, unless Johnny felt like a swim.

He didn't.

Once they had ducked between the gateless brick posts and then into the rough patch of woods that bracketed the drive on the other side, he found he didn't feel like doing anything except getting this over with as quickly as possible.

If Claverton's place hadn't been so beautifully maintained he would have said the architect had been Charles Addams. It was an enormous old house, three stories of Victorian opulence with carefully trained wisteria making graceful looping accents to the lacy white trelliswork that edged the neat portico over the drive at the side.

Keeping to the trees, they worked their way around the lawn to the back of the house. There was a distant sound of a small boat puttering invisibly downriver. A duck or rat made a sudden splash at the marshy edge of the lawn under the veil of willows. The noise made Johnny jump and he bumped into Priddy, who had to grab a willow branch to keep from falling over.

Willow, weep for me, Johnny thought as a long strand trailed damp fingers across his face.

"You wait here, I want to take a look around before we start this thing. Doing it is bad enough, doing it blind is just plain stupid."

Priddy left him and crossed the lawn in a low scuttle, looking like a hunchbacked spider. As he reached the house he switched on a pencil flashlight, keeping the button of light low and moving it in quick sweeps with long pauses in between. There was an occasional wink as it picked up a reflected gleam from the basement windows hidden behind the thick herbaceous borders. Johnny watched until Priddy's shadow disappeared around the far side of the house, then turned to look out over the river. He could see a light in the upper story of a house on the far side, but even as he watched it went out. Good night, sweetheart. There was a faint whisper from the willows as a breeze sprang up from the water and ripples leaped with delicate sucking sounds at the edge of the lawn.

When he'd been safe in the warm comfort of Beth's flat, the idea of breaking into Claverton's conveniently empty house had seemed both simple and expedient. Now that he was actually here, it didn't. He decided Priddy was humoring him again, expecting him to chicken out at the last moment in the face of all this cold reality. He didn't suppose the old man would put him down for giving up. He'd probably be relieved. But he wasn't going to stop now. Before Beth, before Price-Temple, it hadn't mattered so much. Now it mattered just enough to be worth the risk—he hoped.

Suddenly Priddy was back, moving so quietly that Johnny wasn't aware of him until he took hold of his sleeve, making him jump.

"Right," Priddy whispered hoarsely. "Quick lecture. Some people never put burglar alarms in at home, no matter what kind of setup they have on their business premises. Usually they're the overconfident types who think they're untouchable. Claverton qualifies. People who *do* put in security alarms are people with something worth stealing or something to hide. For that, Claverton also qualifies. However, I think he's probably more conceited than careful."

"So no burglar alarm?"

"Oh, I found a burglar alarm all right, about twenty years out of date and as obvious as a zebra in red socks. I took care of that just now." Priddy kept glancing toward the front of the house as if he were expecting someone.

"Well—that's all right, then," Johnny said, as relieved as he could be with feet that were turning cold in every sense.

"Maybe. There might be others."

"Oh, God," Johnny despaired, trying to read Priddy's expression in the darkness. All he could see was the gleam of eyeballs and teeth and wasn't sure whether the teeth were bared in a smile or a grimace.

"You see, security alarms are basically a cry for help. The better they are, the farther away they can be heard. The alarm I put out of action would have waked the neighbors and half the dogs in Berkshire. But bells and horns and buzzers aren't the only kind of noise available.

Maybe the one I cut out was *meant* to be cut out, meant to look old and easy on the outside, but inside it was something else."

"Like what?"

Priddy took a minute to blow some warmth into his cupped hands, still watching the front gate. "A house is just a box, right? A box with holes in it, doors and windows. And an alarm system is usually triggered by sensors in those doors and windows. It could also be hooked into that old alarm. If Claverton *has* a backup system, it's probably through the General Post Office lines. When it's set off it makes an automatic connection to 999 and plays a tape loop that tells the operator to notify the police. Loops usually repeat for about four minutes. Add a couple of minutes for the operator to clear the line and get through to the police, plus their running time out here. Maybe fifteen minutes in all."

Now Johnny realized *why* he was watching the gate. "Then why didn't you cut the phone line from the house?"

Priddy chuckled briefly. "I did. That's the other problem." He blew on his hands again. "Claverton *also* might have a direct line set up, either to the GPO or to a private security firm. That can be set off like the other, through interference with the sensors. But it works on a continuous pulse signal—which means if the line is cut the pulse stops—and *that* sets off the alarm. Heads they win, tails we lose."

"Is that all?" Johnny groaned.

"Hell, no—there's lots of other possibilities." A minute dragged by, taking only an hour to do it. "Want to give up?" Priddy finally asked.

"Of *course* I want to give up," Johnny said through

clenched teeth. "But I'm not going to until you tell me it's impossible."

"Nothing's impossible, son—some things are just bloody difficult, that's all. Are you a gambling man?"

"I'm here, aren't I?"

Priddy grunted. "Well, I still have a few friends in the insurance business, so while I was waiting for you to get out here this afternoon, I made a few calls to people who should know better than to tell me what I wanted to know."

"What did they tell you?"

"According to the records, Claverton has an alarm warranty requirement on his house contents policy. But the girl I got to tap into the computer doesn't know her ass from her elbow, so she couldn't tell me what system they specified. They code that information, and they change the codes every six months or so, automatically. She doesn't have access to them."

"I see. So we forget it?"

"We could, we could. Thing is, this warranty hasn't come into force. They demanded an alarm system, but they haven't verified the installation yet, so he's still paying top whack for his cover. That could mean it hasn't been installed, or it could mean it *has* been installed but he hasn't got around to letting them take a look at it—seeing as he's had a few things on his mind lately, such as getting rid of you."

"Oh." They still seemed to be in the woods.

"That's where the gamble comes in, see? Is Claverton clever, is he careless, or is he lazy? Was the alarm I neutralized the one and only one in the place or wasn't it?"

Priddy looked at his watch, holding it up close to his face

to read the faintly luminous numerals. He sighed. "I haven't got a lot to lose, son, but you do. Cops see B and E as B and E, whether you're after the Crown Jewels or a recipe for chocolate cake. If we're caught, we could go to jail for it. So, last chance—do we go in there or don't we?"

Johnny looked at the dark shape beside him, at the house, at the front gate, then out across the river. "If what you did set off some alarm, they'd be here by now, wouldn't they?"

"They would indeed."

"And they aren't."

"They aren't."

He was shaking so badly with cold and fear he could hardly get the words out, but they finally came. "Let's play it out."

The back of the house had a wide roofed porch running its full width. In the center a set of shallow steps led down onto the rear lawn. Priddy tested each step before putting his full weight on it, and did the same with the wide, weatherbeaten floorboards of the porch itself, playing his flashlight beam along the inner edge of each before he trod on it. He stopped at each window to inspect the frame, and cupped his face against the panes to work out what lay beyond. He finally settled on a pair of French doors about two-thirds of the way along. After going over every inch of the frame with the minute care of a zealous exterminator looking for woodworm, he muttered something Johnny didn't catch, then pocketed his flashlight, adding to the heavy bulges that were already dragging his coat down. Then he reached into his jacket and took out his wallet, extracted a credit card, and inserted it between the doors, running it slowly up and down. Johnny assumed he was going to use it to spring the lock in some way, but he didn't. He put it away, then got a roll of two-inch-wide, transparent tape out of another pocket. After taping the pane of glass closest to the handle of the door, Priddy took off his shoe and gently broke the glass, taking care to ensure the glass was fully stuck to the tape before removing it and putting it down neatly on the floor. He reached through and turned the handle, but the door didn't open.

"Bolts," he muttered. "You've got longer arms than I have. There's probably two, one top, one bottom." He stepped aside and waited while Johnny groped blindly. Finally he located and managed to pull the bolts. It was difficult not only because he was shaking so badly, but also because of the thin rubber gloves Priddy had made him put on. When the bolts were free, Priddy pulled the door open. One of the heavy curtains billowed slightly toward them, then fell back into place. Johnny started to step through, but Priddy grabbed his arm. Pushing the curtains aside, Priddy suddenly ran into the dark room. Johnny started to follow, and Priddy nearly knocked him flying as he came darting back out onto the porch.

"What . . . what . . .?" Johnny gasped, staring at him.

"Hmmm?" Priddy didn't seem frightened at all, so Johnny couldn't understand what had sent him out as fast as he'd gone in.

"What's the matter?"

"Nothing, yet."

"But—"

Priddy hunkered down on the floorboards and looked at his watch again. "Got a cigarette?" He looked up at Johnny's agitated expression and sighed. "Ultrasonic

sound and motion sensors are one of those other possibilities I mentioned. If he hasn't wired the doors and
windows, he might have wired the rooms instead. Saves
setting the thing off every time you forget and open a
window at night for a breath of fresh air. No bells . . . so
it may be a direct continuous pulse system on a buried line
for all I know. So we wait again. If you hear anything—
and remember they won't exactly advertise their arrival—
make for the river and swim a few houses down before you
get out. At least five, if you can manage it. You *can* swim?"

"Yes, can you?"

"Enough."

After fishing out his cigarettes and handing them to
Priddy, Johnny began shifting from one foot to the other,
nearly ready to scream at Priddy's slow and cautious
progress. "Do *all* burglars take this much trouble?" he
hissed.

Priddy smiled. "Only the ones who haven't been
caught." He took a tube of quick-setting putty out of yet
another pocket and began to replace the taped pane of
glass, his smoldering cigarette dangling from his lip so that
he had to tilt his head back to avoid the smokestream.

"What are you doing *that* for?" Johnny demanded, and
was annoyed to hear his voice break like an adolescent's.

"No sense being messy about this," Priddy said, pressing the putty smooth with his thumb. "That's why I used
clear tape—he might not notice it right away."

"What if we make a mess inside?"

"I have no intention of making a mess inside if I can
help it," Priddy said quietly. "Why warn him when a day
might give us the time we need to check out anything we
find?"

"Couldn't we take some things to make it look like an ordinary theft?"

"We could. We may have to. Let's just go along a step at a time, all right?"

"Jeeesus wept," Johnny muttered, wishing he didn't give a damn about being caught, and torn between being grateful for and annoyed by Priddy's fussbudget approach.

Priddy glanced at his watch again. "Guess we can risk it now," he said, getting up and brushing off his clothes. He pulled out his penlight again, switched it on, and stepped through the curtains. After a moment, Johnny followed him. Priddy closed the French doors and made sure the curtains were overlapped before flashing the beam around the room. It picked out a massive antique desk, book-lined walls, a couple of deep-buttoned leather club chairs, a richly brocaded drop-end sofa, and a beautifully carved satinwood sideboard with a tantalus and crystal glasses waiting beside it on a silver tray.

"Looks bad," Priddy grunted.

"Bad?" It looked beautiful to Johnny, the kind of room every man should have. Every man but Claverton, that was.

"Bad for us. I figured his study was our best bet, but I doubt whether we'll find anything here but travel brochures, household accounts, and old love letters. Still . . . you never know. You go through the desk. We'll want his address book, a diary if there is one, bank statements, so on. Anything that looks out of place—anything that looks like business."

Dutifully, Johnny did as he was told, switching on the small green-shaded desk lamp after Priddy told him it was all right. He found an address book and took it. The desk diary appeared to be purely social, but he took that too, just in case. When he closed the last drawer and looked around, he thought for a minute Priddy had run out on him. Then he felt a bump against his leg. He looked down and saw Priddy trying to crawl into the kneehole of the desk, his face laid practically flat on the carpet.

"What the hell . . .?" Johnny whispered, moving aside. After a moment Priddy emerged from the desk and stood up. He looked at Johnny and shrugged.

"No wallsafe . . . thought he might have one set in the floor. No break in the carpet, though. Nice and smooth."

"I guess that's it, then," Johnny said, defeated. But Priddy wasn't listening, he was headed toward the door to the rest of the house. "Where are you going?" Johnny asked, following him nervously.

"There are other rooms. It's a big house."

It was, too. Johnny hadn't expected it to be such a big house. He hadn't expected it all to take so long, he hadn't expected it to be so complicated, and he certainly hadn't expected to be nearly wetting his pants every step of the way, either. As they crept along he realized what he *had* expected was to find a nice big box sitting in the middle of the floor with a tag on it reading, "My Criminal Enterprises, J. Cosatelli for the attention of." The hall was a boulevard of broken dreams.

Priddy only stopped in the reception rooms long enough to ascertain whether any of them had a concealed safe. He was heading toward the stairs to try the bedrooms when he suddenly stopped, causing Johnny to lurch into the back of him. Priddy was staring at the front door. Or more precisely, something on the wall near it. A carved wooden panel that looked as if it had been "liberated" from some church. He stepped over to it, ran his fingers along the edge, which was boxed in, and with a click released the panel itself. It swung back slowly to reveal not a painting of some bland Madonna, but a gray steel panel set with an array of switches and a small red light. When Johnny came up beside him he saw that in the glow of the light Priddy's face was pale and a little sweaty along the upper lip.

"Is that—" he began, and Priddy nodded.

"*That* is what I spent so much time trying to avoid," he answered raggedly. "It's all here . . . every window, every door, every room, sensor circuits, sonic movement detectors, all hooked into a separate direct continuous pulse system . . . the bloody lot, mate. The latest, the best . . . and the most expensive."

"But it didn't work . . . or did it?" Were they out there? Was the place surrounded, were they waiting?

"No," Priddy sighed, closing the panel very gently. "It didn't work."

"Why not? Is it faulty, is it—"

"No fault in the system, it's live. The fault was in the switch." Priddy glanced at him and wiped his face with his sleeve. "The stupid bugger went out and forgot to turn it on."

Johnny felt his knees begin to sag, started to reach out to catch his balance, and touched the carved panel. He jerked his hand away, could have sworn he felt it burn. Priddy smiled without amusement, then turned again toward the stairs. When they were halfway up, a grandfather clock in the hall below went off, striking twelve and taking an equivalent number of years off Johnny's life. Priddy didn't even flinch, and he wondered if the old man was past the point of being afraid. Aside from the few beads of sweat he'd seen on his upper lip, Priddy seemed as he had from the beginning, smooth and careful and efficient. And very quiet. Beside him Johnny felt like an arthritic elephant.

They spent as much time in the master bedroom as they had in the study, but with even less to show for it. Priddy only made a cursory inspection of the other bedrooms, none of which seemed to be in use. The third floor was obviously used as servants' quarters, two of the rooms for sleeping, one as a living room. Those remaining were given over to empty suitcases, stacks of linen, rejected or broken furniture, and dust. Priddy halted at the top of the stairs, looking down.

"Basement," he said abruptly. Johnny groaned and looked at his watch. They'd been in the house for over an hour and had achieved nothing, found nothing, seen nothing. But he obediently followed Priddy's shadow down to the ground floor and along the hall to a door under the back of the stairs. It was the first door they'd seen with anything other than conventional locks—there were two here, both Yale, one high, one low.

"Should have come here first," Priddy grumbled, feeling in yet another pocket and producing what looked like a couple of crochet hooks, except the ends had been filed to thin points. Obviously Priddy had done more that afternoon than make a few phone calls. He inserted one of the picks into the top Yale and probed about for a minute, then began to curse.

"I thought you could open those with a credit card," Johnny said as Priddy put the picks away.

"You'd just end up with a broken card and the things

still locked," he said. "TV stuff—load of crap. These are new locks . . . less than three years old, anyway. Take me half an hour to open each one—if I was good, and I'm not." He had the penlight out again and was sending the beam along the baseboards. "You notice an electrical outlet any— Ah, there's one." He plunged his hand deep into the inside lining of his coat and handed Johnny a plastic package containing a reel of electrical cord with a socket at one end and a plug at the other. "At least he's had the place rewired. Put it in, will you?"

Johnny stared at the reel. "What are you going to do?"

Priddy looked at him in disgust. "Do? I'm going to make a bloody great mess, that's what I'm going to do. Plug it in." Johnny did as he was told, playing out the cord back to the door, where Priddy was waiting with something in his hand that looked like a gun, but wasn't. It was, in fact, a very small portable saw with a long thin blade attached to the head. Muttering, Priddy switched it on, slid the vibrating blade into the narrow gap between the door and the frame, and began to cut around the lock. In the dark silence of the big house the noise was incredibly loud, and set Johnny's teeth on edge. Priddy worked steadily. "Thing is, no matter how strong or complicated a lock might be, the door you put it on is still just wood, usually. He should have put in a steel door, but I guess he figured nobody would get this far. These are just to keep the plain folks out."

He cut two semicircles around the locks, switched off the saw, then turned the handle of the door and opened it, leaving the locks in place against the frame. He looked down at the sawdust scattered over the carpet. "Messy but effective." He flashed the beam of his light down the stairs. At the foot was a small foyer, paneled in pine, with two more doors. Neither had locks, just ordinary aluminum doorknobs. "Okay, reel it in," Priddy directed, disconnecting the saw and removing the blade. He coiled its cord around the handle while Johnny wound up the extension reel. "Now let's see what Mr. Claverton has so carefully hidden."

A minute later they found themselves in Mark Claverton's *real* office. It looked like the bridge of the Starship *Enterprise*.

The walls were pine-paneled, but little of the wood could be seen because an elaborate computer covered one of them, tape storage racks and files spanned another, and the far wall, the one behind the big gray-painted metal desk, was covered with a glassed-over world map. The glass was covered with black grease-pencil lines and a number of different-colored discs. They went across to look at them and found that each had a series of numbers written on them in small, crabbed handwriting.

"That explains two things," Priddy said.

"What two things?"

"The heavy-duty electrical cable running to the house, and Claverton's entry in Who's Who. I wondered why a guy with a doctorate in mathematics had gone into the antiques business."

"Claverton holds a doctorate in mathematics?" Johnny gasped.

Priddy didn't answer. He'd begun pawing through the desk drawers. Finally, with a small grunt of satisfaction, he took out two small black leather loose-leaf notebooks. "Master codes, probably." Johnny peered over his shoulder as he flicked through them.

"Does that tell you anything?" he asked.

"Not me, son. You'd need an expert to wade through all this. The police have lots of experts."

"The police? You mean you're turning this over to them?"

Priddy regarded him thoughtfully. "It's too big for you. Too big for either of us."

Johnny stared at him. "You know what all this is for, don't you?"

"I've got a pretty good idea. Let's see what's behind that other door."

The other room took up what remained of the basement area. It seemed filled with crates and boxes. At one side there was a long workbench covered with all kinds of objects. Clocks, vases, inlaid boxes. They looked like antiques, but some of them seemed to be in the process of being built—or rebuilt. Just in front of the bench was a deep, beautifully carved oak chest, with its lid back. The interior was filled with what looked like tapestry. Priddy went over to it and lifted one corner of the material to inspect the stitches. There was a dull sound from the folds, like bottles clinking together. Priddy bent down and picked something up, directing his penlight beam onto it.

"What's that?" Johnny asked.

"Didn't you do National Service? That is a hand grenade. Just like John Wayne used to throw at the Japs on Iwo Jima," Priddy said with what sounded like satisfaction.

"Put it down," Johnny said, stepping back.

"Perfectly safe," Priddy said, but he put it back with care and in the glow of the beam his face looked a little pale.

He turned to the workbench and began poking at the things on it. Johnny came over to stand beside him, making a wide detour around the oak chest. Priddy had picked up a long, slender piece of metal tube with a bump at the end. It was gilded. Leaning over, he placed it into a groove on the door of an ornate tallboy that stood at the end of the bench. It fitted perfectly.

"What's *that?*"

Priddy was squinting along the metal rod. "Well, I haven't got my reference books handy, but I'd guess it was the barrel of a carbine," he said.

He moved along the bench and picked up a small box, scraping a fingernail over one of the lozenge-shaped carvings on the lid. Raising his penlight beam to the racks behind the workbench, he located a small bottle marked "turpentine" and unscrewed the top to pour some of the liquid over the box. He rubbed it again on a bit of rag and held it out to Johnny. "Ever see an emerald?" The penlight beam brought out the deep green fire of the stone, its facets gleaming where the coating of gilt paint had been rubbed away. When Johnny looked up he saw that Priddy was hefting a large blue and white oriental vase.

"Looks like Ming—probably isn't, though," Priddy said, his voice reverberating hollowly as he tilted the vase to look inside the wide mouth. He shoved his penlight under his arm and started to reach inside. "I think—"

Suddenly they both stopped thinking anything.

A glare of light flashed past one of the small windows high in the front wall of the room. There was a heavy throbbing sound, too heavy to be a car engine. More like a truck. When that engine stopped, they heard another, smoother one whose sound had been masked and then that, too, stopped. It was replaced with the sound of voices . . . several voices.

Johnny grabbed Priddy's arm in panic and the vase slipped and smashed against the edge of the workbench, sending up clouds of sawdust and a flutter of wood shavings. Johnny sneezed and sneezed again as he backed up against Priddy and they both fell across the bench in the darkness.

Choking and gasping, Johnny held on to Priddy.

"*That's* why he didn't turn it on, dammit. He knew he'd be back tonight," Priddy cursed, and also started sneezing. They were still raising sawdust and crunching through shards of porcelain with every move they made.

"We've got to get out . . ."

"The only way out is the way we came in . . . maybe we can—" Priddy said, starting toward the open door. But he was wrong.

At the far end of the big room the ceiling suddenly began to open. As it did, there was the whir of an electric motor and one of the big dark shapes began to rise.

Priddy moaned. "Lift . . . had to be . . . how else would they get some of these things out? The gravel under that portico must be fake. *Damn!*"

Overhead they heard steps coming down the main hall.

"Uh-oh, too late," Priddy gasped. He backed against the bench, sending up another cloud of porcelain dust. "Maybe they'll think we've been and gone . . . come on . . ." He grabbed Johnny's arm and pulled him back into a corner, behind a big pair of packing cases. Johnny thought they bore an unpleasant resemblance to two coffins. They crouched down, sweat running under their clothes. Johnny wondered if perhaps Claverton would smell them out. Although he couldn't smell anything himself he knew they must be giving off the bitter scent of panic in clouds. Suddenly Priddy giggled, and he turned to stare at him in the darkness. After a moment, it struck him as funny, too, the two of them sneaking around the house for hours uninterrupted and then getting trapped like rats just when they'd found what they were after.

"Shhhhh," he spluttered. "They'll hear you."

Priddy giggled again, but more quietly. There were flashlight beams being shone down from outside, now, and the lift began to descend, with two pairs of legs visible on it. They looked like big legs belonging to big men.

"Let's jump 'em," Priddy suggested in a hoarse whisper. "How many can there be, forty, ninety, a hundred and eleven?"

"Count the legs and divide by two," Johnny suggested. He felt very fond of Priddy, suddenly. After all, he wasn't such a bad old sod to die with. Game, too . . . helping him break into this bastard's house the way he had. And it was a bastard's house, too, wasn't it? That bastard Claverton who had killed Lisa—probably because she knew about the Starship *Enterprise* and he wouldn't take her to the moon, the old meanie. He began to hum "Fly Me to the Moon."

"I thought you played the piano, not your nose," Priddy said, digging him in the ribs.

"I forgot to bring it with me," Johnny apologized.

The men had got off the lift, now, and were flashing their lights around the basement room. One of them indicated a big crate that was standing next to the lift, apparently waiting to be shifted. They began to wrestle it onto the platform. They didn't look all *that* big, Johnny decided. Just kind of medium big. In fact, they were getting smaller all the time.

While he was getting bigger.

Much, much bigger.

He was also getting very bored sitting behind this dumb crate. They were finished here, weren't they? They'd found out what they wanted to know about Claverton, found a way to put an end to all this business. Why should he sit here like some scared kid hoping nobody would notice he'd stolen some apples from the tree?

"Listen," he whispered to Priddy as the lift started upward with the crate and the men on it. "Why don't we get some of those grenades out of the toy box and blast our way out of here?"

Priddy considered this. "Somebody might hear us," he objected.

"Oh. I suppose so. Don't want to wake the neighbors," Johnny conceded. Click, click. His mind was spinning over, click, click, click. He'd think of something in a minute, he had to. Click, click. Or was that just his teeth chattering? Why should they? He wasn't scared anymore, just fed up.

There was a shout from the head of the stairs and suddenly the basement lights came on, making them both blink. They were still hidden by the crates, and Johnny turned to peer at Priddy. "You're not ready to receive visitors. You're a mess." Priddy seemed to have fallen into a barrel of talcum powder and wood shavings. Sweat had made tracks through the white dust on his face. Johnny looked down and saw he, too, was covered in the stuff. He plucked at the front of his sweater and a little cloud drifted up, almost making him sneeze again. There was a lot of shouting going on, now, and the lift had started to come back down.

"Maybe if we walk fast nobody will notice," Priddy said.

Johnny risked a peek around the edge of the crate and wished he hadn't. The men on the lift were craning their heads down to see what all the noise was about. He glanced to the right. Claverton and Manvers were standing in the splintered doorway and George the gorilla was right behind them.

They're lining up for us, Johnny thought. I suppose we ought to give them a show, seeing they've come so far.

He was off and moving before he even knew he'd started, his head seemed to be either way ahead of or way behind his body.

"Geronimo!" he bellowed, running toward the group in the doorway and turning slightly sideways to launch himself into one of Pascal's best sabot flyers. He jerked his body together, used his forward motion to curl in a perfect arc, right foot high, legs bent to deliver the vital thrust.

And missed.

He sailed through the doorway and crashed against the far wall, taking the impact flawlessly with his drawn-up legs and then rebounding onto the floor behind George, who, for some reason, didn't seem all that interested in his superb display of expertise.

In fact, he didn't even look down, just kept staring through the door into the storeroom from which Johnny had just taken flight. And after he'd done it so beautifully, too.

A little piqued, he inched forward a little and bit George in the leg. The big man yelped and jerked away, but he didn't look down. Johnny considered biting him again, but remembered just in time that he was a vegetarian. Instead he got up and looked to see what was so fascinating in the other room.

Ah.

It was John Wayne, thinly disguised as Rex Priddy, dusty but nonetheless impressive, standing there with a big fat grenade in his hand. He seemed to be enjoying himself.

"Just step right in, gentlemen," he was saying to Claverton and the others. "You on the left, too . . . just come along nicely please, no whispering or giggling. That's right . . ."

Claverton and Manvers were shuffling forward, cautiously. Priddy was standing right next to the oak chest, and in the bright light from overhead Johnny could see he'd gathered several other grenades into a little heap on top of the rumpled cloth. They looked quite cosy, lying there, nestled together. Priddy glanced at him. "Have you finished your flying demonstration, John, old son?"

"I *was* a thing of beauty, wasn't I?" he said, pushing past George, who looked at him in a kind of wondering horror. What the hell—he didn't look *that* bad, did he? "Boo!" he said suddenly, and George jumped back involuntarily, then scowled and started forward.

"No . . . no!" Manvers said shrilly. "Don't push him . . . can't you *see*—"

See what? Johnny frowned. Lisa had liked him, Beth liked him, his mother liked him . . . what was so terrible about him, all of a sudden? They all looked so damn funny standing there that he had to laugh, though. He was still laughing when he got to the oak chest and picked up one of the grenades. "How do you turn on these things?" he asked cautiously.

"Never mind . . . one will be enough," Priddy said, nudging him toward the far end of the storeroom. "Get on the lift, we're going up."

"Up, up, and awaaaaay!" Johnny shouted, tossing the

grenade up and catching it deftly. Oh, he was good at that. He did it again and heard a low moan from Claverton. He looked over at the old creep and remembered.

"You killed my girl," he accused, pointing. "My *old* girl," he amended carefully. "She knew all about the Starship *Enterprise* and she was going to tell, wasn't she? Hmmm?"

"No . . . no . . ." Claverton protested hoarsely. "She knew I was getting out, getting a divorce so we could get married, go away, finish with all this."

Johnny stopped. "Oh?"

"*Shut up, Mark,*" Manvers said tersely.

"Forget it, old son," Priddy said, reaching for the lift button.

"No . . . wait a minute . . ." Johnny said. Click, click, click. His mind was going along so fast he could hardly keep up with it. He looked at Claverton and then switched his attention to Manvers.

"Did you know that?" he asked.

"No," Manvers said.

"Of course he knew," Claverton said. "I'd told him I was tired of being Routemaster, tired of everything. I just wanted to—"

"Routemaster?" Johnny asked, as Priddy pulled him backward onto the lift platform. "What's that?"

"It's—" Claverton began, but Manvers jerked at his arm.

"If you went, would *he* be Routemaster?" Johnny asked, gesturing toward Manvers with the grenade.

"No . . . he doesn't understand the—"

"Wait a minute, dammit," Johnny said as Priddy

reached for the lift button. He kept staring at Manvers. Suddenly he laughed. *"There's* your killer, Claverton," he said, pointing his bandaged hand at Manvers. "I don't know what the hell a Routemaster is, but if you're the only one around then he needed you, didn't he? With Lisa out of the way, there would be no reason for you to leave, would there? Nothing would change, everything would just go on nice and profitably . . . right? *Right?"*

"Don't be ridiculous," Manvers protested. "I had nothing to do with the girl's death, Mark, he's only trying to—"

But Claverton was staring at Manvers, wide-eyed and pale. "He's right . . ." he whispered.

"Damn right I'm right!" Johnny shouted, feeling absolutely brilliant as the lift started to rise. "Ask him, Claverton," he called, bending down to keep them in view. "Ask him what he had to gain by getting her out of the way! You've been after the wrong guy all along . . . and I bet he encouraged it, too. Bet he kept telling you how rotten I was, how I'd better be got rid of in case Lisa had talked to me . . . told me something dangerous— didn't he? *Didn't he?"*

The lift bumped to a stop and he saw they were standing under the portico. It was pitch black there, with only the light shining up around the edges of the lift. Priddy was tugging at something in his hand . . . he tossed the grenade onto the lift platform, pushed the button, and, grabbing Johnny's arm, began to run down the drive.

*"Didn't he?"* Johnny screamed over his shoulder, and then the grenade went off. A gout of flame shot up through the opening, concurrent with a clap of thunder

that was everything John Wayne could have wished for. He thought he might mention to Price-Temple the advantage of adding a few grenades to the end of the 1812 Overture, even though the crack of the explosion might shatter the eardrums of the first four rows.

"Heigh-o-silver!" Johnny shouted as he and Priddy ran down the drive toward the gate. After the obscene blast of the grenade the night seemed very very quiet, except for the crunch of their feet through the gravel. Johnny looked back and saw smoke billowing out of the lift opening, swirling and twisting in the light of flames from below. He saw something else, too.

George must have ducked up the cellar stairs while he and Priddy were rising on the lift. He was rounding the corner of the house and coming after them.

Johnny thought he looked a little irritated.

He began to run faster, following Priddy out between the gateposts and heading up the street toward the cars. They split without a word at the end of the cul-de-sac, and he managed to pull the keys to the Spitfire out of his pocket as he ran, which didn't surprise him as he felt pretty well capable of anything, now. By God, that had been fun. Seemed a shame to leave . . . but Beth would be worried. Couldn't have Beth worried.

He got into the Spitfire and the engine caught immediately. What else? He threw it into gear, let out the brake and clutch, and felt the little car leap forward eagerly. As he passed the opening to the cul-de-sac he saw George stop, stare, then turn and start back toward the house.

Maybe he'd left a tap running.

He sailed past Priddy, who was struggling with his car door. He blew the horn cheerfully and waved.

Good old Rex.

\*   \*   \*

Priddy had just got his car door unlocked when he felt somebody's hand grab his shoulder and he was whirled around. A very angry man stood behind him, bellowing. Maybe they'd waked the neighbors after all.

"Hi," Priddy said cheerfully. "Nice evening, isn't it?"

"You bloody horse's ass!" the man shouted at him. "What the hell do you think you were playing at . . . do you realize you've just—"

"Just what?" asked Priddy, genuinely interested. The man seemed too furious to explain further, just stood there opening and closing his mouth like a fish. Another man joined them, then a third. They *all* seemed to be very cross.

Suddenly Claverton's Rolls roared out of the cul-de-sac and went past them, following the red wink of Cosatelli's taillights as they rounded a distant curve and disappeared.

"Is your name Priddy, by any chance?" one of the angry men suddenly demanded, distracting Priddy from the sight of the Rolls also rounding the bend and disappearing into the dark night.

"Rexford Austin Priddy, at your service," he said firmly. "And you, my good man?"

"David Anthony Ellis, Customs and Excise," the man answered, showing him a badge. "You're under arrest."

"*Splendid!*" Priddy enthused, waving one arm expansively. "Take me to your leader!" The dramatic effect of this was spoiled somewhat by his bursting into a fit of uncontrollable laughter.

"What the hell's the matter with him?" one of the men asked.

Ellis peered at Priddy, reached out and ran a finger over his face, gathering up some of the white dust that caked it, then put his fingertip to his tongue. His eyes widened as Priddy stared at him drolly. "He's covered with *cocaine*. He must have breathed in enough to blow off the top of his head. No wonder he's so full of himself."

"What about the other one . . . Cosatelli? He looked just like old Dusty, here."

Ellis stared down the road. "The other one, too," he said.

# 18

Gates covered the receiver with one hand and turned to Dunhill. "They can't get him to stop laughing," he said in exasperation. He took his hand from the telephone. "See if he's got anything on him . . . anything at all . . ."

He'd been getting a tirade from Ellis for the past fifteen minutes on how *his* suspect had blown *their* midnight stakeout for covering Claverton's entire operation from start to finish. How they'd been waiting to follow the truck and its distribution pattern with an elaborate car and helicopter network—they'd even put a man into a tree over the entrance to the drive to toss a splash of luminous paint onto the roof of the truck as it left so they could track it from above. And now . . . *now* . . .

Gates sighed. They had Priddy but had lost Cosatelli. And Cosatelli was not only a danger to himself but everyone else on the road. They knew he was driving a dark blue Spitfire, but hadn't got the registration number.

He stared blankly at Dunhill, who was standing on the other side of his desk. "No, I don't mean that kind of thing . . . a notebook or something. Yes . . . see if there's

269

anything about Cosatelli in it. Ellis, I don't give a monkey's about your goddamn operation, it's been a pain in the ass from the beginning . . . no, we've already got that number. Anything else?" He grabbed for a pen and began to write. "388-0908 . . . no, that's a new one." He wrote it again and tore off the page to hand to Dunhill. "Get an address on that," he directed, then began to nod impatiently as Ellis continued to complain into his ear. Finally he broke in. "Look, Ellis, I don't really see the problem, you've got Claverton and the evidence right there in your hand. He's doing what?" Gates' eyes widened. "Accusing Manvers? That's a new one. Go on. Maybe he knows something we don't . . ." There was a pause in the conversation from the other end and he stared down at the new number they'd read out from Priddy's notebook. Was it somewhere that Cosatelli would go or just Priddy's tailor? Ellis came back on the line. Priddy had just collapsed, apparently. They had a doctor and were getting him to the nearest hospital. The excitement and the overdose of cocaine had been too much for his heart, but the doctor called it a minor attack. Ellis said if it was he'd hate to see a major one.

"What does your doctor say about Cosatelli?" Gates asked. His face darkened as he got another earful. "I *know* he's my problem, he has been from the beginning. Thank you *very* much."

He slammed the phone down and looked at his watch. Nearly two o'clock. They'd alerted the freeway patrols. It seemed logical that Cosatelli would head back to London, but logic might not apply to a man unwittingly high on cocaine. From what Ellis *had* passed on he knew that Cosatelli was covered in the narcotic dust, which was almost pure, and that if Priddy's condition was anything to go by he was not only higher than a kite but would continue to stay that way. Every time he moved he would give himself another blast as the powder drifted up from his clothing into his face. In that condition there was no telling how he'd react. According to the doctor he'd feel wildly confident and would overreact to everything. He'd be a menace in a closed room, much less driving around in a sports car. Generally he would be cheerful, but if crossed he could turn nasty very fast.

Dunhill came back into the room, looking harassed. "They're running the number through the computer now, shouldn't take long."

Gates picked up the telephone and dialed the number.

It rang and rang and rang.

But nobody answered.

# 19

"Well, folks, it's a lovely night here on the M-4," Johnny announced in ringing tones as the Spitfire slewed slightly down the ramp to the freeway. "A little misty, it's true, but certainly nothing for Our Intrepid Hero to worry about, no indeed. We see him now, skillfully . . . oops . . . maneuvering his trusty 53-cylinder Lagonda toward the towers of old London Town, filled with the knowledge that before long he is going to be screwing the panties off Mrs. Beth Fisher, grass spinster of that parish." He patted his pocket, looking for his cigarettes, and sneezed as another cloud of dust billowed upward. "God bless you, my son."

There was very little traffic on the freeway, just a few trucks and an occasional car. He pressed the accelerator down and went around the flank of a truck carrying a load of tomatoes destined for, if the lettering on the tailgate were to be believed (and he had no reason to doubt it) Gino's Trattoria.

Now, that was quick work. Gino had only left school a few days ago and already he was in business for himself.

Clever kid. They were all clever, especially himself. If he'd left it to Gates, Claverton would have gone on getting up people's noses forever, especially John Owen Cosatelli's.

"John Owen Cosatelli," he sang in a rich basso profundo.

He glanced into the rearview mirror. Headlights were coming up behind him. It must be Priddy, catching up at last.

"About time, boyo," Johnny shouted at the mirror, then looked ahead again just in time to avoid a truck that had pulled out to pass.

"Oops!" he chuckled as he overcompensated and the right front fender of the Spitfire came into a brief and blazing contact with the metal fence in the center strip and rebounded. "Always loved fireworks," he said as he gripped the wheel for control and ignored the fact that his hand was hurting like hell. He didn't mind—it had absolutely nothing to do with him. He was above such petty considerations. Absolutely.

The more he thought about what he and Priddy had achieved with a little independent initiative, the more he enjoyed the prospect of seeing the look on Gates' face when he told him about it. So much for Mr. Plod the Policeman.

The car behind was coming up close—too close. Its headlights reflected from the rearview mirror into his eyes and he squinted, taking his bandaged hand from the wheel and holding it up to block the glare.

"All right, Rex 'old son,' if you want to lead the parade, go right ahead," he grinned, moving over into the center lane. The car behind moved over with him. Annoyed, he tapped the brake several times to get Priddy off his tail, but the car held its position and began to blink its headlights at him.

"Dammit, back off!" he shouted, turning slightly and waving his arm. Another cloud of dust rose from his pullover and he sneezed, the Spitfire wobbling slightly at his involuntary jerk of the wheel.

The sneeze seemed to clear his head for a moment and he squinted into the rearview mirror again. That wasn't Priddy's car, it was a Rolls Silver Cloud. The little figure on the hood was unmistakable—she seemed to be coming after him like an avenging angel. He'd *never* liked skinny women, and now this one was getting aggressive. The front bumper of the Rolls touched the rear of the Spitfire. And again, harder.

Suddenly he knew who was behind him, and for a moment was very aware of the solid bulk of the Rolls as opposed to the small and relatively fragile Spitfire. He tried to cheer himself up by turning into W. C. Fields.

"Baz, m'boy, something tells me we're going to need a few repairs if I'm not careful." He pressed down on the accelerator and the little sports car leaped forward. "'Bye, 'bye, birdie," he said to the silver figure in the mirror.

After a momentary hesitation, the Rolls again came up behind him, steadily, inexorably. The glare of the higher headlights was so bright that it was only a dark and menacing silhouette until they passed another truck and the Rolls was lit from behind, revealing the equally menacing silhouette of George at the wheel. Again, the bumper of the Rolls nudged the Spitfire and Johnny felt the pressure increase, a steady heavy thrust that made controlling the sports car extremely difficult. He looked down at the speedometer—he was doing seventy-five already. Knowing Baz, the engine was probably due for a carbon job. Still . . . he floored the accelerator and shot away from the Rolls. He was doing a hundred now, but even as the needle hovered at three o'clock, the Rolls came on. It was no good. No matter what acceleration he developed, the Rolls could eat it up with steady power, catching up with him every time. At the top of the Spit's capacity, George would still be yawning.

Where were all the cops?

A string of several cars passed on the other side of the center strip, the one in the lead with its high beams on, and he was momentarily bracketed in a double glare. In another second George would get it.

He turned the wheel and skidded into the left lane, only to have to swing out again as he rushed up on yet another slow-moving truck. Ducking around it, he took his foot from the accelerator and settled down just a few yards in front of it, allowing the gap to narrow until there wasn't room for the Rolls to get between them.

Now George was running abreast of him, looking over with a glower on his bull-face, and leaning over to reach for something. Johnny smiled and waved, keeping his backside nice and close to the enormous refrigerator trailer truck. He'd definitely give *all* his grocery business to Gateway after this.

Now George was straightening up again and looking down momentarily at something on the seat beside him, fiddling with it, keeping one hand on the wheel. He touched something on the dashboard and the electric window began to glide down, the sudden breeze whipping George's curls wildly. And then Johnny saw what George had found so interesting on the seat.

He'd got a gun out of the glove compartment and was pointing it straight at Johnny. He was smiling, too.

"Goddamn playground bully!" Johnny shouted and touched his brakes. The driver of the big truck behind him hit the airhorn as he was forced to decelerate abruptly or ride right over the Spitfire. But the first shot missed as the Rolls moved ahead. And then, when George slowed to draw back even again, Johnny hit the accelerator and went ahead. Not quite fast enough, however. The window starred just behind him. Even as he involuntarily put up his arm, several jabs of pain told him that some of the glass had hit his face. Just glass, however, not the bullet. The Spitfire slewed with only his bandaged hand holding the wheel, and the entire cockpit was littered with twinkling diamonds of glass as they came up to the lights of an exit approach. George was raising his arm to fire again.

At the last possible minute, Johnny wrenched the wheel to the left and shot down the exit ramp, nearly losing control entirely as his rear wheels caught the warning rise that divided the main road from the deceleration lane. The big truck hooted furiously again and as he fought the rocking Spitfire he saw the taillights of the Rolls flare crimson, and then his vision was blocked by the overpass. He braked just inside the Yield line at the bottom, and the Spitfire skidded on the road surface that was just wet enough in the thin mist to give him a free ride over the rainbow. The car whumped into the grassy central rise of the traffic circle and fishtailed but held as he accelerated to regain control, following the circle and going under the freeway.

He gradually slowed as he continued, trying to read the signs and find out where the hell he was. No, he didn't want to go to Slough, Staines or Wales and the West. He brushed some of the glass off his lap and wiped his face with his bandaged hand, bringing it away streaked with red. There went his last chance to be Mr. Universe. Smiling, he thought of the enraged George continuing helplessly along the M-4, unable to get off until the next exit.

Or would he have sense enough to pull over and wait for Johnny to go by again? Maybe Wales and the West *was* a good idea. His father was probably bigger than George's father. He'd passed the entrance to the westward side of the freeway and so continued around the traffic circle to come up on it again.

And found he'd been wrong about George.

Instead of driving on, then pulling over to wait, he'd simply let the trailer truck move ahead, then driven the wrong way back down the entrance ramp for London. The Rolls was, in fact, sitting facing Johnny as he came around the bend, the big headlights glaring, ass-backwards to London and blocking the access road completely.

Johnny was deeply shocked. George obviously had no respect for the Highway Code.

He accelerated past the Rolls and saw it glide in behind him, moving up. Picking up speed, he made a partial circuit of the traffic circle and ducked down a road into darkness away from the lights of the interchange. The Rolls stayed behind him, and he saw they'd come almost immediately into countryside. A few houses on the side of the narrower road, a gas station closed and dark, the glow of some sleeping village ahead. Pressing down hard on the accelerator, he prayed to God nobody else was out joyriding tonight, waited until the Rolls came up behind him, then moved over into the wrong lane. As he'd expected, George followed, simply intent on his obliteration. Gritting his teeth, Johnny took his foot from the accelerator, slowed until he couldn't stand it anymore, then grabbed the handbrake with his bandaged hand, wrenching the wheel around at the same time. His scream of pain and the scream of the tires combined, but the Spitfire stayed upright as it spun across onto the shoulder, clipped a fencepost and then regained the road facing back the way it had come.

Bigger, heavier, and far less maneuverable, the Rolls plowed on, the brakelights blazing as George tried to stop. But Johnny was moving away, now, back toward the freeway, his eyes streaming tears of pain as he released the handbrake and clamped both hands on the wheel to keep from ending belly-up in a ditch. It would take George time to stop, reverse the big car in the narrow road, and start after him again. Not much time, but some.

The lights of the freeway loomed up ahead and Johnny curved into the traffic circle and took the access road to London, moving out into the freeway rocking and rolling all the way.

The wind came in the shattered window beside him, cycloning around the cockpit and playing games with the glass fragments. He could see them skittering around the seat and floor, like crystallized ants in a frenzy, the vibration of the car increasing their agitation. It was pretty, in its little way, all that glittering motion. If only George would back off he thought he might even have time to enjoy it.

With a crack that jarred his bone structure, the Rolls rammed the rear of the Spitfire just off-center and sent it sideways into the center-strip fence.

A spray of sparks went up as the entire side of the car scraped metal, and Johnny felt the heat right through the door. He swerved away from the fence and shot right across the three lanes at full throttle, riding up onto the rising bank beyond the emergency lane and then skidding back onto the freeway on two wheels, the chassis of the little car juddering in protest as first one side and then the other was subjected to abuse. The torn tendons of his left hand, already beginning to swell again beneath the bandage, tore again and a pain no one could have ignored, not even Superman, enveloped his arm clear back to the elbow. He screamed again, half sob half curse, and as the Spitfire rocked and skidded on the slippery road, the cockpit was suddenly filled with the incongruous sound of the First Brandenburg Concerto. Somehow the impact had set Baz's cassette deck going.

"Jesus God, Johann, don't sit there fiddling, tell me what the hell to do!" he shouted as he managed to steady the car into the middle lane. George was waiting for him. But, as they were now getting closer to London, even at this hour of the night, the traffic on the freeway was increasing. Ahead Johnny could see several cars and, lo and behold, the tomatoes bound for Gino's Trattoria yet again. He must have passed me while I was surveying that country road, Johnny thought. I wonder what he's going to do with all those tomatoes, anyway?

He shot between Gino's truck and another car, straddling the white line, utilizing a gap that was too narrow for the Rolls to gain a little yardage. The driver of Gino's truck was so startled by this that he swerved toward the other car, a Renault 5, closing the gap even more, then swerving again and opening it up as he realized what he was doing.

And let the Rolls through.

"Thanks a lot, Gino," Johnny called.

He began to use the other cars on the road as allies, much to their consternation, by darting back and forth, in and out, weaving a long and hopeless tapestry of evasion, trying to get away from the big silver Rolls that simply thundered on.

He couldn't get away. He just could *not* get away from the goddamn thing. Suddenly, out of the corner of his eye, he saw a big green sign showing Service Area and realized he was approaching the Heston Plaza.

Maybe they'd both feel better after a sandwich and a cup of coffee.

Counting down the warning markers, he waited until the last possible moment before turning onto the exit ramp.

The Rolls followed.

He could see the glow of the restaurant ahead, shot into the parking lot, still going too fast, and raced between the widely spaced cars angled to the pedestrian walkway.

The Rolls followed.

A driver, dismounting from the cab of his truck, jumped back just in time to save himself and his door from being ripped off and sent to heaven on a Silver Cloud.

Ahead Johnny could see the low bank that separated the restaurant from the gas station. He was up and over it before he could stop, landing with a crunching thud on the other side, skidding into the corner of a closed Wall's ice cream stand. A tin sign that had been affixed to the front of the little hut showing multicolored cones and flavors of ice cream sliced across the top of the Spitfire, laying open the fabric as it went. Now he had another tornado to contend with, as well as the Rolls, which wavered just a little as it ran over the bits of wood that had once been a corner on the ice cream shop. But it didn't waver much.

And it kept coming.

Now he was up to the gas station, and he turned to the right, going between two of the lines of hooded pumps, the overhead lights again rainbowing all the glass fragments as they danced to the music of the Brandenburg. He had a quick impression of a dozing clerk behind the window of the pay booth suddenly leaping up as he roared by, and then he was through and into darkness again. Across the deep river-trench of the freeway he could see the companion plaza floating in the thin night mist like a gauzy bubble of light. He could even see a few people inside, crouched over their meat pies and chips, and one standing at the end of the long self-service counter handing something to the cashier. He was so enchanted by the sight that he nearly missed the access road and turned just in time. He glanced into the rearview mirror and saw the Rolls wasn't there.

It was ahead of him.

He jammed on the brakes and felt them grab on one side only. In a whirl of motion and music and screaming rubber, the Spitfire went out of control, jerking the wheel from his hands. He clipped the side of the advancing Rolls and then he was skewing the other way, ricocheting back and forth between the curbs and banks that edged the road and finally coming to rest with a lopsided crunch across the access road itself.

The engine continued to throb.

The Brandenburg continued to play.

And he saw the Rolls gavotting in perfect time to the music, almost lazily turning and sliding across the pump area of the station, narrowly missing the last hooded pump in the line and finally plowing sideways into a parked yellow Automobile Association van.

The empty van lurched, started to go over, then righted

itself and burst into flame as the Rolls rammed it along the bank, cutting a deep black gouge in the grass as it went. He could see flames from the van licking at the gleaming silver flank of the Rolls, and a snake of burning gasoline slithering across the pump area. The attendant who'd been in the pay booth came out and started running like a madman across the parking area for trucks toward the restaurant. Johnny didn't blame him. *He* didn't particularly want to stay around a gas station with a fire on top and twenty thousand gallons of gas and diesel fuel underneath, either.

Despite his fondness for fireworks.

What he found even more unsettling was the sight of George stirring inside the Rolls. He was still alive, and for all Johnny knew, so was the Rolls.

Enough sightseeing.

He put the Spitfire into reverse with an ominous coffee-grinder complaint from underneath the hood, turned it only to hear something fall off and clatter onto the concrete behind him, then pressed the accelerator to get away. It was hardly necessary.

With a blast that literally catapulted the small car forward, the snake of burning gasoline from the van reached and ignited the first of the line of hooded pumps. A roiling cloud of flame and debris volcanoed high, high, high into the night sky. He felt a wave of heat pass over the torn canvas top of the Spitfire as he skidded down the access road and regained the freeway, narrowly missing a red Mini. He wrenched the wheel straight and—

Not Gino's Trattoria. Not *again.*

In his rearview mirror he could see the billowing flames illuminating the entire service area as brightly as day. On either side of the freeway cars and trucks were screeching to a stop as their drivers caught sight of the unexpected early sunrise, and after a moment it seemed as if he were the only one moving.

No, that wasn't quite right.

The Rolls was moving, too.

Blackened on one side by the burning van, it was following him again, but slowly, slowly. Fair enough, he didn't seem to be making such good time, either, now. He didn't know whether he or the Spitfire was in worse shape. His entire body was chattering to him, shaking and jabbering bone to bone, muscle to muscle, tendon to tendon. He felt as if he were sitting in a hollow in the middle of all that noise, as if everything inside him had suddenly evaporated. He was a clockwork man, tick, tick, ticking his way toward London.

A pair of police cars came down the other side of the center strip, presumably to hand out parking tickets to the drivers who had stopped to watch the Heston Service Plaza self-destruct. In fact, there was even a police car coming toward him down the *wrong* side of the freeway, lights flashing and siren wailing.

There seemed to be an awful lot of crazy drivers out tonight.

Well, let them get on with it, he'd had enough. He swerved across the path of the oncoming patrol car and down the next exit. It screeched to avoid him, its brakelights blazing, and he saw the Rolls come up and pass it on the far side, wobbling slightly.

He took the next few turns at random, going this way and that without knowing why he was doing it or where he was going . . . or even who he was. He pulled into a driveway that curved behind a hedge, turned off his headlights for a moment because their flickering was beginning to annoy him, and thought things over.

The police car went by on the other side of the hedge in a blare of noise and light that gradually faded. After a moment he reached down and switched off the Brandenburg concerto, which was also beginning to get on his nerves, then peered at himself in the mirror.

The light here wasn't very good, but he thought the dust-coated face, streaked with blood and sweat, looked vaguely familiar. He wiped some of the dust off, getting quite a lot of it into his nose and mouth, and looked again. After a minute or so, it came back to him.

He was Johnny Cosy.

He was going home.

And about time, too.

# 20

There was a crackle from the radio and Dunhill reached for it. "Triumph Spitfire, dark blue, Registration GAE 494S, sighted on M-4 just east of Heston Service. Exited freeway, believed heading into London."

"*Believed* heading? Don't they know?" Gates asked.

Dunhill replaced the mike after a few questions. "Lost him. They've got that fire under control and they're holding the driver of the Rolls . . . he gave them a good run, though."

"Cosatelli may not realize that—he may still think he's being chased and just keep on going in circles."

Dunhill shrugged. "He can't drive around London without *somebody* seeing him. We've got a car at his flat and another at the Savoy, we're watching his agent's place, and every patrol car has the registration number of that Spitfire, now. Only a matter of time."

"It always has been."

"Well, we've got our murderer, anyway," Dunhill said.

"Manvers is saying nothing very loudly," Gates grunted. "Ellis says he's just sitting there with his arms folded, demanding a solicitor, while Claverton is spilling

285

his guts in the other room." He turned out of Camden High Street. "What was that number on Delancey?"

"Seventeen. There it is."

A patrol car was waiting for them. One of its uniformed officers came up as Gates cut the engine and got out. "We can't get an answer, sir, but the lights in the flat are on." He pointed up at two brightly lit windows on the top floor of the three-story building.

"Have you got me any information on Elizabeth Fisher?" Gates asked, moving across the pavement and staring up at the windows.

"I know her personally, sir. She's a social worker, in and out of our place a lot. Nice woman."

"Is she the type to stay out all night and leave her lights on?"

The uniformed officer glanced at his partner with a frown and shook his head. "No, sir . . . very practical type, she is."

"She's not answering her phone, either," Gates said. "Does that strike you as odd?"

"I guess it does."

"Me, too," Gates said reflectively.

He pushed the button marked Flat 5 and waited. No reply. "How long have you been trying?" he asked the uniformed officer.

"About five minutes . . . we only just got here a little while before you and—"

There was the sound of a laboring engine and they all turned to see a dark blue Spitfire slowly turn into the street and finally come to rest opposite Gates' car.

"Well, well, well," Dunhill said. "Anybody got any Scotch tape?"

The Spitfire was minus a rear fender and most of its top was torn to ribbons. The front end was battered, the entire body on the right side was scored and gouged down to the metal, and the driver's window was completely gone. As Gates watched, the door opened and one of the hinges snapped. Cosatelli got out and stood there trying to get it to close again. After a minute he made a gesture of disgust and walked away, leaving it hanging open. He came across and looked up at the four men standing on the top step.

"Don't build cars worth a damn anymore," he said with a grin. Dunhill started to say something but Gates nudged him and smiled back at Cosatelli.

"How are you?" he said in a friendly voice.

"Oh, I've been better, but not bad, considering," Johnny answered, brushing at his clothing. Gates saw that most of the cocaine had blown away or begun to melt in the damp air, giving a varnished effect to Cosatelli's jacket. But where the jacket had protected it the sweater underneath was still heavy with dust and some puffed up. Johnny choked on it. "Seem to be catching cold, though," he sniffed. "Can't smell a thing and I keep sneezing. You know anything good for that?" He came up two of the steps. Dunhill whispered something to the two uniformed men beside him and their eyes narrowed a little as they looked down at Johnny.

"In your case, I think a—" Gates began, but Johnny interrupted him.

"What the hell are you doing *here?*" he wanted to know, the sight of them suddenly striking him as peculiar.

"We were waiting for you," Gates said. "A lot of people are waiting for you, here and there, as a matter of fact. You've got some explaining to do."

Johnny nodded. "I *know* who killed Lisa," he said. "You won't believe this, but—"

Suddenly another voice was added to the conversation

and with a start Gates realized he'd been standing there all the while with his thumb on the button of Flat 5.

"Who is it, please?" said a woman's voice.

"It's me, sweetheart," Johnny bellowed, coming up another step. He winked broadly at Gates. "'s my girl, Beth."

Gates turned to the grille. "Sorry to have bothered you, Mrs. Fisher. This is Detective Inspector Gates of the CID, here. We were looking for a man but he's—"

Suddenly there was a scream from the grille, and then a man's voice roared out at them, transfixing them where they stood.

"Keep away from here . . . get away . . . or I'll kill them both, you hear me? I mean it . . . I'm tired of pushing around and you bastards never—"

There was another scream, and then from above, the sound of a window being raised and a woman's voice calling into the darkness. "He's got a knife . . . he's . . . he's—"

All of them looked up and saw a dark head and shoulders silhouetted against the light from the flat.

"I think you said the wrong thing," Dunhill croaked, as the figure was dragged back and the window slammed down again with a cracking sound. A small shard of glass knifed down past the front of the building and shattered in the basement entryway below, followed by another larger piece that hit the top of a garbage can and showered splinters all around it.

"Who was that man?" Gates demanded of the uniformed officers.

They stared back at him. "No idea, sir," one of them gulped. "Didn't recognize the voice."

"Does it matter who it is?" Dunhill asked, starting

down the stairs toward the radio car. "He said he'll kill them . . . it sounded like he meant it."

"I think I—" Gates said, turning toward Johnny. The steps below were empty, as was the street in both directions. "Where's Cosatelli?"

One of the uniformed men cleared his throat. "He was there a minute ago . . . sir."

# 21

He hadn't realized before that he could fly.

The sensation was unmistakable. Moving down the street and around the corner, he knew his feet could not be touching the ground at all, because he heard and felt absolutely nothing.

Nothing except Beth's scream, which seemed to go on and on in his head, half a tone off A sharp and thin with terror.

The street was long and narrow, the houses silent on either side, and the cars lined up in front of the parking meters like so many crouching dragons moored for the night. The streetlights had a pinkish cast, and a ginger cat sat foursquare on the hood of a red Cortina, watching him fly by.

Good evening, Tom.

Turning at the far end he went along the shop fronts until he came to the mouth of the alleyway he'd gone down once before when she'd cried out to him. And, although it seemed impossible, he thought he'd heard Laynie's voice, too.

A knife. He has a knife, she'd said.

How in the name of God had George managed to get here before he had? Did the Rolls have nine lives like that cat back there? Once again he stumbled through the lumberyard, tearing his jacket on some stacked rolls of wire mesh. Over the fence and into the garden. Above, he could see a faint glow of light in Beth's kitchen window, presumably an overspill from the living room.

He ducked under the scaffolding and tried the rear door, but it was locked. Shoving his shoulder against it, he tried to burst it open, then kicked at it, but to no avail. Some things *were* still built like they used to build them.

Stepping back, he gazed upward again.

The spidery columns of the scaffolding stretched above his head, standing out from the building but reaching right to the top.

He jumped for and missed the first platform, hearing his jacket split up the back. Shrugging it off, he dropped it at the foot of the nearest steel support and swung himself between it and the first diagonal. He had to climb one-handed because the left hand was completely useless, swollen and straining around the constricting bandage, immovable. It didn't hurt anymore. Nothing hurt anymore, at least not on the outside. Just inside, where Beth was still screaming in his head.

As he gained the first platform he could hear a lot of cars going down the streets toward the front of the building. Men were shouting back and forth. He looked at his watch. Five-fifteen. A little early for the rush hour to start, wasn't it? He wiped his face on his sleeve and felt a coldness on his lips and tongue, a fresh numbness that spread down his throat and up into his nose. Honey and lemon . . . was that what his mother used to give him? Honey and lemon for a cold?

It sounded right.

Taking a deep breath, he put his foot between the intersecting steel supports and began to climb again. As he did, he saw some lights come on in the ground floor flat, and then in the flat above. People were stirring and talking behind the curtains, sounding sleepy and confused, and he heard louder voices, firm and impatient, cutting in. As he swung up onto the platform opposite the second floor he saw the curtains in the flat below part and a face looked out. Then the curtains fell together again and he was alone.

Using his left elbow as a lever, he made his way through the forest of steel tubing and wooden boards, slipped once and found himself hanging in midair above the messy garden fifty feet below. If he'd been able to find a phone booth he'd have stripped down to his Superman outfit, but as it was he had to contend with his belt buckle, which kept getting caught as he tried to pull himself up onto the last platform but one. His muscles were quivering and trembling, and he was angry to find they were so undependable when his mind was so clear and strong and functioning so incredibly well.

Eventually he gained the rough splintered surface of the boards opposite Beth's kitchen window and lay there for a moment gazing up at the sky through the gaps in the final platform above. There were a few stars visible, but the sky was brightening a little in the east, and he turned his head to see the GPO Tower outlined against a grayish mass of clouds that were only just visible in the glow from the city below. Or was it the glow of the sun?

Ah. Sunrise Serenade in A flat.

And no time to be lying around humming.

He struggled to his knees and looked at the window in

front of him. The scaffolding was set out from the block of flats, and there was a good three feet of clear space between the platform and the window. Lying down on his stomach, he reached across the gap and pushed at the window. It was a little loose in the frame and opened outward, he remembered, but could not recall for the life of him whether the lever he could see inside went up or down to release the catch. It was also a very narrow window, one of two over the sink. He remembered standing there this morning washing up the breakfast things and staring out through the scaffolding at the activity in the builder's yard.

If he kicked in the window the glass would fall into the stainless steel sink and make a hell of a noise. He'd never much liked steel-band music and decided it lacked a certain panache as background for the entrance of Super-man.

From below he heard low voices and glanced over his shoulder between the network of scaffolding. There were shadows moving in the garden. Somebody called his name in a hoarse, urgent whisper. It sounded like Gates. What was he saying—Coke? Hell of a time to offer a man a drink.

He took a deep breath and began to pull his sweater up over his head, choking a little as he inhaled the dust that still clung to it. There—that was better. Things were sharper now as the cold night air hit his skin. He'd been weakening for a moment, but now he was fine.

Absolutely terrific, in fact.

Right.

He lay down on his stomach again and poked the edges of the sweater into the gap between the window and the frame, working it down as far as he could inside, until the bottom edge of it caught the lever. As he struggled with it he felt the scaffolding shake slightly. Somebody else was climbing up. Well, he couldn't wait to say hello. The sun was down and the tide was out and this was no time for folks to begin to shout. After the third try he managed to snag the lever upward with the sweater. But when he pulled at the edge of the window it wouldn't budge.

Oh, yeah. It opened down, not up.

Wonderful.

He wiped his face on his aching outstretched arms, then began to work the sweater-wrapped lever down. The knitted material stretched and stretched and finally he succeeded in dragging the lever down all the way. There was a dull metallic snick and the window swung outward so suddenly that he nearly went headfirst down between the scaffolding and the side of the building. Only a fast grab at the leading edge of the window saved him, and as he hung there, the blood rushing to his head, he watched the sweater slither over the windowsill and drop limply down the brick wall, catching a couple of times before finally draping itself on the bare stalks of a dead plant on the windowsill of the ground-floor flat. Even as he wriggled himself back onto the platform he heard the pot fall from the window and make a dull crunch of itself on the areaway in front of the back door.

He stood up. Wrapping his right hand around the steel tubing overhead and locking his left elbow around a vertical support, he swung his feet clear of the platform and thrust them through the narrow open window. He hung there suspended, his feet tangled in Beth's kitchen curtains, then let his left arm slide down the vertical steel pipe as he let go of the one above. His shoulders hit the platform with a thump, and then he flailed out with his right hand until he managed to catch hold of the window again. With his backside swinging in midair he pulled himself toward the building, inch by inch. At the last moment his swollen hand hit the platform and, on the wings of pain, he got himself through the window and into the sink.

Now he was up to his crotch in cold water, sitting in the sink with one leg hanging over and the other doubled up on the drainboard. The kitchen was dark but he could see into the hall as far as the edge of the living room door. He could hear Beth crying and a man talking in a frantic, angry voice. He seemed to be making a speech.

Moving as quietly as he could he levered himself out of the sink.

His feet made a slight sound as they touched the linoleum. Bending down, he slipped off his shoes, feeling cold water running down his legs inside his trousers. As long as it was cold he knew he hadn't done anything *else* to disgrace himself.

Out of the corner of his eye he saw a dark shadow on the scaffolding outside. He ignored it and padded across the linoleum and slipped into the hall, keeping as close to the wall as possible.

Through the open door of the living room he could just see Gino, white-faced, on his knees in front of the stereo, his hair hanging down over his face.

Gino?

He moved a little closer and Gino's face turned in his direction, his eyes widening and his mouth opening. Johnny shook his head and waved his bandaged hand. Gino's eyes flicked away, and he looked down at the carpet in front of him. Good boy, good boy. Goddamn, that was a good boy.

The angry voice was still making a speech, and it didn't really sound like George at all. That left only one candidate. More dangerous than George, or less? He'd never seen Pantoni, had no idea whether he was large or small, fat or thin, smart or stupid. In fact, the only thing he knew about him was that he had a knife.

He heard Beth's voice, pleading, begging, telling Pantoni that this was no way to get what he wanted, no way at all. But Pantoni wasn't having any. He sounded wild and desperate and very determined. He wanted no more pushing around, he said. He was taking his family away from this bad country and this bad life, back home, he said, back home where a man was not put in jail for "looking after" his son.

If only Johnny knew where Pantoni was in relation to the door. Facing it or facing away? Was the knife near Beth?

Then he heard Laynie's voice, the flat American accent sounding even more foreign than Pantoni's.

"Beth is right, Mr. Pantoni  . . they'll simply sit outside and wait and wait and wait until you give up this insane—"

"No! I don't wait, me. You open that window, you shout down what I say. You, old lady . . . you tell them I want them to take me to airport, to bring Rosa and Theresa there, fly to Italy right away. *Right away!*"

Johnny almost smiled. He could imagine Laynie's reaction to being described as an "old lady." If Pantoni wasn't careful he might find *her* going for him along with everyone else.

He heard the sound of the window being pushed up, and felt a draft of cold air enter the hall. Pantoni's attention would be directed toward the window, and telling Laynie what he wanted her to say to the police below.

It was now.

He stepped into the open doorway and fixed the scene in his mind even as he moved. Pantoni holding Beth against his right side, the knife in his left hand pointed at her chest. Gino still crouched on the floor. Laynie at the open window, looking down.

He took three running steps across the thick carpet, brought his left leg up, toe extended, and kicked Pantoni's left arm as hard as he could. The knife went flying into the air, hit the wall between the windows, and slid down against the baseboard.

Coming down on his left foot, he threw his weight onto it, swiveled, and then drove his right leg into Pantoni's exposed side, pushing him into Beth, who went down on her knees. Pantoni staggered, grabbed at the air, turned toward Johnny.

Following through, Johnny stepped onto his right foot and brought the following left straight up from the floor and into Pantoni's jaw just under the point of the chin. There was a sharp crack as Pantoni's open mouth snapped together by the force of the blow, and then Pantoni was falling onto the settee, his eyes rolling back. Johnny aimed another kick at the side of Pantoni's head, then fell across him onto the floor. He rolled over, drawing his right knee back, but Pantoni lay inert, blood trickling from the corner of his mouth.

At last, at last he'd done it the way Pascal had taught him.

Beth lay not two feet from him, and she stared into his

face wildly, unable to comprehend either his arrival or his bizarre appearance. He heard a noise behind him and turned to see Laynie drop the knife neatly out of the open window, then lean against the sill with closed eyes.

He looked back at Beth.

"Hi," he panted. "I think I just broke my toe."

# 22

They were having a hard time getting Pantoni into the patrol car. He was screaming in Italian and literally frothing at the mouth, a pinkish foam of spit and blood.

Johnny was standing next to Gates, who had him very firmly by the arm. He felt bloody ridiculous wearing one of Beth's pullovers, but there'd been nothing else available. At least it was plain and dark. He wondered if she'd visit him regularly in prison. There had to be a dozen charges waiting to be laid against him, from housebreaking to reckless driving to involuntary arson.

He hardly remembered, now, the drive down the freeway. Gates had told him about the cocaine, and as the effect of the drug wore off he was beginning to get scared in retrospect at the things he had done, the chances he'd taken, the sheer bloody madness of it. And as for his human fly act up the scaffolding, well, he couldn't understand that at all. He had absolutely no head for heights, never had. Now he was just *tired*. So tired, in fact, that Gates had to repeat his question twice before he heard it.

"What's Pantoni yelling at you about?"

He blinked and tried to dredge up what little Italian Dom had taught him. "I don't know . . . something about the car, I think. Something about my flashy car and my . . . blond whores . . . I don't know. He seems to think I drive around with women at all hours of the night . . . he's just raving. He says he's glad I smashed it up . . ."

"It's not your car, is it?" Gates asked, watching as they finally got Pantoni into the back seat with a uniformed constable on either side.

"No. Something else I've got to make good," Johnny said wearily. Everything he did these days seemed to be so expensive.

Laynie and Beth came out of the door and down the steps. They were holding one another up, but they were smiling. Beth came over to him and held something out. He glanced down and slowly took Cymru from her hand, still warm because she'd been holding it so tightly. He reached for her and pulled her close, burying his face in her thick, tumbled curls.

"Well," Laynie said in a practical voice. "At least you've got your good luck piece back, John. I think you're going to need it, from the look on the Inspector's face."

"Mmmmm," he murmured, wishing he could just go upstairs and get into bed, hold his woman in his arms and fall asleep forever. Gates was talking to someone and had let go of Johnny's arm, so he brought it around and drew Beth closer.

"Maybe if he'd gotten it to you right away, all this wouldn't have happened," Laynie was going on, releasing her tension in a flood of peevish complaint. "He *promised* he would."

"Promised he would what?" he asked, not really caring.

"Take it to you right away. On his way home from the benefit," Laynie said. "*I* don't know . . . you can't trust anybody these days."

Johnny raised his head and blinked at her. She looked as if nothing had happened at all, just small and cross and only slightly unkempt. No worse than she looked at the end of any busy day.

Click, click, click.

He let go of Beth and stared down at Cymru. The little brass dragon gleamed in the pale early morning light, its heavy-lidded eyes still keeping secrets. He looked at the street around them. Everything was edged with a strange shimmer. The police cars were revving their engines, the pavement was filled with staring people, the car holding Pantoni moved off with a rising note from its siren. All the buildings were oddly flat against the pearly gray of the sky. He stood there knowing suddenly what he didn't want to know, and wondering why everything looked so peculiar.

And then he remembered.

Every day, about this time, the dawn came.

Whether you wanted it to or not.

# 23

"A man is helping the police with their enquiries."

He supposed he'd helped. He supposed it had been the proper law-abiding thing to do. He wished it felt right, but it didn't.

It might have been the same room where Gates had first interrogated him. Beth sat beside him now, holding his good hand, knowing he didn't want to say any more after all he'd said to Gates. Knowing he just needed her to be there, part of him, helping to ease the pain.

Not the pain in his hand. That was rebandaged now and numbed by the police surgeon's injections. There were no drugs for the other pain.

If, if, if.

If Lisa hadn't fallen in love with Claverton, then Claverton would have continued to be what he'd always been. The Routemaster. Using his antiques trade to cover his real profession—organizing what had always been one of the biggest problems in crime—getting stolen goods from seller to buyer. Acting as an expediter—computerized, efficient—taking his cut and moving everything from emeralds to cocaine to arms to stolen paintings and stamp collections . . . you name it, the Routemaster moved it from A to B, for a price.

But the "ifs" went on.

If Pantoni hadn't come around regularly to beat up Rosa he'd never have seen Lisa getting into the car that night. If Lisa hadn't been murdered, Johnny would have never had his hand smashed by Claverton's thugs. If they hadn't smashed his hand, he would never have sent the stereo to Gino, and Beth would never have dropped by his flat to discuss it. If Johnny hadn't shot off his mouth at the funeral Manvers wouldn't have suspected he knew more than was safe and given instructions to have him killed instead of just maimed. If he hadn't been shot at he'd have never hired Priddy, and the old man would still be repossessing cars for finance companies instead of recovering from a heart attack.

All of them would have gone on existing in their separate worlds, unaware of one another, never meeting, never knowing the others even existed except as anonymous faces in the street.

Only one sour note had changed all their private tunes to mingled cacophony.

The door opened and Gates stood there. "We have him," he told Johnny. "He didn't give any trouble." Johnny nodded. "He wants to see you," Gates went on. "He wants to . . . explain."

Johnny stood up and looked down at Beth, reached out to touch her face. "I'll be back in a bit," he said.

"I love you," she whispered.

He looked at her for a moment, then smiled a little. "Nearly," he murmured.

He followed Gates down the hall to another room just like the one he'd left and went in. He stood there for a moment. "You okay?" he asked softly.

Baz lifted his head and nodded slowly. "I told you it was too late," he said. "I told you . . ."

"I'm sorry. I should have listened."

Gates closed the door and stood against it. Dunhill and a uniformed constable sat against the far wall, listening, the constable writing everything down in a stenographer's notebook.

"I didn't mean to do it," Baz whispered.

Dunhill stirred slightly, looked down at his hands to hide the boredom of hearing it all start with the same old words, same old tune.

"After the benefit was over I told Laynie I'd bring the dragon over right away, because I knew how important it was to you. But really . . . I needed to talk to you," Baz went on in a blank way, staring at Johnny's face without seeing it. "When I got there your place was dark, and I thought I'd got there before you, so I waited. I needed to talk, Johnny . . . it was bad that night, really bad for me."

Johnny nodded and swallowed, afraid to move.

"I sat there in the car, waiting . . . I don't know how long it was. I didn't want to go home. I knew if I left without talking to you, I wouldn't . . . go home." The blank gray eyes flickered slightly. "I've never, Johnny . . . not once since Bristol. I kept *that* promise, anyway."

"Yes," Johnny tried to say, but no more than a rasp came out.

"Then . . . after a long, long time . . . Lisa came out and I realized you'd been in there all along. She looked beautiful . . . I always did fancy her, Johnny . . . I knew her before you did but there was never anything. She liked me, but . . . there was never anything." Baz blinked several times, then went on. "I looked at her and I thought . . . maybe if I could make it with *her* that night, then maybe . . . then maybe it would be easier for a while, you know? Get rid of the . . . dreams. So I called her over and we sat there for a few minutes, just talking. She seemed . . . I don't know . . . kind of sad and lonely. And then she said why didn't we go for a drive . . . she liked to drive around at night, she said."

Slowly, carefully, Johnny sat down in a chair next to Baz.

"So we drove around for a while and then . . . I stopped. I don't know where it was . . . some place with trees. After a bit I kissed her, started touching her up a little. She was really beautiful, wasn't she?"

"Yes," Johnny said, hoarsely. "She was beautiful."

"She went along with it for a while . . . sort of laughing a little but not . . . anyway, after a while she pushed me away. Not tonight, she said. Maybe another night, but not tonight. So I told her it had to be tonight, it had to be right *then,* but she wouldn't listen. So, I tried to . . . change her mind . . . I kept on, thinking I could change her mind . . . and she got cross, and started to struggle and push me away harder. Not tonight, she kept saying, but I knew if I didn't . . . if she wouldn't . . . right then . . . then I . . . you know, Johnny. You know why it had to be there and then . . . it had to be . . ." His eyes started to glisten and his voice cracked, blurred, running the words together.

"It's okay, Baz . . ."

"No. It's not okay . . . not . . . I got angry, you see. She just wouldn't listen . . . and I took her by the neck and started to shake her, trying to make her listen to me . . . and then she closed her eyes and went limp so I thought it was all right but it wasn't all right . . . she was dead. She was *dead*." There was a trace of astonishment in Baz's voice, only momentary, as if he'd been startled to be so betrayed by a friend. "I let go . . . stared at her . . . I didn't know what to *do*. What do you *do* when somebody . . . when—" Baz choked up, started to shake almost imperceptibly at first, then with increasing intensity. "I got out of the car and walked around for a while. But when I got back in . . . she was still there."

Her perfume in the car the next morning, not on his jacket but on the upholstery, Johnny thought. Not a piece of a brass instrument caught under the seat track but a piece of gold—a charm broken from her bracelet in the struggle.

Baz took a long breath, but the shaking continued. "After a while I started the car and drove to . . . somebody I used to know. Before Bristol—before I promised. And he said he would help me . . . we'd make it look like something else . . . so he came with me and we drove to some place, some field some place, and we got her out of the car into the weeds. He took off her jewelry and put it in her handbag and made me take it. And then he . . . he . . . started kicking her face, her body . . . all over. Bitch, he kept saying, dirty, dirty, bitch. And he made me . . . kick her, too . . . made me . . . made me . . ." Baz gagged, suddenly, and Gates got a wastebasket over to him just in time. When he'd finished vomiting Baz drank some of the tea Gates gave him, shuddered, then went on. "That was bad . . . but afterward . . . afterward . . . he made me go back to his place. He said . . . I had to pay for the favor. So . . . I paid for it the way he wanted. And you know what? You know what, Johnny?"

"What?"

"I didn't want to do it. The minute he touched me it all went away . . . I didn't want it anymore, I hated it, it hurt and he wouldn't stop and it . . . was . . . terrible . . . *terrible.*" He lost the tea in the wastebasket, remembering. The dry retching went on for a long time after it needed to, but eventually it stopped.

"You told me he wanted money," Johnny said.

"Later . . . later he began asking for money . . . but not then. Money wasn't what he wanted then . . . kicking her . . . had . . . made him . . . want to . . . want to . . ."

Johnny didn't know if he could go on sitting there much longer, looking at Baz's agonized face, listening to all this. But if he stood up and left . . . walked out on him . . . he couldn't do that, either.

"Moosh . . ." Baz said, suddenly.

"What about Moosh?" Johnny asked, startled.

"The next day . . . at the session, remember?" Johnny nodded. "He asked me for a loan, I didn't have anything to give him, no cash, anyway. But I said I had some stuff in the car he could sell if he knew where to sell it. I told him it was stolen . . . a friend of mine had stolen it, I said. But he said that wouldn't matter, he knew somebody who would handle it."

Charley Masuto. No wonder he'd been looking for

Moosh. Fencing stolen jewelry is one thing . . . fencing evidence in a murder enquiry something else again. Too much trouble, even for Charley.

"Molly," Baz said in a wretched voice. "Molly . . I want Molly . . ."

Johnny looked at Gates and Gates nodded. Johnny stood up and Baz suddenly touched him, reached out and touched him for the first time. "I never thought they'd suspect you, Johnny. If they'd arrested you . . . I would have told, then. I would have."

"Yes . . . I know you would have."

"When they didn't . . . I thought maybe it would be all right. That they'd just give up, eventually . . . but I'd have had to go on paying . . . and paying . . . and Molly would have wanted to know where the money was going . . . where I was going . . . she'd have kept asking . . ." Baz blinked and the gray eyes filled with self-disgust. "She won't ask, now. She won't want anything to do with me, now . . . not ever . . ."

"Your wife is waiting to see you, Mr. Bennett," Gates said gently. "She came down as soon as she found someone to look after the children . . . she refuses to leave until she's seen you . . . she wants to see you. I'll have them bring her up in a little while." He jerked his head at Johnny and they went out. Gates stopped a moment to have a word with a policewoman and she went down the stairs as he and Johnny started down the hall, away from the room where Baz was finishing his last blues solo.

"What's going to happen to him?" Johnny asked as he limped along.

"He's confessed. He'll be examined by a psychiatrist but I don't think that will help." He glanced at Johnny. "A good barrister might turn it around to manslaughter," he said carefully.

"Then I'd better hire Molly a good barrister, hadn't I?" Johnny said, just as carefully. "And what about Claverton . . . and Manvers?"

Gates rubbed the back of his neck and looked a little guilty. "Well . . . the fact is, we haven't mentioned to Mr. Claverton that we have Lisa's murderer down here. He still thinks Manvers ordered her death, and he's telling all he knows. He knows a lot, and they sort of hate to interrupt him while he's going on so well. We'll get Manvers on attempted homicide anyway because the chauffeur has admitted he tried to kill you on Manvers' say-so. You didn't tell us someone took a shot at you on Waterloo Bridge."

"I didn't think you cared . . ." Johnny stopped and looked at Gates. "It was Manvers behind it all, wasn't it?"

Gates nodded. "Looks that way. Claverton had the mathematical expertise to organize the Routemaster business, but it was more an intellectual exercise for him than anything else. I'm not saying he didn't like the money it brought in, but I don't think he let himself really think about just *what* he was sending from A to B. Manvers told him to move a consignment and he moved it. Claverton isn't really a villain, not compared to some I've arrested."

"I know," Johnny said. "Lisa wouldn't have loved him if he had been. That's why I could never understand what was coming down on me from his direction, once I saw him face to face. His grief was the real thing, and he didn't seem the type to . . . dammit, I kept feeling *sorry* for the bastard, all the time I was supposed to be hating him. I think half the reason I wanted to break into his place was to get him out of the mess as well as myself. Does that make any sense?"

"From anyone else but you, Cosatelli, no. You don't look like a bleeding heart, but you keep acting like one."

"And you're another."

"I told you once before, we should start a club," Gates grinned. "But don't count on my heart bleeding all the time. Sometimes I can be just plain nasty."

Johnny sighed. "I wasn't counting on anything. Where do you want me to go now?"

"Where do you want to go?"

"Aren't I under arrest? Don't I have to—"

Gates shook his head. "The way I see it, you've more than paid your way, Cosatelli. We've got everybody we were after. You might get *sued* by a few hundred people, but you won't be arrested. Not by me, anyway. Or anybody else, if I can stop it, and I think I can."

"Thanks."

Gates looked embarrassed, then concerned as Johnny began to sway with exhaustion and relief. "You want to go to the hospital, after all?"

"No. I'm . . . okay. If it's all right with you I'm just going to take my lady home and sleep for a week. Maybe on Sunday I'll take her down to meet my folks. After that I'll go back to the doctor and find out if he can still get my hand into shape. If he can, then maybe I'll start arguing with a fat man about a concerto."

"And if not?" Gates asked.

Johnny stopped at the door of the room where Beth was waiting, looked down at his rebandaged hand, then shrugged.

"I can always give piano lessons."